PRAISE FOR ED GAFFNEY'S

Premeditated Murder

"Full to the brim with thrills, spills, and chills . . . Electric, tingling fare." —*Los Angeles Times*

"Great characters in a gripping story, wild twists, and— surprise—big laughs! I love this book!" —*New York Times* bestselling author Suzanne Brockmann

"[A] unique thriller filled with intrigue and non-stop action." —*Romantic Times Magazine*

". . . a fast-paced, dramatic ride through the decisions that affect everyone's life since September 11. In a first novel, Ed Gaffney does not disappoint as a storyteller. He paints a picture that is vivid and taut with tension. Readers who enjoy legal thrillers or political suspense will enjoy this novel." —freshfiction.com

"This is a deep legal thriller that is at its best in court scenes and when the lawyers meet with their client. Ed Gaffney writes a fabulous tale that grips readers from the moment Judge Cottonwood shows his bench bias, and never slows down. . . ." —*Midwest Book Review*

"A fascinating plot . . . *Premeditated Murder* is recommended reading this summer or at any time that you want to scope out the next thriller that is written 'outside the box.'" —*I Love a Mystery*

Suffering Fools

Ed Gaffney

A Dell Book

SUFFERING FOOLS

A Dell Book / June 2006

Published by Bantam Dell
A Division of Random House, Inc.
New York, New York

Dell is a registered trademark of Random House, Inc.,
and the colophon is a trademark of Random House, Inc.

ISBN-13: 978-0-440-24283-3
ISBN-10: 0-440-24283-5

Printed in the United States of America
Published simultaneously in Canada

www.bantamdell.com

OPM   10 9 8 7 6 5 4 3 2 1

This book is dedicated to my son, Jason. In a world where truth and honesty seem to be in sharp decline, I am proud that he is a champion of both.

ACKNOWLEDGMENTS

Thanks again to my editor, Kate Miciak, for her terrific suggestions and enthusiastic support.

Thanks also to my agent, Steve Axelrod, for his excellent instincts and guidance.

Thanks to the entire Bantam team for all of their talents.

To Tina Trevaskis and Kathy Lague, the research staff—again with my gratitude.

To fellow author Virginia Kantra—thanks so much for the duct tape story. You saved me an interesting conversation with my son.

Thanks to the first-draft reading Dream Team: Suz Brockmann, Fred and Lee Brockmann, Deede Bergeron, Scott Lutz, and Patricia McMahon.

As always, special thanks to Eric Ruben, whose passion and humor are the inspiration for Terry.

Thanks to everyone in the Tribe for their friendship, and their endless and boundless support.

And to Suz, thank you for everything. I love you.

Suffering
Fools

PROLOGUE

AT THE PRECISE MOMENT THAT HE FELT HIS trusty crowbar connect with her head, Elmo knew he owned her.

And then, everything turned to shit.

She reeled away a few feet from the force of the blow, and then she crumpled to the ground like a sack of crap, just like she was supposed to. She was obviously out like a light, so Wally went over to help pick her up and throw her into the back of the car. But the minute he got down to where her feet were, she shot her leg up viciously and kicked him square in the balls.

Now all of a sudden it was fucking complicated. Wally was doubled over, clutching his crotch with one hand and pulling up his ski mask with the other, puking on some poor sap's front lawn. Meanwhile, the stupid woman was lying there, holding her head and groaning. Good thing the only light at this end of the street was coming from the moon. The longer this took, the better the chance that somebody would see them. This wasn't exactly supposed to be a public event.

Elmo needed the woman alive, at least for a little while, so he hadn't brought his gun. Besides, shooting her in the middle of the street would have been too noisy anyway. So he raised the crowbar again, approaching her carefully. He sure didn't need a kick in *his* balls.

She was on her back, with her hands over her face. Blood was pouring from a huge gash the crowbar had left, and she sounded like she might have been crying, or whimpering, or something. Whatever she was doing, she sure didn't look like she was going to be kicking anyone in the balls anytime soon. But Elmo wasn't taking any chances. He lined himself up so that he was close to her head—well out of range of her legs—and started to swing. When he hit her this time, he was really going to clean her clock.

But son of a bitch, she twisted out of the way at the last second, and as the crowbar thunked harmlessly into the ground about three inches from her left ear, Elmo's momentum threw him off balance, and he stumbled forward just enough to give her the opportunity to grab his ankle as he staggered by. Before he knew it, he was on his face in the dirt.

Excruciating pain tore through Elmo's bad right leg as he fell, and he grabbed it with both hands. It felt like somebody had just stabbed him with a knife.

To make matters worse, that stupid little bitch was still trying to get away. She had managed to roll over, get onto her hands and knees, and was now up and running—actually more like stumbling—away from him. With his shitty knee, Elmo was no good in a footrace. If she got away, he was really fucked.

Thank goodness for Wally. He had stopped throwing up long enough to see what was going on, and just as she started to make her way past him, he nailed her in the mouth with a clean right cross. Wally was about twice her size, and the bitch went down like a ton of bricks. No way she was getting up after that shot.

Wally was standing over her, and was so pissed off that he tried to kick her in the ribs for good measure, but all he ended up doing was hurting himself again. He grabbed his groin and staggered over to lean against the car. Poor bastard.

But Wally wasn't the only one who was pissed. This thing should have been over a long time ago. Instead, Wally looked like he was ready to start heaving again, and Elmo was flat on his ass in some stranger's yard. His hands were scraped, his knee was on fire, and his hostage was nowhere near tied up and in the back of his car. Damn it all to hell and back again.

He rose slowly and limped over to the unconscious woman. Her left arm was trapped beneath her, and her right was stretched out straight. She was lying on one side of her face. Her eyes were shut, but her mouth was open. She was bleeding now, not only from her head wound but from the split lip that Wally had given her.

The danger was over, thank God.

Elmo closed in once again, this time taking out the roll of duct tape he was carrying so he could get her bound and gagged and into the fucking car already. He worked enough of the tape free so that he could get started with her hands, but just as he bent over to start taping her up, she flipped onto her back, whipped her left hand across her body, and hit him right in the face with—what the hell was that? A rock? Shit! Was she holding a rock in her hand when she hit him like that?

Elmo staggered back and put his hand up to his cheek. It stung, and it was wet. He pulled his hand away, and sure enough: The bitch had drawn blood with that one. And it felt like she might have chipped one of his teeth in the bargain. Goddamn her.

"Get over here, Wally, and hold her down," he said, spitting blood and wiping his mouth with the back of his hand. He reached into his pocket and pulled out the bottle of liquid he had brought, and twisted off the top. Fuck this shit. She was done now.

Wally came over, grabbed her by the front of her shirt, and son of a bitch if she didn't try to knee him in the balls again. But this time he was ready, and turned, deflecting the blow. She didn't have much left, anyway. "Cut it out, goddammit," he said, slapping her in the head. Then he flipped her onto her stomach and yanked her hands behind her.

Elmo limped over and quickly taped her wrists together. She was still struggling, and tried to say something that he couldn't make out. Then Wally rolled her over onto her back, tore off a piece of tape, and started to gag her.

But before he could finish, Elmo stopped him, jammed the bottle into her mouth, and started to pour the liquid down her throat. She twisted her head away, spitting and trying to choke out God knows what—*I'm dying*, or some bullshit—until Wally smacked her again, a good one, and she finally stopped struggling. Her eyes started rolling around in her head, and there was no more resistance when Elmo poured the rest of the drink into her. She coughed a lot, and about half of it ended up spilling down the front of her shirt, but she swallowed plenty before the bottle was empty. That was fine. The guy who gave it to him said that it wouldn't take much.

While Elmo retrieved the crowbar, Wally finished taping her feet together. Then he tried to hoist her up over his shoulder, but that only hurt him again, and he cried out in pain and dropped her. It didn't matter. Bitch was out cold and didn't feel a thing.

Elmo limped over as Wally dragged her to the car,

opened the back door, and shoved her in headfirst. Then they got in the front, and just as Elmo started the car, she started groaning again.

"I shoulda finished gagging her outside," Wally said, tearing off another piece of tape and turning around to lean into the backseat.

"Please, I'm dy—" the bitch moaned, just before Wally finally taped her mouth shut.

"Yeah. Fuck you, you crazy little shit," Wally said. "You ain't dying. Not yet."

ONE

ASSISTANT DISTRICT ATTORNEY LOVELL: *Detective, were you working on the evening of March 19?*

DETECTIVE JOHN MORRISON: *Actually, I was off duty that night.*

Q: *I see. Do you have a specific memory of that night?*

A: *Yes, I do.*

Q: *And why is that?*

A: *Because that was the night that I walked into the Nite & Day Convenience Store and the clerk told me he'd just been robbed by a guy with a knife.*

Q: *Can you describe the condition of the victim when he told you this?*

A: *Yes. He was obviously very upset. He was nervous. His hands were shaking, and he kept looking around, like he was expecting—*

ATTORNEY WILSON: *Objection.*

DETECTIVE MORRISON: *—some surprise or something.*

ATTORNEY WILSON: *Objection. Move to strike.*

THE COURT: *The answer is "He was upset and nervous. His hands were shaking, and he kept looking around." The rest of the answer is stricken.*

ASSISTANT DISTRICT ATTORNEY LOVELL: *Did you have any further conversation?*

DETECTIVE JOHN MORRISON: *I asked him if he knew who had robbed him, and he said that he recognized him as a regular customer, but that he couldn't remember his name.*

Q: *What happened next?*

A: *I suggested that he come down to the station with me to look at mug shots, but then the clerk remembered that the robber had been in the store a few days earlier at the same time as me.*

Q: *Did you remember this incident?*

A: *Not at first. But then the clerk started to describe the guy to me—long, stringy hair, kind of slouched all the time, looked down a lot—and then suddenly he shouted, "I remember! His name is Babe! Babe something." And then I knew exactly who he was talking about. Babe—uh, Rufus—Gardiner.*

(Commonwealth v. Gardiner, Volume IV, September 10, 2004,
Pages 61–63)

April 5, 2004
Five months earlier

ATTORNEY TERRY TALLACH KNEW THAT IT WAS
the obligation of every lawyer to take certain cases for free.
The bar association called it taking a case pro bono, which
translated from the Latin as "for the good." God, lawyers
couldn't even be nice without being pompous.

From one perspective, it made sense for Terry's partner and best friend, Zack Wilson, to decide to take the
Gardiner case without charging. Rufus himself had no
money—he was living hand to mouth when he got ar-

rested. And his mother, who had called to ask them to look into the case in the first place, was barely making ends meet as it was.

But when Terry saw their new client present himself to the MCI–Wakefield prison guard for a final search before their first meeting, he couldn't help but turn to his partner and say softly, "I'll buy you a pizza if you change your mind about this one."

Zack said nothing as Rufus entered the attorney/client visiting room. As he turned to close the door behind him, he fumbled with the file folder he had been carrying. Somehow, the papers in the folder managed to fly all over the place. He bent down to pick them up. "Make it two," Terry whispered.

Rufus Gardiner was technically an adult—he had turned thirty early last month—but he still managed to project the image of a recent high school dropout. His waxy skin and watery eyes were unhealthy looking, his shoulder-length greasy hair was a mess, he breathed through his mouth, and he carried himself in a perpetual slouch. He looked fundamentally stupid, but worse than that, he looked spectacularly guilty. Of everything. He didn't make eye contact, he mumbled, and he shook hands like he was afraid that such intimate contact might allow you to read the dirty thoughts that kept running through his tiny mind.

He was the walking, talking embodiment of the worst defendant in the world. If he was on the witness stand and testified that the sky was blue, half the jury would think he was guessing.

The other half would think he was lying.

Zack, of course, acted as if Rufus was just like every other defendant he'd ever met for the first time. Innocent until proven guilty. Entitled to Fifth Amendment protection against self-incrimination. Encouraged to help in his own defense. Relied upon for honesty in communications. Protected by the attorney-client privilege.

Rufus just stared at the table as Zack went through his new-client spiel. He might as well have been speaking Swahili with a Chinese accent. At the end, Zack said, "I know this is a lot to take in all at once, Rufus, so if there's anything you don't understand—"

"Can you call me Babe?" Rufus asked, looking up and establishing eye contact for a full half second before lowering his gaze back to the table. "Instead of Rufus. Nobody calls me that anymore."

Except your mother. And the court system. Oh—and the prison administration, too.

"Uh, sure," Zack said. "Sorry."

Terry couldn't wait any longer. He clicked his pen and pulled his legal pad in front of him. "So, Babe, let's talk about how all this happened."

"I picked it myself," Babe replied, with a shy smile as he shuffled the papers he'd brought to the meeting.

There was a prolonged silence as everyone tried to figure out what the hell had just happened. Babe certainly didn't look crazy. "What?" Terry asked.

"My name," Babe explained, looking up for a second. "I picked it myself. That's how it happened."

Terry ground his teeth and tried to speak slowly and calmly. "Not your name." Numbnuts. "The charges against you. How did all *that* happen? What were you doing that night? Why did you get busted for robbing the convenience store?"

"Oh, yeah. That night." Welcome to the conversation, Babe. "Did my mother show you that tape from the store? I didn't do it."

Well, that certainly cleared things up.

"We haven't met with your mother yet," Zack replied.

"She has health issues," Babe offered into the silence.

Who was this guy? Rain Man?

"Let's put aside the tape for a second," Zack said. "I think what Terry is asking is if you can tell us what you were doing that night. Starting from after work. Your mom said you work at a factory or a warehouse, right?"

"Yeah," Babe said. "I got through with work around five, and then I drove to this restaurant called The Burger Barn to have dinner."

Terry was familiar with most of the restaurants around Springfield, but he hadn't heard of that one. "Where's The Burger Barn?" he asked.

"It's like a little place off of Route 22," Babe said. "Up past Norton."

That's why he hadn't heard of it. *Up past Norton* was code for "indoor plumbing optional."

"Okay," Zack said. "Walk us through the evening. You left work around five and went to The Burger Barn. When did you get there? Do you remember?"

Babe was now using a well-chewed pencil to make doodles in the margin of a piece of paper on the table in front of him. "Uh, I dunno. I guess it was about six. Maybe quarter of. I dunno. It's kinda hard to remember."

"Well, it's kinda important for you to try to remember, Babe," Terry said, wondering if the sudden sharp pain in his head meant that it was going to explode right off his neck, or that he was just going to have a stroke. "We're trying to establish whether you have an alibi for this crime."

Babe stopped doodling. Probably to concentrate extra hard. It didn't work. He returned to the doodling. He seemed completely befuddled.

Zack jumped in. "We want to know exactly where you were, and when, that night, so that we can figure out if it was even possible that you committed this crime."

Babe struggled with that one for a minute and then explained, "But I *didn't* commit this crime."

At least he was consistent.

"Right," Terry said. "We know that. But what we also want to know is what you *were* doing while you weren't committing this crime."

There was a moment of processing, and then new understanding washed over Babe's incredibly unappealing yet remarkably expressive face. Dawn breaks on a vacant building.

"I was home," he said.

"Great," Zack said. "When did you get home? Did you go home right from The Burger Barn?"

"I'm not sure," Babe answered. His eyes shifted away, and suddenly his body language proclaimed "I am not only the biggest liar in the world, but the worst one, too." How could he not be sure whether he went straight home? Was he confusing this night with the several other nights he was accused of armed robbery?

Terry put his pen down. At the rate this was going, they'd all die of old age before the trial even began. Would the local gun-shop owner waive the waiting period for buying a pistol if Terry promised to shoot himself before he left the store?

"Why don't we do this," Zack suggested. "Babe, you just tell us the story, as best as you can remember, of what you did that night. From when you left work until you got home and went to sleep. Try to tell us details, but it's okay if you don't remember everything. Just do your best. Whatever you recall."

Babe was back to doodling. Whether that was a sign of comprehension or a complete psychological collapse was anyone's guess.

Zack continued. "Meanwhile, Terry and I will do our best just to take notes and not interrupt you. Then, the next time we meet, if we have any questions, we'll ask you about them. How's that sound?"

The doodling continued. Babe had filled up all of the blank space on the top page of his stack and had moved on to the margins of what looked like a copy of a disciplinary report. Maybe he was writing his memoirs. *I Named Myself Babe*.

Babe finally set the scarred pencil down, and then he nodded to the table. "Okay," he said. "I think I can do that."

Terry took a deep breath, exhaled very slowly, and picked up his pen again. With any luck, they'd be done by his next birthday. He had plans to go out that night.

DETECTIVE VERA DEMOPOLOUS WATCHED WITH satisfaction as thirty feet down the sidewalk the small can of baked beans hit the escaping thief right between the shoulder blades. He yelped in pain, reaching awkwardly behind him as if to touch the spot that would later be marked by an ugly bruise, and then stumbled forward, tripping and falling to the ground. Vera was already sprinting toward him and shouting over her shoulder to Dotty to call 911.

At least she still had her aim.

It figured, though. Her first real police work since she'd moved to Massachusetts, and it was with a can of vegetables.

She had just finished her morning run—a little ahead of schedule, because the nightmare woke her up an hour early today—and was cooling down, walking to her neighborhood store for a quick cup of coffee before showering and heading in to the station. As she entered Bo's Big Grocery, which was neither big nor owned by anyone named Bo—go figure—a scruffy teenager was at the front counter, paying for a newspaper.

Five seconds later, the owner's sixty-eight-year-old mother, Dotty, was screaming and falling backward into a rack of magazines, the kid was tearing through the door with a handful of money that the family business could not afford to lose, and Vera was looking around for something about the size and weight of a softball.

Now, thanks to the baked beans, she was only a few steps behind the creep, and moving in fast. He had no wind, and was wheezing as he staggered ahead. Vera closed the remaining distance between them and tripped him from behind, taking care to land on the small of his back with her knee as he fell onto his face.

Her dad always told her that size was overrated. That was good, because this kid was over six feet tall, and Vera was about five-five on a good day. But with the wind knocked out of him, and now with his right arm twisted up behind his back, and the crescendoing wail of the cruiser's siren as it pulled up to the curb next to them, the kid wasn't going to give her any grief.

The uniforms jumped out of the black-and-white, cuffed the suspect, threw him into the back of the car, and then chased after Vera as she ran back to make sure that Dotty wasn't seriously hurt.

Any grief would come from Vera's own conscience, later, when she started coming down on herself about how she should have realized that no scruffy-looking teenager would be up at six-thirty in the morning, buying a newspaper.

Was she ever going to get her instincts back?

ENOUGH TIME HAD PASSED. HE HAD TO GET RID of the evidence. This was going to be the most important part of the whole mess. Elmo was going to have to be very, very careful if this thing was going to work itself out.

He was alone in his workshop. Well, to be fair, it wasn't really a workshop. It was actually a garage.

And if you were going to be picky, he wasn't really alone, either. Not if you counted the dead body in the trunk of the car in front of him.

He lit a cigarette, took a drag, blew out the match and threw it down on the floor.

It was good that his partner was in on this, because he needed the help—he'd fucked up bad. But that's what partners were for. They watched out for each other, and helped clean up each other's mistakes.

Luckily, Elmo didn't have anything planned for tomorrow, because this was probably going to take a while. If he rushed the job, or was sloppy, he'd make the situation worse. He had a couple of shovels, lots of extra plastic bags, duct tape, a few bottles of different kinds of cleaners, rubber gloves, rags, a cooler full of beer, and some of the other stuff, which he really shouldn't be using, but it was nice just knowing it was around if he needed it.

Like his partner said, the main thing was just to take his time and do the job right. Everything would work out. It had to.

He finished his cigarette, put the gloves on, put the cooler of beer in the front seat, threw the rest of the stuff into the trunk with the body, started the car, and drove off into the night.

TWO

Dear Sharon,

I just heard about Bernie from my mother, and I tried to call, but I can't get through. I'll keep trying until I do, but I just wanted you to know, in case you get this before I reach you, that I'm thinking about you and praying for both of you.

He's very strong. He's going to make it.

Love, Vera

April 20, 2004

"AND THEN I LEARNED THAT THE MINIMUM SEN-tence my son could receive is fifteen years in prison. I couldn't believe it."

Terry watched as Katerina Gardiner paused for a moment and slowly crossed her right leg over her left.

Damn.

If this were a movie, the woman sitting across from him would be a tall blond bombshell, wearing high heels and a skirt so short that watching her cross her legs would risk blindness. But in the real world, leggy blondes weren't frequent visitors to the law offices of Terry's longtime friend and partner in criminal law, Zack Wilson. And watching Mrs. Gardiner cross her legs risked nothing. Except maybe an onset of depression.

If you squinted a little, it was possible to imagine that Mrs. Gardiner, a lifetime or two ago, might not have been bad-looking. But twenty or thirty years of handling her son's crap and, well, it was pretty clear that worrying about how she looked had fallen off her things-to-do list.

How much longer was her story going to last? Her son got indicted for the armed robbery of a convenience store. The victim had ID'd him. What else was there?

Terry turned toward Zack. He sure didn't look like one of the best criminal defense lawyers in the state. As usual, Zack was sporting his I-look-like-I'm-on-vacation look. Linen shirt—sleeves rolled up, of course, probably just to piss Terry off—jeans, and boots.

But despite his stubborn refusal to look the part, Zack always seemed to be surrounded by this golden aura of professionalism. He walked into a courtroom, smiled like he couldn't believe how lucky he was just to be alive, and juries instantly fell in love with him. It was like some kind of genetic accident had left him with an overabundance of charm.

Unfortunately, Zack also had an overabundance of patience. Mrs. Gardiner had already been talking for more than twenty minutes. She was earnest, and obviously intelligent, but Zack had already agreed to take the case— what more was there to do here? A group hug?

But Zack just sat there, nodding and listening—a mountaintop temple of peace and reassurance. While Terry felt like a downtown firehouse fifteen seconds into the first alarm. *If an oversized, curly-haired, five-o'clock-shadowed, loud and impatient criminal lawyer could be a firehouse. Mrs. Gardiner, believe me—we will work our asses off for Babe. We will run down every lead, we will file all the motions, we will sing and dance for that jury until our voices are hoarse and our feet are blistered. But you should assume that your son is already pretty well fried. With his latest boneheaded felony, Rufus will be lucky to get just fifteen years. With the wrong judge, he could easily be looking at twenty or twenty-five.*

At least she hadn't claimed that Babe was innocent.

"And I know that you've probably heard this a thousand times before, but my son is innocent."

Oh well.

It was almost like the parents of these jerks felt it was their sacred duty to tell the world that regardless of what anyone—especially police officers, judges, and juries—said, their kid was just in the wrong place at the wrong time. Terry didn't have the heart to ask her if Babe was innocent of the crimes he had pleaded guilty to four years ago—breaking and entering a junkyard and stealing a car radio. Jesus Christ. That must have been an arrest for the ages.

This is the police. Put the cheap-as-shit-stereo-equipment-that-nobody-in-his-right-mind-would-ever-try-to-steal down, step away from the car, and place your hands on top of your head.

The guy even had a loser criminal history.

That was one of the reasons ol' Babe was looking at so much time. Massachusetts had recently enacted a three strikes and you're out rule—on your third felony conviction, you get fifteen years at a minimum, no matter what the crime. About five years ago, Rufus had been caught with enough marijuana to roll a small joint. Thanks to a genius lawyer, in exchange for a guarantee that he wouldn't spend any time in jail, Babe had pleaded guilty to a felony—possession with intent to distribute. Strike one.

Then, a year later, he made his little shopping trip into the junkyard, and suddenly, the count was oh and two.

Terry turned again toward Mrs. Gardiner. She looked tired around the eyes, like she hadn't slept much lately, but her gaze was clear and direct. And despite the strained circumstances, she was reasonable and pleasant, without coming off like she was kissing up to anyone. From the look and sound of her, it was hard to believe that Babe had gotten himself into trouble because of something she did or didn't do as a mother.

But holy shit. That washed-out, ankle-length dress really uglied up the whole room. And what was with those shoes? Did she actually spend money on them? "Rufus really is a good person," she confided, smiling somewhat sadly. "And he's my only son."

Thank God Terry didn't have any kids. He spent a lot of time with Zack and his six-year-old son and saw how tough it was to be a parent. And Justin was an awesome kid with a terrific attitude and a great sense of humor. What in the world would it be like to raise a mean little snot-nosed creep running around in dirty diapers for years, only to see him grow up to star in *My Big Fat Felony*?

"I brought something for you," Mrs. Gardiner continued, "that will prove he didn't do it." Terry looked over at Zack, who shrugged. He knew whatever dumb thing the defendant's mother was going to yank out of that oversized canvas bag she was digging through wasn't going to be worth diddly.

And what a bag it was. Lime green, about the size of a suitcase, and for no discernable reason, sporting the days of the week stenciled at odd angles and in several different bright colors and typefaces across its sides. Was it possible to get queasy looking at a canvas bag? The headache was a given.

After far too long, Mrs. Gardiner pulled out a videotape. "Here," she said, with a strange mix of grim satisfaction and uncertainty as she handed it to Zack. "It's going to take some work, but I believe this single piece of evidence will win the case."

Sure it would.

"What is this a tape of?" Zack asked.

"It's an exact copy of the videotape the police took from the security camera at the Nite & Day," she replied. "It proves that Babe didn't rob that store."

"HEY, DETECTIVE. NICE WORK THE OTHER morning."

Vera smiled and thanked the sergeant as he left the kitchen. It was amazing how quickly word had spread about how she'd initiated an arrest with a fastball to the middle of a bad guy's back.

Not that she minded. More people had talked to her in the past two days than in the two weeks since she'd started as a detective with the Springfield Police Department. If it took throwing a can of baked beans to break the ice around here, then so be it.

Now she filled her mug from the half-empty pot on the burner in the station kitchen. Cup number three, and it was only ten-thirty. Jeez, she was tired. If she didn't watch out, by the time she went home she'd have had an even dozen. Her doctor would not approve at all.

But she had to do what she had to do. She'd been awakened by the nightmare again, and had gotten a total of two hours of sleep.

Like all of her bad dreams, it started out innocently enough. She was back in Fairbanks, as a rookie uniformed cop. It was late spring, and the Alaskan air was crisp. The lines that the evergreen trees and puffy clouds made against the bright blue sky were sharp as she climbed into the passenger seat of the patrol car.

But unlike reality, the driver of her patrol car in the dream was Bernie Washman.

When Vera actually had been a rookie on the Fairbanks force, Bernie was a sergeant, and typically didn't patrol. He spent most of his time in the station house. But that didn't stop him from flying out of the squad whenever backup was called for. Bernie's was almost always the first additional cruiser on the scene, adding not just another body but an experienced officer into whatever potential jackpot was brewing.

In her dream, Bernie was stopped at a traffic light and in the middle of inviting Vera to dinner with his wife, Sharon, and their twin daughters, when all of a sudden there was a crack, and Bernie stopped talking abruptly. He turned to Vera with a quizzical look on his face and said, "Hey, tell Sharon—" just before he slumped forward, over the steering wheel, revealing a hideous bullet wound in the back of his neck.

Of course, that's not what had really happened.

"Hey, Vera, I left something for you on your desk."

Her new boss, Lieutenant Carasquillo, had joined her in the coffee room, and was opening the little refrigerator. He was one of the only cops Vera knew that didn't drink coffee. Instead, he had these energy shakes. They looked awful.

"Oh. Okay. Thanks, Lieu."

She had to stop daydreaming. It was bad enough to be plagued at night by what had happened. Bernie would be pissed if he knew it was bugging her on the job.

Vera returned to her desk and couldn't believe her eyes.

There, right next to the embarrassingly tall stack of ancient case folders that promised to occupy the next several days—if not weeks—of her life, was a file with a note attached to the front cover. *Vera—Here's a new one for you. Lt. C.* Yes. Finally a chance to get up off her rapidly expanding butt.

When Vera had first transferred into the squad, Lieutenant Carasquillo had assigned her to review some of the older open cases to help her "transition into the atmosphere" of her new job. While it was certainly far from the most glamorous police work, Vera had assumed that the lieutenant was simply biding his time before getting her into the normal routine of a detective.

But for two straight weeks at Springfield Police Headquarters, Vera had found herself saddled with just about every possible assignment that didn't involve catching real cases. Reviewing old files. Making phone calls on missing persons cases that were colder than a morgue. Serving as the department's representative on the citizen review board set up to monitor police misconduct.

Transitioning herself into the new atmosphere. Oh come on.

Sure—her arrival made her the only female detective in this squad, and at twenty-eight she might have been a little young to have the rank. But two weeks of desk duty? Please.

To be fair, it didn't seem like the other three detectives were overwhelmed with fieldwork right now. Willy Grasso had been around for decades, and although Lieutenant C. was technically responsible for assigning cases to the detectives, every one went to Grasso first. He'd look at the file, decide if he wanted it, and if not, drop it down to the next most senior member of the squad, Ole Pedersen, the man with ears almost as big as Uncle Monty's. Which was really saying something.

If Ole wasn't interested, or was too busy, the file went to the hero of the force, Detective John Morrison.

Morrison looked just too good to be true. Like some movie star had taken a wrong turn and ended up in an actual precinct instead of a Hollywood soundstage. Thick chestnut brown hair, deep blue eyes, dazzling smile, cleft chin, broad shoulders—he was the complete visual package.

And as if that weren't enough, according to Willy, three or four years ago Morrison had just about single-handedly broken up a nasty cocaine-distribution network that had been plaguing the city. He also had a reputation for carrying a very heavy caseload and knowing everything that was going on in the Springfield underground.

And since a case only went to Vera if everybody—including Detective Perfect—passed on it, that just about guaranteed that anything that made it to her desk would be deadly dull.

Vera opened the thin folder. It was another missing persons case, but unlike the dozens of others she had been wading through over the past two weeks, this one had been opened in the current century. There was actually a chance that she might be able to do something useful here.

She read the first few lines of the report. David Zwaggert. Age twenty-five. Reported missing by his parole officer on March 24. Vera felt a little excited. This case was going to give her some real detective work to do. She quickly turned the page and found his criminal history.

Zwaggert had been committing crimes from at least the age of thirteen, when he first got busted for joyriding. Since then, he had spent most of his time getting arrested and convicted of a string of low-level misdemeanors, gradually escalating in severity until he finally managed to get himself eight months in a county lockup for hitting somebody over the head with a beer bottle during a bar-room brawl.

But at nineteen, he'd gone pro. Armed robbery with another guy at a gas station in Springfield. That had gotten him his first state time. Five to ten years. He'd made parole on his second try, and had a decent job on an electronics delivery truck when, all of a sudden, he'd stopped coming to work. His employer had called his parole officer, who had unsuccessfully looked around for him, and gotten a warrant issued.

Vera tried to call the parole officer, but he wasn't in, so she left a message. Then she copied down Zwaggert's employment information onto the notepad she carried with her, shrugged on her jacket, and headed for the door.

Maybe if she could make some headway in this case, people around here would finally start treating her like a real cop.

April 23, 2004

ATTORNEY ZACK WILSON LED HIS PARTNER, Terry Tallach, into the living room, where they planned to view the videotape that Katerina Gardiner swore would prove her son was innocent.

"I'm really looking forward to seeing this," Terry told Zack as he sat on the couch. "Because as everyone knows, grand juries indict people all the time for armed robbery when the police have videotapes that show they are innocent."

Terry's attitude wasn't exactly a surprise. Ever since they'd met, back in high school, the question for Terry wasn't whether the glass was half empty. It was whether what was inside the glass would kill him or just make him sick.

Now, twenty years later, they were successful law partners, and Terry still looked at the world through doom-colored glasses.

Zack inserted the tape into the VCR.

"In fact, if that thing does what Mrs. Gardiner says it does," Terry said, "I will place it between two pieces of rye bread with lettuce and mustard, and I will eat it for lunch."

"Just make a copy before you do," Zack said, picking up the remote control and pressing the play button. "Here we go."

The television screen flashed once or twice, and then a remarkably grainy image of the inside of a convenience store appeared. The picture was about as bad as if it were being transmitted live from the surface of the moon. There was a time code running in the upper left corner of the recording. It read 11:44 P.M.

A few shelves of goods ran from the bottom of the picture to the top. The clerk's counter, on which sat the usual stuff, including a cash register and a lottery machine, was on the right side of the screen. Farther up the right side of the screen there was an open door, which looked like it might have led to a storage room of some kind. There were some freezer cases running across the top of the screen, although that, like just about everything else appearing on the low-tech video, was kind of hard to make out.

No one was in sight. It was as if the store was completely abandoned. And then a figure appeared at the bottom right of the picture. He was holding a newspaper. As he walked on the checkerboard-patterned tile floor toward the counter, he was looking to his right, so his back was to the camera. It looked like he was dressed all in black. Why in the world would a business use a surveillance system so bad you couldn't even tell what kind of clothes the bad guy was wearing?

"Is that a ski hat?"

"Yes," Terry replied. "Or he has hair."

The clerk came out from the storage room to handle the customer. Although he was facing the camera as he approached the register, his features were virtually indistinguishable. He was probably white. Beyond that, it was anybody's guess what he looked like.

The customer put the newspaper on the counter and, a second later, handed some money to the clerk. The pair seemed to engage in some discussion.

Then, all of a sudden, the guy ran around behind the counter, grabbed the clerk, and pushed him into the back room. The struggle took only a second, and a candy display case blocked the camera's view of the bad guy's face.

"When he comes out of the room, we'll get a nice, snowy, unfocused, useless look at him," Terry said. But when the robber emerged from the room a few seconds later carrying a bag, it wasn't even that good. He wasn't wearing a ski hat—he was wearing a ski *mask*. He was completely unrecognizable. Ski Mask went behind the counter, opened the register and grabbed the cash from the drawer, took some lottery tickets, stuffed it all in the bag, and then bolted out of the store. The time stamp read 11:47 P.M. And then the screen went blank.

Zack clicked off the television and sat back with a sigh. Terry looked over at him and said without the slightest emotion, "I would just like to say I am shocked and disappointed to learn that the videotape that was supposed to prove that our client was innocent is in fact totally useless to us."

Terry kept talking, but Zack's attention had been pulled away from his partner by a piece of paper on the coffee table by their feet. It was a drawing of two triangles and a circle that Justin had made the other day. Something about those triangles looked familiar.

Zack's son was closing in on the end of the kindergarten year, and so far, the little boy seemed to have three undeniable strengths: making friends, drawing geometric figures, and getting bloody noses. The first time Zack had gotten called by the school nurse, his heart started racing so fast he thought *he* might be the one headed for the emergency room.

After the second incident, they took a trip to the doctor, where they learned that the problem was nothing more than dry sinuses. It was on the way back from that doctor's visit that Zack realized Justin was going to be fine—it was he who was going to struggle to make it through elementary school.

Suddenly, Zack remembered why the triangles on Justin's drawing had gotten his attention. He stood up, turned the television on again, and then said to Terry, "So how much trigonometry do you remember?"

THREE

ASSISTANT DISTRICT ATTORNEY LOVELL: *When was the last time you saw the victim?*

DETECTIVE JOHN MORRISON: *The night of the robbery.*

Q: *You mean you didn't do a follow-up interview after that night?*

A: *That's correct.*

Q: *Why not?*

A: *Because I never saw him again.*

Q: *Well, do you recall the last conversation you had with him?*

A: *The only conversation I had with him.*

Q: *Yes.*

A: *Sure. I had already ascertained that he had suffered no physical injuries. I asked if he needed transportation anywhere, and he said that he had his car and that he was going to close the store and go home.*

Q: *So what did you do then?*

A: *I drove to Babe Gardiner's house to arrest him.*

Q: *You knew where he lived?*

A: Yes. We live in the same town. I pass his home on a regular basis.

Q: When you drove to Babe Gardiner's home, what happened?

A: He wasn't there. His car wasn't there, and no one answered the doorbell. I was very concerned, and I immediately drove to the station house and put out an APB for the defendant.

Q: Why were you very concerned?

A: Because the clerk told me that after Babe pushed him into the back room, Babe told him that if he squealed on him, he would kill him.

(*Commonwealth v. Gardiner*, Trial Volume IV, Pages 82–84)

Hostage

HER EAR WAS THROBBING. NO, THE WHOLE SIDE of her head was throbbing. Her shoulders ached. Her throat was raw. Her lips were burning. And something was on her mouth.

Where was she? Wow. What a headache. She opened her eyes, and all she saw was an unfamiliar floor. She was sitting in some chair, but she had no idea where.

Then the memory of a man's voice came into her head. *Well, happy freakin' birthday to you.* She couldn't remember who had said that. Or why.

She decided to pull off whatever was stuck on her mouth, but she couldn't move her hands. They were tied together, behind her, to the back of the chair. Her legs were tied, too, to the legs of the chair.

Fear gripped her. What had happened? Where was she? She tried to call out, but she was gagged. What was on her mouth? Some kind of tape? That's probably what her hands and feet were tied with. That's why her lips burned. The adhesive of the tape. Oh my God.

Her right temple was pounding. Panic flooded her. She looked from side to side. She could see no one else. How long had she been here? Where was she?

She fought the panic. *Panic only digs the hole deeper.* Someone had told her that once. She couldn't remember who. Her head hurt so bad she wondered if she was going to throw up. But her mouth was taped shut. *Please don't let me throw up.* She'd choke to death on her own vomit. Oh my God.

No panic. No panic. Calm down. Get organized. Get a plan. Figure out what she knew and what she didn't know, and make a plan.

Okay. Calm down. Breathe. What did she know?

She was bound and gagged in a room she didn't recognize. Her headache was severe, and the throbbing on the side of her head and face was probably from some kind of injury. And since she was bound and gagged, she must have been attacked. She didn't remember, though. She couldn't remember being hit in the head.

What else did she know? She was alive, she was alone, and she was scared. And what a headache. Forget the headache. Focus on something else. Okay—she was seriously thirsty. And she had to go to the bathroom.

She pulled again against whatever was tying her hands to the back of the chair. Her shoulders were sore, but that was because her arms were stretched back in an uncomfortable position. They were okay. Her hands felt cold— probably lack of circulation—but they weren't damaged. She could move her fingers. The tape, or rope, or whatever it was—was tightly wrapped around her wrists.

She tried to move her legs, and although they were tied to the legs of the chair, they didn't feel injured. She tipped her face forward and looked down—God, her head was killing her—she still had her clothes on. She probably hadn't been raped.

No harm in you looking for the good news, as long as the bad news was looking for you.

Who used to tell her that?

Happy freakin' birthday. And who had said that? Why was she remembering that?

She tipped her head back slowly and looked up. The low ceiling was made from acoustical tile. It was old—the once-white tiles were yellowing. There was a simple frosted-glass fixture attached to the middle of the ceiling, through which a single low-wattage bulb shone, casting the entire room in a dim gray light.

The walls in the room—the one to the left side of the chair, the one across the room to her right, which had some kind of old paneling on it, and the one directly in front of her with the cheap-looking glass sconce and a door that led to what might be a little bathroom—didn't look like anything special. They didn't have any windows. With the exception of the paneling, they were painted off-white.

There was an old couch with torn and stained upholstery against the wall. A tall, thin, ugly metal floor lamp stood beside it. Between her and the wall in front of her, a rickety-looking folding chair was pulled up under a fake wood card table, where somebody had left the remains of their lunch.

The room smelled musty. No. Make that nasty. Moldy, with some stale cigarette smoke and old beer thrown in. And some body odor. Frat house minus. Probably the basement of some home.

She looked past her right leg at the floor. Some kind of gross green-and-gray vinyl tile, with lots of litter. Cigarette butts, a brown-and-blue paper coffee cup that had been used as an ashtray, a beer can, three beer bottles, an old newspaper, a bag from a sandwich place.

Okay. So that's what she knew. Now, what didn't she know?

She had no idea where she was. She didn't know how she got here, but it sure looked like somebody hit her and brought her here, unconscious, and tied her to the chair. But she had no idea who would want to kidnap her.

And then a slow, unpleasant realization began to force its way slowly into her throbbing brain. What else didn't she know?

Everything.

Another wave of nausea passed through her, and again she fought the urge to throw up. There was something wrong with her mind. Something was blocking her memory. It was like a wall or a curtain was denying her access to the simplest things. Parts of her memory that she needed. She was really scared.

Because she couldn't remember *anything.* The day of the week. Where she lived. What she did for a living. Who her parents were. Whether she was married. Whether she had kids.

Oh my God.

Her name.

May 14, 2004
Approximately four months before the Babe Gardiner trial

THE BLOND LAWYER, ZACK, WAS DOING MOST OF the talking, which was good. Because the big one, Terry, looked like he got up on the wrong side of his cave, and was much more interested in his coffee than in this meeting. And Mrs. Gardiner, well, she just looked so—tired.

Maria Gallegos began to take notes on one of the purple legal pads that her boss, Anthony LoPresti, insisted on buying for the office. Maria looked up at him for a second. Like always, he was overdressed—a dark blue pin-striped suit, a white shirt, and a red silk tie, along with his gold watch, cuff links, and a pinky ring. He kept what little hair he had on his head cut very short, like his closely trimmed goatee and moustache. Anthony had to be the weirdest private investigator in the world. He looked more like an in-shape forty-year-old manager of some fancy restaurant.

"Terry and I met with Babe the other day," Zack said, "and it turns out that he doesn't remember too many of the specific details of his activities on the night of the robbery."

Terry blew out a quick, humorless laugh. "Yeah," he said. "Not too many."

"Anyway," Zack continued with a quick glance at his partner, "as far as we were able to piece together, at around five o'clock that night, Babe left Ibis Industries in Laurelton, where he works as a janitor. He drove from there to a restaurant called The Burger Barn, up past Norton, and arrived a little before six. He had dinner there, alone, and then things get a little fuzzy."

Maria looked down at the picture of Babe Gardiner that his mother had given to Anthony. Maria and her friends had a code regarding men. They described them in terms of food. A man with real husband potential would be a nice big chicken dinner. A player with a sharp ride who might be fun for a little while would be an ice cream sundae. And if he was really good-looking, he'd have sprinkles on top.

Babe looked more like last week's taco.

"Was he drinking?" Anthony asked.

"The safe money is riding on 'yes,'" Terry replied, clicking his pen repeatedly. "But 'oh yes' is also an excellent possibility." Now the big lawyer looked like a bear whose caffeine had just kicked in.

"I think it's fair to say that Babe had a little trouble be-ing, uh, forthcoming about what he did or didn't do from that point forward," Zack said. "But The Burger Barn does serve alcohol, Babe did have the following day off, and the arresting officer said he smelled alcohol on Babe's breath."

"And after we asked him about fifteen times, he told us that he *might* have had a small beer with dinner and that he *might* have gone to a bar after dinner." Terry clicked his pen a few more times. "But, of course, he didn't exactly remember the details. Except the one about the beer being a small one. After we talked for a while, he got pretty confident of that."

As Terry spoke, Mrs. Gardiner nodded but stayed silent. She did not look happy. If there was ever a woman who needed some good news, she was the one.

Anthony saw it too. "This case shouldn't be too much of a problem," he said. "We'll go up there, ask around. I'm sure somebody will remember seeing him."

Then Maria asked, "Mrs. Gardiner, you don't happen to know if Babe uses a credit card?"

Mrs. Gardiner looked over at her and then back to Anthony. "I, um..."

"Maria handles most of our administrative work, but she also supports me in field investigations from time to time," Anthony said. "She has my complete trust. Please feel free to share with her anything you would share with me."

Anthony may have been weird, but Maria loved it when he said that to new clients.

Mrs. Gardiner nodded and spoke directly to Maria. "I'm sorry—I know this is public information, but I still tend to be a little overprotective of Rufus. He's made some bad decisions, but his heart is almost always in the right place. I've had some medical problems, and he's always..." She took a shaky breath and let it out. "I'm sorry. This is just... hard."

"I understand," Anthony said.

Mrs. Gardiner took another breath and began again. "After he pleaded guilty the last time, Rufus had some problems with credit card companies and ended up filing for bankruptcy. He doesn't use credit cards anymore, at least to my knowledge."

"Babe was in jail?"

"No, he got a suspended sentence and a three-year term of probation."

"And when was this?" Anthony asked.

"About four or five years ago," Mrs. Gardiner replied. "And the bankruptcy was about a few months after that. Around Christmas."

"I see," Anthony said. "Is there anything else we should know?"

Zack looked down at some notes. "Just one more thing..."

AS DETECTIVE VERA DEMOPOLOUS STARTED TO take on more cases, her search for fugitive parole violator David Zwaggert slowed down considerably.

Her visit to Zwaggert's employer had generated only a weak lead—apparently Zwaggert had talked to one of his coworkers about spending a lot of time in the past at a bar named Froggy's. And as Vera had expected, David Zwaggert's name and picture had not generated a great deal of enthusiastic recognition among the people who were hanging out in Froggy's when she had arrived. So she took the name and number of the owner of the place, gave her card to the only waitress on duty, and sat down to eat.

The good news was that Froggy's had a dinner menu.

The bad news was that the only two things on the menu that weren't fried were beer and ketchup.

If she hadn't been so hungry, she would have waited to get a bite to eat on the return trip, but there wasn't anywhere to stop on the way home for thirty miles, so she decided to roll the dice and try a burger and a Diet Coke.

And when the waitress brought Vera's meal to the table, it didn't look as bad as it could have. The pickle was a little small, but hey. Maybe she'd get lucky with the rest of her dinner. She took a bite of the burger.

Maybe not. But food was food. As Vera washed the questionable mouthful down with some soda, the waitress came back over. "When did you say that guy might have been in here?"

Vera swallowed, and then checked her notepad. "March nineteenth. We think if he came here, it was probably that night."

The waitress nodded. "Okay. That was Friday, right? It gets kind of busy here Friday nights, so Irene would have been working with me then, too. Maybe she'll be able to help you. She's been working here for years." She handed Vera a slip of paper. "I wrote her number down for you, in case you needed it."

Vera thanked the waitress, wiped her hands, took out her cell phone, and dialed the number.

A minute later, she was speaking to Irene Quarrels.

Who knew Davy Zwaggert real well, and had seen him about a month or so ago. Yes, it could have been on the nineteenth.

But before Vera even had a chance to put her cell phone away, it rang again.

Suddenly, she had another case. Detective Morrison had been accused of assault.

FOUR

THE COURT: *All right, Mr. Tippett. I understand that you've talked to your attorney and want to change your plea to guilty.*

THE DEFENDANT: *That's right.*

THE COURT: *Fine. I will accept your plea after the prosecutor reads the facts into the record. Mr. Prosecutor.*

ASSISTANT DISTRICT ATTORNEY JONES: *The facts of this case are quite simple, Your Honor. On February 7, police officers responded to a report of shots fired near Clark's Corner in Springfield, a neighborhood they knew to be a high-drug neighborhood. At that time they proceeded to 50 Eagle Terrace.*

Upon arrival—

THE COURT: *I'm sorry. Was that Eagle Terrace?*

MR. JONES: *Yes, Your Honor.*

THE COURT: *Thank you. I'm sorry. Go ahead.*

MR. JONES: *Upon arrival, the officers executed a search of the premises, and in a closet discovered seventeen and one quarter kilograms—that's a little over thirty-eight pounds—of a powdery white substance, which was later determined to be ninety percent pure cocaine. They then arrested the defendant.*

THE COURT: *Is that correct, Mr. Tippett?*

THE DEFENDANT: *Yeah.*

THE COURT: *Fine. The court accepts the defendant's plea of guilty and will now hear the Commonwealth on sentencing...*

(*Commonwealth v. Warren Tippett*, Plea Hearing, July 18, 2003, Pages 14–15)

June 2, 2004

"MR. LOVELL? CAN THE COMMONWEALTH LIVE with the defendant's suggestion? Straight possession, eighteen months in the house of corrections?"

Assistant District Attorney Louis Lovell liked to think of himself as an ethical man. And so Judge Park's question—no, this entire conference with the defendant's attorney in the judge's chambers—was driving him crazy.

If he accepted Warren Tippett's offer to plead guilty, Louis would ring up another conviction for the office, which his boss would really love.

And an eighteen-month sentence was appropriate for the typical drug-possession case.

But in Warren Tippett's case, the sentence was far too lenient. It was simply wrong.

And the whole reason Louis had decided to work as an assistant district attorney was because he wanted to do what was right.

The entire case was like a nightmare. A terrible criminal—the man distributed untold pounds of cocaine to a city already overwhelmed with poverty and despair. A terrible job of police work—and an overintrusive search which was very likely to have been unconstitutional. And thanks to an inexperienced prosecutor and a burned-out judge—

both of whom had moved on to other careers, thank God—a terrible and now somewhat infamous guilty plea.

Before Tippett's case had become news, the rule in Massachusetts was that if you wanted to plead guilty to a crime, you had to follow certain procedures at a public hearing. The Massachusetts procedures were stricter than those of many other states, and so Massachusetts plea hearings took a little longer than normal. But that was okay. In some places, guilty plea hearings were nothing more than a few routine yes-or-no questions and answers asked and answered by a judge and a defendant who were obviously just going through the motions. Louis had personally seen at least three such hearings in other states where he was sure that the defendant had no idea what was going on, except that he was going to jail without a trial.

And that made no sense. Nobody wanted people to plead guilty without understanding their actions. And the Massachusetts rules actually made it harder for a defendant if he later attempted to withdraw his guilty plea—and it was amazing how many tried—because he'd get nowhere unless he could show that the appropriate procedures weren't followed. If the guilty plea hearing went as it was supposed to, the record of the hearing—the actual words said at the time, transcribed by the court reporter—would conclusively establish that the defendant fully understood and accepted his decision to plead guilty. And the record of the hearing was critical, because it was the only thing that all parties officially agreed to. Police reports, conversations out of court, plea negotiations—none of those things mattered.

But the judge and the prosecutor in Tippett's case had bungled everything. They might have been distracted, or maybe it all seemed so obvious to them as a result of the negotiations that took place in order to arrive at the plea bargain, but for whatever reason, the record of the hearing on Tippett's plea was a joke.

For one thing, in order for the guilty plea to be constitutionally acceptable, the record had to establish that the defendant committed a crime.

In Tippett's case, it wasn't even close.

The prosecutor never bothered to mention that the cocaine the officers had seized was owned by Tippett. He didn't even manage to explain that the address where the cocaine was found was where Tippett lived. If you read the record of Tippett's guilty plea hearing carefully, you'd see that all the defendant admitted to was that the police came to an address that apparently had no connection to Tippett, grabbed some cocaine, and then arrested him.

In the eyes of the Constitution, you couldn't plead guilty to the crime of possession of drugs when the Commonwealth didn't even allege that you possessed drugs.

So when Tippett challenged his guilty plea, despite the fact that everybody in the world believed that he was actually guilty—the courts were forced to allow him to withdraw the plea and grant him a trial.

The media had a field day. Louis's boss, Francis "F.X." O'Neill, the state's most blatantly politically motivated district attorney—which was saying something—spent about a week in an apoplectic rage, waving around a newspaper with the banner headline: "Confessed Drug Dealer Gets New Trial on Technicality."

Worse still, the appeals court was so embarrassed by how thoroughly the judge in Tippett's case had messed everything up that they swung the pendulum way over in the other direction. They decided that for any future guilty pleas, Massachusetts would require only a few, very simple, very general questions to be asked and answered at every guilty plea hearing. If the answer to all of the questions was yes, the defendant's guilty plea was assumed to be "knowing and voluntary."

Regardless of whether the defendant was a Rhodes scholar or a hapless dolt.

Add to that F. X. O'Neill's and the local police department's shared philosophy on conservation of prosecutorial and police resources—a guilty defendant closed a case forever—and the chances of a guilty plea perverting the justice system were getting bigger by the second.

And so now here they were. Tippett had successfully withdrawn his guilty plea and had been awarded a new trial. His new lawyer properly recognized that the Commonwealth's case against him rested on some very shaky evidence. So she telephoned Louis and gave him two options. He could accept a new plea bargain where Tippett would admit that he only possessed a fraction of the pounds and pounds of cocaine the police had found in his apartment. That would result in a conviction, but a much shorter prison term than Tippett's original one, which would mean he'd be back on the street in merely a few months.

Or Louis could reject the new deal and actually try the case. The problem with that was there was a real chance that all the charges against Tippett would get thrown out, because the cops probably violated his constitutional rights when they rushed into his apartment and broke into locked containers in a closed closet where the cocaine was hidden.

The judge cleared his throat. "Mr. Lovell? What is the Commonwealth's response?"

MARIA CHECKED HERSELF IN THE MIRROR. SHE did not look good.

Anthony had sent her home early with three crisp one-hundred-dollar bills and instructions to stop at the mall, where she was to get some casual clothes from Banana Republic, wash them so they didn't look brand-new, and wear them tonight. They were going to do fieldwork, and she was to be his preppie girlfriend. What a trip.

Now, four and a half hours later, she stood there with her hair pulled back in a straight, lame ponytail, wearing a pink-and-white-striped oxford button-down shirt open only at the collar, khaki pants, and boat shoes.

God hadn't given her much of a shape to start with. Other women with this body might look slender and sleek, but Maria managed only to look sexless. And this outfit made things worse. She put a small, plain gold stud in each ear and a thin gold chain around her neck.

And as Anthony had requested, she wore no makeup.

If there was an award for dullest look of the year, she'd need an acceptance speech.

She left her bedroom and found her ten-year-old brother, Felix, alone at the kitchen table, doing his homework. The apartment was small, so she spoke quietly. "Is Mommy asleep already?"

Felix looked up from the worksheet he was filling in. "She started to watch television, but then she felt bad again so she went to bed." He filled in another blank on the page and couldn't keep from smiling. "She said to have fun on your date."

The doorbell rang. It was seven-thirty. Anthony was right on time. "It's work, not a date," Maria said as she used the intercom to tell Anthony she'd be right down. "Do I look like I'm going out on a date?" Felix did not answer. "You know I don't." She fished her keys out of her purse. "I'll be home late. No TV until your homework is finished, and—"

"And bedtime is nine-thirty. I know," Felix said with a

heavy, calculated sigh as he laid his head down on the table.

"If you or Mommy need anything, I've got my cell phone with me," she said, picking up the ugly blue sweater that completed her outfit and opening the door. "Be good."

Maria turned the key in the lock behind her and headed down the stairs of the two-family house.

Things had really changed fast since the three of them had moved into this apartment last year. They had been so optimistic when they finally found a way to get out of their old place. Their new home was a little small—Felix had to sleep in the living room—but it was in a decent neighborhood, and Felix's school was good. The problem was that Mommy just kept getting worse and worse. It had been weeks since she'd been able to go to work, and Maria's salary just barely covered the rent, utilities, and food. Forget about anything else. Felix was already growing out of his clothes, but they couldn't afford new ones. And if anything unexpected came up, they were going to be in real trouble.

Anthony stood waiting for her in the little entryway at the bottom of the stairs. It was amazing, but he looked even worse than she did. He was wearing a dark blue polo shirt tucked into bright green shorts, and loafers with no socks. His calves looked stronger than Maria would have guessed. The rest of him looked like a complete dork.

"Good job shopping," he remarked as they left the building and walked toward the—what was that thing, a Volvo?—parked out front. "Did you remember to get something to eat?"

"I had a sandwich at the mall. Which reminds me." She took an envelope out of her purse and handed it to him. "Here are the receipts and the change. I was able to get most of this stuff on sale. The whole outfit, including the shoes, cost less than two hundred." She got in the rented car and closed the door. Leather interior. Not bad.

Anthony climbed into the driver's seat, started the car, and handed the envelope back to her. "When we do overtime fieldwork, you get additional compensation. You can start by keeping this. We'll figure everything else out later."

He would never have any idea how welcome that extra money would be. "Thanks," Maria said, returning the envelope to her purse. "But don't you need the receipts? You know. To show the client for reimbursement?"

"We're on this one for free," Anthony explained as he turned down Main Street and headed for Route 2.

And just like that, Maria's good feeling about the extra money vanished. She wanted to reach over and just smack her boss on his stupid bald head.

Maria had been working for Anthony for six months. In that time, they had taken on about ten cases. In at least three of them, Anthony didn't charge the client anything. *Anything.* And many of the others were such small jobs— one day of surveillance, research into a scary boyfriend's past, that kind of thing—that they hardly paid more than a few hundred dollars. A thousand at the most.

In fact, the only job that was really a good one was the Upton case, which was the one Anthony was working on when he hired Maria. He was gone for weeks at a time doing a lot of sophisticated surveillance. The client was a big corporation, and they paid every invoice on time, with a nice, big check and no complaints.

But the Upton job was finished, and since then, Anthony had been spending much more money than he had been taking in. If this kept up, he wouldn't be able to stay in business. And Maria would be on the street again, with little or no chance of finding a job good enough to pay her family's bills.

She'd really been encouraged when Anthony took the Gardiner case, because it was clearly going to be more than just a quick phone call or two. Anthony had already gone to The Burger Barn to try to find someone who'd seen Babe Gardiner on the night of the robbery, but he'd struck out. So he decided to talk to the store clerk who had been robbed.

But when Anthony checked with the owner of the convenience store, he learned that the clerk—his name was Steve Hirsch—had stopped showing up to work. The owner actually suspected that Hirsch might have been in on the robbery. So Anthony thought it would be best to go looking for him undercover.

Maria had done some asking around, and learned that Hirsch liked to go drinking at this place called Yellow Belly's. She did a little more research, got hold of a copy of his high school yearbook, and Anthony decided that he and Maria would head for Yellow Belly's and try to get in touch with Cousin Steve about their impending wedding.

But now that Maria knew that all this work was just more and more charity, suddenly the case seemed a lot less desirable. Being nice was one thing, but going broke was just plain stupid. She was going to have to take care of this problem, but carefully. If she came off too pushy or bossy, Anthony would probably fire her. But if she didn't do something soon, it wouldn't matter.

After what seemed like a reasonable time had passed, she said, "Can I ask you a question?"

"Sure."

She hoped she could strike just the right tone—curious, yet respectful. "Have you ever thought about doing work for insurance companies?"

Anthony smiled. "That's funny. I was sure you were going to ask why I told you to get something to eat before we went out to dinner."

"I just figured if we weren't hungry, we wouldn't run up such a big bill at the restaurant," she responded. Mommy had taught her that trick years ago.

Anthony laughed. "That's not it. You can order as much as you want. I'm just not sure that you're going to want to eat a lot there. From what I've heard..."

"It's a dump?" Maria suggested.

Anthony exited onto a smaller road. "Well, dump-like, anyway. Let's just say that I don't expect to discover great cuisine here." He pulled into a parking lot across the street from a dark building with an old, painted sign that read *Yellow Belly's—Eating, Drinking, and Everything in Between.*

For a place out in the middle of nowhere, Yellow Belly's had a surprising number of cars in the lot. Anthony pulled into one of the few open spaces, and they got out and started to walk toward the restaurant.

Before they made it out of the lot, though, a group of four or five guys ran across the street toward them. All were obviously coming from the restaurant, pretty loud and real drunk.

The momentum of one pair propelled them toward Maria, and she backed up against one of the parked cars, but not quite far enough to avoid contact. It was nothing, but the one who had bumped into her, a skinny kid who was wearing a very ugly pink-and-green shirt, started to make a big deal out of it. "I'm really sorry," he said, regaining his balance by reaching out and grabbing on to the car with his right hand. His buddy, a big, tough-looking kid with really pale blond hair, immediately appeared on his left, directly in front of her, effectively blocking her path.

"It's fine. Excuse me," she said, trying to step around the blond one. But he grabbed her arm and pushed her back against the car, holding her there, saying, "Whoa, cutie. What's your hurry? My friend here just apologized."

Then ugly-shirt guy started to giggle and said, "Yeah, cutie, how 'bout a little kiss," as he stepped even closer to her. But before Maria even had a chance to react, the blond guy suddenly flew backward and landed on his ass in the dirt. And then there was Anthony, spinning the other one around and throwing him on top of blondie, like that was the part of the parking lot where you were supposed to pile up the drunken fools. "What the fuck?" the blond one sputtered, trying to push ugly-shirt guy off of him.

In two strides, Anthony was next to her. "Are you okay, Maria?"

She barely had a chance to say "I'm fine" before the two idiots had scrambled to their feet. Anthony turned to face them. Their three friends were standing near a car on the other side of the lot, watching. They were either smart, or chicken. Maybe both.

Blondie sneered, "What's your problem, dude?" and then stepped toward Anthony, pulling back his right fist. He was taller and heavier than Anthony, and he had murder in his eyes. Almost faster than Maria could see, Anthony shot a left jab at the kid, hitting him square in the nose and stopping his advance cold. "Ow. Fuck!" he yowled, grabbing his bloody face and staggering away. "Motherfucker!"

"You asshole!" the other one shouted, running at Anthony as if he intended to jump on top of him. But Anthony merely hunched down a little, stepped quickly to the side, and before the jerk could change direction, hit him square in the middle of his ugly shirt with one strong punch. The kid grunted, grabbed himself around the waist, took a step back, and vomited all over the place.

Maria had already pulled out the little bottle of

pepper spray she carried in her purse, but she obviously didn't need to use it. She stepped around the mess and walked with Anthony across the street to the restaurant. As he looked over his shoulder at the two beat-up drunks climbing into their friends' car and driving away, he said, "When you write up the report for our activities tonight, you have my permission to say that we made a big entrance."

FIVE

ASSISTANT DISTRICT ATTORNEY LOVELL: When you spoke to the Nite & Day clerk who had been robbed, Detective Morrison, did he give anything to you?

DETECTIVE JOHN MORRISON: Yes. He took the security videotape that had been recording when the robbery took place, and gave it to me.

Q: And I am showing you now a videotape that has been marked D for identification. Do you recognize this tape?

A: Yes. This is the videotape that the clerk gave me that night.

ASSISTANT DISTRICT ATTORNEY LOVELL: At this time I'd like to offer this as an exhibit, Your Honor.

THE COURT: Any objection?

ATTORNEY WILSON: Yes, Your Honor. There's been no showing of a chain of custody.

THE COURT: Mr. Lovell?

ASSISTANT DISTRICT ATTORNEY LOVELL: When you were handed the videotape, Detective, what did you do with it?

DETECTIVE MORRISON: I brought it to the station house, made a copy, and placed a sticker on the original

*with an identifying number. I then wrote the number and
the description of the item on the evidence log we keep at
the station. And then I locked the videotape in the area of
our building where we keep evidence collected from crime
scenes. I retrieved it from the locked area this morning.*

ASSISTANT DISTRICT ATTORNEY LOVELL: *Your
Honor?*

THE COURT: *The tape is admitted as Exhibit 5.*

(*Commonwealth v. Gardiner*, Trial Volume IV, Pages 112–113)

Hostage

SHE OPENED HER EYES AND REALIZED THAT SHE
had fallen asleep again. Or lost consciousness. Whatever.
God, did her head hurt. And she really needed to pee.

She blinked repeatedly, but things stayed out of focus
longer than usual. Her right eye felt funny. She took turns
looking out of one eye, then the other. The right one was
definitely having a problem. It was probably swollen.
Somebody must have really hit her hard.

Wait. There was a man. A big guy, with a mask. He
had come into the room after she awoke the first time.
When he saw her look at him, he left the room, came back
in with a cloth in his hand, and stuck it over her nose.
That's it. She'd been drugged.

Okay. That didn't explain how she'd gotten here in the
first place, but at least she remembered how she could
have fallen asleep after she became aware that she'd been
kidnapped.

Kidnapped. Her stomach fluttered at the thought and
she involuntarily took in a sharp breath through her nose.
How had this happened to her? How was she going to get
out of here alive?

She forced her mind back to the masked man. What was nagging at the back of her mind about when he last came into the room. He had entered from a door behind her. When he opened it, she could hear a voice. Not like the voice of somebody in the room he had come from. It was more like the sound of a radio. No. It was a television.

But that wasn't what was tugging at her memory. It was something about the man with the mask himself. She tried to visualize him. He was a pretty big guy, wearing a ski mask, jeans, boots, and a sweatshirt. He smelled like he'd been drinking. What was it that she was trying to remember? Did she recognize him? Wait—it was something about the mask.

Okay. Think. The mask. It was a pullover ski mask, with holes cut out for the eyes and mouth. It was black. Knit. Probably some kind of blended fabric. What difference did any of that make?

Brain boomerangs. Those little parts of your memory that suddenly sail off into space, and then, just as suddenly, fly back to you out of nowhere. That's what this mask thing was. A brain boomerang. It would come back to her.

But, Grandma, who throws brain boomerangs?

That's one of the fun mysteries you get to have when you're alive.

Well, at least she remembered that she had a grandmother. That was something.

There was something about that mask that made her feel—what? Safe? That was crazy. She had been kidnapped, and her masked captor gave her a feeling of security? Maybe she was losing her mind. What does it feel like when you lose your mind? Do you know you're losing it? Or does it just sort of drift off...?

What was she doing, daydreaming? She was awake,

she was alive, some nut with a ski mask was holding her hostage. She had to get out of here.

She looked around the room again. There had to be something here she could use to get herself free.

Garbage on the floor at her feet. The other chair, set in front of the table. The clutter on the table—beer cans and bottles, a pizza box, a coffee cup, a bag from a sandwich place, and something small and red. It looked like the end of a piece of plastic, and it looked very familiar.

The sandwich bag was in the way, and she couldn't get a good look. She leaned over a bit to the left—God, her head was killing her—to get a better view. Now she could see that the piece of plastic was actually three or four inches long. There seemed to something coming out of one end....

Oh my God. Could it really be? Despite the ferocious headache, she craned her neck around even farther to the left to be totally sure.

And there, with its shiny red handle and its bottle-opener tool extended, was the most beautiful sight she could have hoped for.

A Swiss Army knife.

June 3, 2004

ZACK WATCHED AS TERRY WALKED INTO THE office, dropped a notepad onto the table that Zack had pulled in front of the television, and said, "I'm pretty sure that right now, Perry Mason is laughing his ass off at me."

Zack turned on the VCR and paused the videotape of the robbery to the point where the robber's body, head to toe, was in the screen. He had arranged on the table some graph paper, a ruler, a couple of pencils, a calculator, and a trigonometry textbook.

"And the convenience store clerk—who was h-h-h-hot, by the way—was not giving me a lot of love as I wandered all over her store with a step stool and a tape measure."

"Perry Mason is fictional, so I wouldn't worry too much about him," Zack said. "And what you were doing was collecting data for a very important trigonometry exercise, so I'm sure that one day, the h-h-h-hot convenience store clerk will understand." He sat down, opened the textbook to the tables at the back, and looked up at Terry. "If I remember what Mrs. Greer taught us." He took a look at Terry's notes. "This is how far up the wall the camera was?" he asked.

Terry joined him at the table. "Nine feet, three inches," he said, "which was a pain in the balls to measure, by the way, even with the step stool. And the other two numbers are from that wall to where the guy was standing, and then from the wall to the other place you mentioned. Although why that makes a difference remains a great mystery."

"Here," Zack said, drawing a rough sketch on one of the pads. "I hope I'm doing this right." He drew a right angle. "Imagine that the vertical leg of this angle is the wall of the store, and the horizontal leg is the floor."

"Gotcha, Einstein," said Terry.

"Okay. You measured that the camera was nine feet, three inches high. That's"—he multiplied nine times twelve on the calculator and then added three—"one hundred eleven inches." He wrote 111 next to the vertical leg of the triangle.

"Now look on the videotape and imagine a straight line coming out of the camera, just grazing the top of the robber's head, and continuing on down to the floor. See where it would end?"

Terry looked at the television screen. "Just where you asked me to measure," he replied.

"Right. And you said that was"—he checked Terry's notes—"eighteen feet, eight inches from the wall." He used the calculator again. "Two hundred twenty-four inches." He wrote 224 under the horizontal leg of the right angle. Then, about halfway along the horizontal line, he drew a crude vertical stick figure.

"That's the robber?" asked Terry. He looked over at Zack. "Whoa. You suck at drawing."

"I know," Zack said. "Shut up. It doesn't matter. It's just a sketch." Then he drew a straight line from the top of the vertical line to the end of the horizontal line, grazing the top of the stick figure, making a large triangle.

Terry pulled the paper over in front of him. "And now you're going to do something with this sketch which is going to prove something."

"Exactly," said Zack, filling in the last figure on the sketch from Terry's notes—the distance from the wall to where the robber was standing. "Since the wall and the robber are both vertical, these two lines are parallel, which means that these two angles are equal—"

"You know what?" Terry interrupted, getting up. "Mrs. Greer was scary enough. You just do whatever it is you're going to do. When you're done, let me know if Babe's the robber, or whether he was only lying about everything else. Meanwhile, I'm going out to get us something to eat." He headed off, probably to the deli.

Zack flipped back to the chapter he'd read earlier that day. If his sketch was correct, all he had to do was plug the numbers Terry had gotten into some formulas, check the tables at the back of the book, and he should be able to figure out the robber's height. According to Babe's booking sheet, he was just a little bit over six feet tall. If the robber turned out to be significantly taller or shorter than that,

Zack and Terry would have a powerful piece of evidence to use at the trial.

Zack started up the videotape again. It was hard to judge, but as the robber moved around the store, especially as he stood at the counter before he pulled the clerk into the back room, he didn't seem tall at all. In fact, as he grabbed the clerk, he looked like he might even have been an inch or two shorter than him.

When they got a chance to speak to the clerk, that would be another way they could check whether Babe was the robber.

Zack turned off the television and started doing math. In a few minutes, this case might be over.

WHEN TERRY RETURNED TO THE OFFICE WITH sandwiches and beer, Zack was leaning back in his chair, staring vacantly at the ceiling. The table he had been working on was littered with papers on which he had made dozens of sketches of triangles, most with several multiplication and division problems squeezed into the margins, several of them crossed out. Two pieces of graph paper had fairly accurate, at least for Zack, drawings of the inside of the convenience store, complete with a rough representation of a camera mounted on a wall.

Terry sat down across from Zack, pushed aside enough of the papers to put down the bag he was carrying, and said, "You ready for this?"

Zack blinked a couple of times, smiled his I-must-not-be-as-smart-as-everybody-thinks-I-am smile, and started gathering up the papers. "I am really ready for that."

Terry started opening up the bag. "How'd the big math problem turn out?"

"Well," Zack responded, "as I was doing the calculations the first time, I was feeling pretty confident that the height of the robber was going to come out significantly shorter than six feet." He sifted through his work, pulled out a piece of graph paper, and looked at it for a second. "And it turns out, I was right. According to my initial calculations, the height of the robber was exactly two feet four inches."

Terry took a couple of beers out of the bag and gave one to Zack. "So you figured maybe you made a mistake, and you did it again."

"Right," said Zack, taking a swig. "And sure enough, I got a different answer. Two feet *three* inches tall."

Terry nodded, then reached into the bag for the sandwiches. Zaney's Deli made the best chicken salad, ever. He passed one to Zack—no tomatoes—and said, "So you did the calculations again."

"Yes I did," Zack said, opening his sandwich. "And you know what? I was right the first time."

Terry took a bite of his sandwich and washed it down with some beer. "Leading to the conclusion that this convenience store is located in the merry old land of Oz?"

"Or maybe we aren't going to win this case with trigonometry," Zack said.

IF IT HADN'T BEEN SO LATE, VERA WOULD HAVE had less trouble keeping her mind off the accusation against John Morrison. This kind of thing was predictable—sometimes suspects resisted arrest, and then got indignant when they got hurt as the police took them into custody. And sometimes cops lost it, and went overboard after securing a suspect. But a cop like Morrison didn't get the reputation he had from beating up perps in handcuffs.

But Vera had to return her focus to her missing fugitive case. Irene Quarrels was only too happy to talk to Vera about Davy Zwaggert. So the Morrison thing was going to have to wait.

"I think he is such a sweetie," the large young woman said, letting Vera into her cluttered, airless first-floor apartment. "He was always really nice to me. Like a real gentleman." Irene had a pleasant, roundish face, with pretty blue eyes and thick, wavy black hair. There was something about her that had a kind of Oprah Winfrey quality—if Oprah had been poor and white, and wore dark purple sweat suits and bright yellow socks with cats on them. "I was hoping—this is silly, I know"—she took a big breath—"but I was thinking that he might have been getting ready to maybe ask me out on a date or something. Before he stopped coming to Froggy's, I mean."

An overflowing laundry basket had been dropped in front of a tired-looking green couch on which sat a pile of folded shirts and a tabloid open to a story about a twenty-year-old movie star's divorce settlement. On the television, a young man in a tuxedo sang in a horrible voice. Irene used a remote control to mute the TV as they both sat down. "I really hope he's okay."

A big, hairy white cat that had been sleeping on the floor stood up, rubbed itself against Vera's leg, and then jumped onto the couch and curled up in Irene's lap. "This is Cleo," she said in a baby voice, as she stroked the cat and kissed it on the top of the head. "She hopes Davy's okay, too. Don't you? Yes you do. I know you do. You hope he's okey-smokey. You do." Cleo's response was to take a bored swipe at her owner with her claw. Irene just chuckled and kept mumbling baby talk. Something about scratchy-watchy Mommy's face.

The young woman was clearly a nice person, but wow. Did she have any idea how ridiculous she sounded talking to the cat like that? Vera tried to keep her face neutral. There was a lot going on here. Irene obviously cared about Davy, and it didn't make any sense to upset her, even though the odds that Davy was okey-smokey were dropping with every passing moment. Vera had to be honest, but Irene was the kind of person who would respond to sunshine and daffodils much more quickly than to a thunderstorm. "It could be nothing," Vera said carefully, "but since Davy is on parole, it's very important that we find him as soon as possible. For his sake."

Irene nodded solemnly. "I know. That's all Davy needs—for the police to think he's running away."

Well, whether Davy needed it or not, that's exactly what the police were thinking. Or that he was badly hurt. Or dead. "Exactly. So we're talking to the people who knew him, you know, to see if we can figure this thing out quickly."

Irene sighed. "I wish I could help you. Davy is such a good person inside. Do you know that one time he gave me a twenty and told me to keep the change on a twelve-dollar check?" Poor Irene's crush on Davy was so obvious, Vera felt like she should slide over on the couch to make extra room for it.

"When's the last time you saw him?"

"Not since that Friday night at Froggy's. He came in for dinner, like he usually does—"

"He's a regular?" If Davy really was a recovering alcoholic, going to a bar often enough for a waitress to know you by name was kind of dumb.

"Not really regular regular, if you know what I mean," Irene responded with a smile. Cleo began to lick her paw. "I mean, he'd come in usually once or twice during the week, just for a burger and fries, stuff like that."

"Okay." The young man on the muted television had been replaced by a twelve-year-old girl wearing a low-cut evening gown that managed to make her look both trashy and pathetic. She was singing into a microphone as if she'd been doing it professionally since she was three. "So that night at Froggy's, was Davy alone?"

"Yeah," Irene said. "A lot of times he came in with a friend or two for dinner, but this time he just got a small table by himself."

Vera started to reach for her pad and pen, but at the last minute merely shifted her weight on the couch so she was facing Irene more directly. She didn't want to interrupt the flow. If the waitress could remember something significant about these other guys, Vera would have time to write it down later. "Would you recognize Davy's friends if you saw them again?"

Irene thought for a minute. "I think so. But I'm not sure." She blushed a little. "I'm afraid I was paying more attention to Davy." She sighed and shook her head. "I'm so sorry. I'm not helping at all, am I?"

"You're helping much more than anyone else I've spoken to," Vera said. Technically, that was true. In fact, technically, Irene was helping quite a bit. It was just that she was at the beginning of her helping. The trick was to keep it going so that the helping actually produced something.

Cleo jumped down and stalked out of the room. Almost immediately an orange striped cat appeared out of nowhere and followed her. "That's Malcolm," Irene explained. "He's not very social. Bye, Malcolm," she called out as the cat left without the slightest hint that there was anyone else in the house. Irene turned back to Vera. "I don't think his first owners took very good care of him."

Vera nodded. Irene's cats were the last thing on her mind, but as long as the waitress was comfortable talking to her, she was happy to hear about them. Vera waited a minute, and then asked again, "So did you have any idea why Davy was alone this night, instead of eating with his usual friends? Did he do something or say something unusual? Was he acting strange in any way?"

Irene took a moment to refocus. "Oh no," she said, "nothing like that. I mean, Davy was eating dinner—he always gets a number six—extra Swiss cheese, no pickle, with a large Coke. . . ." She smiled, glanced down, and then looked back up at Vera, almost shyly. "My manager said I memorized the menu faster than anybody he's ever seen. I don't know."

Vera smiled back and, after a moment, gently said, "So Davy was having a number six. . . ."

"Oh yeah, silly me. He's just having his dinner, and then all of a sudden, this other guy comes right in and sits down with him."

What? "I thought you said Davy was alone that night."

"Oh I'm sorry, sweetie. I thought you wanted to know if he had come in with friends. He came in alone, but he left with another man." Irene thought for a minute. "I'd never seen him before. I remember that real well, because this man had a goatee, and I like goatees. But for some reason I didn't like this guy. I'm sure he was perfectly nice, but I don't know. He just gave me a funny feeling, you know?"

Now Vera reached for her pad. It had been quite a while since she'd seen one, but if she wasn't mistaken, Ms. Irene Quarrels, career burger waitress, had just presented her with a bright, shiny lead.

SIX

ASSISTANT DISTRICT ATTORNEY LOVELL: *What is your occupation?*

ROBERT SULLIVAN: *I am the owner of three convenience stores in the Springfield area.*

Q: *Including the Nite & Day Convenience Store in New Wilton?*

A: *Yes.*

Q: *Can you tell us how you learned about the robbery that took place at that store on March 19?*

A: *The police called that night and left a message. I didn't get it until the next morning.*

Q: *And what did you do?*

A: *I went right to my store.*

Q: *What time was that?*

A: *I got there around six-thirty in the morning.*

Q: *What was the condition of the store when you arrived?*

A: *Well, first of all, Steve wasn't there, and he should have already opened up. And besides that, it was obvious that something had happened. I mean, the place wasn't locked up, the alarm hadn't been set. Besides* *that, the door to the office was open, and the cash register was empty except for some change.*

Q: *Who is Steve?*

A: *He's the guy that was on duty when my store got robbed. Steve Hirsch.*

Q: *And he was supposed to open the store the morning after the robbery?*

A: *Yeah. Actually, Steve wasn't exactly the world's greatest employee, so it wasn't a big surprise to me that the store wasn't locked up that morning. In fact, at first— well, I probably shouldn't say that.*

Q: *Are you talking about what you said to the police?*

A: *Yeah.*

Q: *That's okay. You can tell the jury.*

A: *Well, at first I told the police that I thought Steve was involved. You know. In the robbery. But that was before, you know.*

(*Commonwealth v. Gardiner*, Trial Volume II, Pages 80–82)

July 1, 2004

EVERYBODY KNEW THAT THE SIMPLEST PLANS were the best plans, and so Elmo took a lot of pride in the way that he was hiding the body. It was so simple it was brilliant. There was no way it could go wrong.

He pulled his car into the space behind the trailer where Dewey kept his office, and got into the—whatever the fuck this was—holy shit, a Dodge Reliant—threw the cooler into the front seat, and off he went.

Elmo had made an arrangement with Dewey, a decent guy who ran a junkyard. They shared some history through the criminal justice system, which made working with Dewey easy. All Dewey knew—all Dewey needed to know—was that about twice a week Elmo would call and ask Dewey to leave some old car unlocked with the keys in it. A few days later, it would be returned to the same place with a twenty-dollar bill in the glove compartment. No questions asked, no questions answered.

What was so simple about the plan was that the body would never get discovered, and all Elmo had to do was a little bit of driving. That was no problem, because even before everything had gotten so crazy and he'd ended up killing that guy, Elmo would spend hours every night, usually between around midnight and four in the morning, driving all over the county on his own private patrol—with a case of Budweiser and his friend Captain Jack Daniel's at his side. He would listen to those morons on talk radio, or sometimes he'd tune in to the lite rock station, not that rap noise and whatever the hell else passed for music these days. And sometimes he just drove in silence, figuring out what he was going to do when he finally hit the lotto.

Elmo reached into the cooler and grabbed another Bud as he passed Route 14 on his way up toward Finnesburg. He liked taking this route because even though it wasn't that wide, it was so rarely traveled by anyone, including cops, that it didn't matter if he drove down the middle of the road.

It was a damn good thing Elmo had come up with this new plan, because that first night he'd almost killed himself trying to bury the stupid body in the woods. He'd driven down a dirt road he'd discovered some years ago when he'd been patrolling out in the middle of nowhere, parked the car, turned the high beams on, and started digging where the car lights made it easy to see the ground.

But the goddamn rocks and roots and whatever other bullshit was all over the place made it impossible to dig a hole deep enough to bury the corpse. Exhausted, and maybe a little the worse for wear from the extra drinking he'd done—anybody would've needed a little more help than usual from Captain Jack on that fuckin' day—Elmo had returned to his car and fallen asleep behind the wheel before he'd even had a chance to drive home.

That was dumb, because if anybody had found him there, he'd have been screwed. But when he woke up, after he'd had a beer to clear his head, he realized that he didn't have to bury the body. That was good, because you always see some dog or some kid or some busybody uncovering some poor jerk who was buried in a shallow grave out in the woods.

The answer had come to Elmo in an inspirational moment just after he'd taken a leak behind that pine tree with the roots that had been such a pain in the ass the night before. As anyone knew, the safest place to keep a dead body was in the trunk of a car. But it would be too suspicious if Elmo left a car in a parking lot day after day. The cops would impound it, pop the trunk, and then the shit would really hit the fan.

The answer was to rotate cars! Elmo had been driving over these past nine—or was it ten already?—years to tons of places where he could park a car for a couple days without raising any suspicion. And Dewey's cars were always in such shitty condition that there was no chance that anyone would ever think to steal one.

There were two slight hitches with the plan. The first was that the body was so goddamn heavy. Elmo almost threw out his back the first time he tried to pick that load up out of the trunk, and his bum knee was not getting any better.

But then he'd figured out a way to position the cars so that it wasn't so bad—back-to-back, angled a bit so he had enough room to stand between the cars. All he had to do was hoist the body up so that one end was resting on the edge of the first car's trunk, then he could swing the other end up and out of the first trunk and drop it into the second one. After that it was easy to lift and dump the other end of the body into the second car, close both trunks, and drive away, clean as a whistle.

The other hitch was that he had to choose places where his cell phone worked. Because once he ditched the car with the body in the trunk in a new location, he had to call Wally on the cell phone to taxi him back to where the first car was stashed in the last location. Then he'd drive that car to Dewey's, drop it off, pick up his own car, and head home.

He took another slug of beer just as he veered hard right at the stupid fork off of Middleboro Street onto Sachem Drive, which was so dangerous it was almost criminal. Did somebody have to fly off the road and crash into that tree before they put up a warning sign, or what? He must have had two or three close calls himself, and he knew this road like the back of his hand.

He finished the Bud and decided to have a shot of Jack just to get the juices flowing, because this trip was going to be a little tricky. The last time he'd stashed the body—it was funny, he didn't even remember what kind of crap car it was in—anyway, the last time he'd not only been enjoying his usual case of Bud and a few shots of Jack, but he'd also done some coke. He wasn't proud of that, but shit. Sometimes a guy was forced to go out of his way to keep body and soul together.

Anyway, he'd done more coke than he'd planned, and so he forgot to leave the car in a good place for the cell phone. So he'd had to walk quite a ways before he reached Wally. And now he was having a slight problem remembering exactly where he stuck the car with the body in it. He took another swallow from the pint bottle of Jack and flipped on his brights. Goddamn country roads were so dark they could be treacherous sometimes.

Anyway, it was no big deal. He knew he left the car somewhere in the town of North Borden—at least he was pretty sure it was in North Borden—because it had tons of little country roads running through lots of hills and woods with plenty of dirt path turnoffs that he could use as temporary parking places. The thing was, he always—well, almost always—took a minute to make a mental note of where he ditched the car before he called Wally to bring him to the car that he would return to Dewey's. The thing was, the last time Elmo left the car he was a little too wasted to remember to make a mental note, so now he was just working on straight memory.

Which shouldn't be so bad. Hell, there weren't that many places he could have left it, were there? He passed the *Welcome to North Borden* sign on Route 89 and took the first right up the hill into a little rinky-dink development, and then past the entrance to the state forest.

Did he leave it in there? No way. Even though it had plenty of good places to stash a car, there was always the possibility that a state worker would stumble onto it, call the cops, and all hell would break loose. One night a couple of years ago he was patrolling around here and actually fell asleep for a second and ended up rolling off one of the dirt roads and bumping into a small tree. Good thing he wasn't going fast and that he didn't hit a bigger tree or he would have really fucked up his car good.

Anyway, as soon as he woke up he realized that he needed to get out of there, and about fifteen seconds after he was back on the road heading out of the state forest—and doing quite nicely, thank you very much—he passed a statie just rolling through. Man, that was close.

Now he drove another five minutes and suddenly passed a sharp turn to the right that led up a fairly steep hill. He had to stop the car and back up so he could make the turn, but there was no one in the road, so it was no problem.

He didn't have a specific memory of taking this route, but it just felt right. As he looked both left and right, he hoped that some particular detail might jump out at him and jog his memory, but there were no streetlights, and the goddamn night was so dark he could barely see his hand in front of his face.

And then there it was. A little nothing church stuck up on the side of the hill to the right of the road. He specifically remembered thinking last time that whoever picked that location for a church must have belonged to the dumbest religion in the world. No place to park, hard to get to, not much to look at. Guaranteed that God thought it really sucked.

He pulled into the tiny lot, took a shot of Jack Daniel's, chased it with a good belt of Bud to celebrate, and then walked around the side of the church to take a leak. As he stood there, he noticed that the paint was peeling near one of the doors. What a shithole.

But hey. Whatever. That was their problem. The real story was that now he knew he was getting close to where he'd left the body. He zipped himself up, got back into the car, and headed toward where he knew sooner or later he'd find a left turn into the woods. But then, before any left turn presented itself, he found himself at the end of the road, forced to turn right or left onto Route 44—a state highway that did not go into the woods.

That didn't make any sense. He was sure it was a left into the woods just after passing the church. So he made a left, figuring that maybe he'd just forgotten about Route 44.

But there was no left turn into the woods off of Route 44—it turned away from the heavy forest and opened up into a small commercial area. There was a gas station, and an old broken-down diner called Mel's Fat City, which he surely would have remembered. Shit.

He pulled into the gas station to turn around, and headed back in the opposite direction on Route 44. Maybe last time, after he passed the church he had taken a right on 44 and then made a left into the woods. That must have been it.

But it wasn't. Off to his left were a series of streets into a residential area. Not very nice houses, but even in this crappy neighborhood he'd never have left a car with a body in the trunk. Somebody would have called somebody.

He reached for the Jack, but as he tipped it up to pour the delicious liquid into his mouth he realized that it was empty. Goddammit! He rolled down the window and fired the bottle out onto the road. Why did this crap always happen to him? He grabbed another Bud from the cooler and took a long pull.

He stayed on Route 44 rather than turning off onto a smaller road that headed back into the woods. He needed to think. He needed a plan.

Elmo knew he remembered that shitty little church. Who could forget how pathetic it was? But now that he was thinking about it, was he remembering it from the last time he ditched the body, or was it from another time he was out on patrol? Fuck.

This was not good. He took another swallow of beer. What he needed was a map. He always kept a map book in the backseat. He'd just turn to the page with the map of North Borden, and if he had to, he'd drive up and down every goddamn road in the town.

He pulled over, left the blinker flashing for safety, and got out of the car so he could check the backseat. But the ground was so crappy that he stumbled as he exited the car, and scraped his hand as he fell. At least he hadn't hit his bad knee. But when he pulled himself up he saw that his pants were torn, and his good knee was bleeding and dirty. Shit. That was going to hurt like a motherfucker tomorrow.

He opened the back door to check for the map. But there was nothing in the car except empty beer bottles and a coffee cup. What the fuck? The backseat didn't even look familiar.

Then he remembered. This wasn't his car. It was one of Dewey's. Shit. He was going to have to do this without a map.

He closed the door and got back into the car. He was beat. Maybe the best plan was to rest for a minute, then start looking again. Yeah. He'd just close his eyes for a second.

SEVEN

ASSISTANT DISTRICT ATTORNEY LOVELL: *Would you please state your name for the court?*

MICHELLE KASPERIAN: *Michelle Kasperian.*

Q: *Where do you live, Michelle?*

A: *664 Old Country Road, Overton, Massachusetts.*

Q: *And how old are you?*

A: *Fourteen.*

Q: *What grade are you in?*

A: *Ninth.*

Q: *You go to Overton High?*

A: *Yeah.*

Q: *And last spring, were you going to Overton Middle School?*

A: *Yes.*

Q: *Okay, Michelle. Now I'd like to speak to you about something that happened this past summer, sometime in July. Do you remember coming upon something unusual around that time?*

A: *You mean when I found that abandoned car near Shelby's Pond?*

July 7, 2004

MARIA WANTED TO MAKE THE PERFECT IMPRES-
sion, so she took a lot of time getting ready for work that
morning. She wore her most professional-looking outfit—black pants with her comfortable but good-looking
boots, white pullover, and gray pin-striped jacket with the
longish cut that managed to look both sharp and casual
at the same time. She also paid extra attention to her
makeup. She didn't put on any more than usual—she was
just a little more careful than on other days. She wanted to
look like a serious businesswoman, but not like a sexless
robot. And, of course, not like a cheap hooker.

Normally she started work a half hour early. Today
she made sure that she got in to the office forty-five minutes early.

It wasn't that Maria was trying to come on to her
boss. Not that she would have had any problem if it
turned out that Anthony was attracted to her. He seemed
like a very decent man, and the good Lord was well aware
that Maria and her family could use someone like him in
their lives. But if her boss had any interest in Maria other
than as an employee, he was certainly taking his time letting her know about it.

No. Maria wanted to make an especially good impression today for very non-romantic reasons.

Anthony was coming in just as she arrived. He was
wearing a black turtleneck, a tweed jacket, tan pants, and
loafers. "Well, you look like you're ready for something
special," he said, opening the door for her. "Got a date
tonight?"

"No," Maria replied as they entered the office. "I was
just hoping that we could talk at some time today, about,
um, a few things."

"That sounds pretty serious." Anthony walked over to

the little kitchen area and started to make a pot of coffee. One of the good things about working here was that Anthony didn't skimp on the coffee. It tasted so good that last Wednesday Maria wasn't paying attention, had three or four cups before she'd even noticed, and got so wired on caffeine that she spent most of that night staring at the cracks in her bedroom ceiling.

When the coffee was ready, Anthony poured them each a cup, and they went into his office. He sat down behind his desk, took a sip, and said, "So, I'm guessing that you've come to tell me that you've found another job."

Nothing like getting off on the totally wrong foot. He couldn't have been further off if he'd tried. Maria didn't know whether to laugh or to cry. She took a sip of coffee, and her hand was shaking. This was a little harder than she'd thought it was going to be.

"Oh no, that's not it," she said. "I, um, actually, I wanted to talk to you because I was afraid that one of these days you were going to tell me that I had to go look for another job."

A puzzled look came over Anthony's face, and then he smiled, a little carefully. "So, then, just so we're on the same page. As I understand it, right now, we are on two completely different pages." His smile grew a little broader. He put his mug down and sat back in his chair. "Tell you what. Let's make a deal. You tell me what you wanted to tell me, and I'll try not to blurt out any stupid guesses about what you're going to say. How's that sound?"

Maria smiled. One thing about Anthony that she really liked was how he could be humble about his mistakes and still seem like he was totally confident about himself. It was a trick Maria hoped to learn herself. She hated making mistakes.

"Okay," she said. "Here's what I wanted to say." She looked over at him and hesitated. He seemed so sure of himself, so under control. What right did she have to question whether he was running his business into the ground?

Then an image of Felix and her mother packing their things and moving out of their new place back into the old neighborhood came into her head, and whether Maria had the right or not, she had to speak up. She took a deep breath and blurted out, way too fast, "I wanted to say that I'm afraid you aren't earning enough money to keep the business going."

Anthony just sat there, waiting. He might have been nodding a little. At least he wasn't firing her. Yet. So she continued. "And I'm scared when you spend all your time, and even some of your own money, on cases where people don't pay you, and I'm afraid that one of these days you're going to go to the bank and find that there isn't any money left, and even though you're a really good private investigator, and even though I've worked really hard for you, you're going to have to fire me because you can't afford to keep paying somebody to work for you when you don't have any money coming in."

Anthony still sat there, looking at her like he didn't know that she was finished. Maria couldn't tell what he was thinking. Well, it was too late to take any of it back, even if she'd wanted to, which she didn't. So she just kept on talking. "And I know I shouldn't have said all that, but I like it here, and I really need the job, and I hope you won't fire me for saying all of this, but I just figured if I was right and the company was in trouble, and I didn't say anything, you were probably going to have to fire me anyway, so..." Her voice trailed off. She had started to babble. The message was delivered. If he was going to fire her, this was the time. She took another deep breath and prepared for the worst.

Anthony took a sip of coffee, cleared his throat, and

put the mug back onto his desk. "Okay. First of all, I just want to tell you that I really appreciate the fact that you shared all of that with me. It was, well, I'm a little surprised, but I probably shouldn't be. Anyway, it sounded like it wasn't the easiest thing you've ever done. So thank you for that."

That sure didn't sound like an introduction to getting fired, but there was obviously much more to come. Maria tried to sit still while Anthony paused before speaking again.

"I started this business on September 8, 1998. I can remember the exact date because it was the one-year anniversary of my partner's death."

It took a moment for Maria to process that, mainly because it didn't make sense. "You started this company a year *after* your business partner died?"

"Not my business partner," Anthony said, with a sad smile. "My life partner." He reached around and took a framed photo from its place on the credenza behind his desk and handed it to her.

"I thought that was a picture of your parents' wedding anniversary," Maria said, looking at the group shot. An older couple was at the center of six people who stood smiling, shoulder-to-shoulder, arms around each other's waists. Anthony was at the end on the left side of the photo. He looked no different than he did today. Well, okay, he had more hair.

He was standing next to another young man with a great smile wearing a button-down striped shirt. On the opposite side of the group a college-aged boy and girl stood beside each other. Those two looked a lot alike.

Anthony came out from behind his desk to stand next to her. "It is. My parents are in the middle, and my brother and sister—they're twins—are on one side of them. I'm on the other side, and this," he said, pointing to the smiling man with the striped shirt, "that's Joe. My partner, Joe Hillary. We met in our last year in business school, and we started living together after we graduated."

"Wait a minute," Maria blurted out. "You're telling me you're gay?"

"That's right," he replied. He had an odd smile on his face. "Gay as a banana daiquiri."

Talk about surprises. Anthony was gay? He sure didn't look gay—at least not like her cousin Emilio, who didn't listen to anything except show tunes and Barbra Streisand CDs and wore skintight pink pants and pastel scarves 24/7. An image of Anthony punching that guy in the face in the parking lot came into Maria's mind. It was hard to image Emilio getting into a fistfight.

Whatever. The fact that Anthony was gay actually explained an awful lot. Why the best-dressed private investigator in the world would have no girlfriend. Why he treated Maria like a perfect gentleman. Maybe why he wanted purple legal pads in the office.

But it sure didn't explain why he needed to bankrupt his business.

"Joe and I had been a couple for seven years when that picture was taken. Five days later, he was killed by a drunk driver on the Mass Pike. That was on September 8, 1997."

"Oh my God, that's terrible," Maria said. Her head was spinning. Anthony was gay. And a widower. Widow. Whatever a gay person was. How awful.

"Anyway, Joe and I had a lot of money," Anthony explained. "We hit it big in the dot-com investment boom."

"You worked on the Internet?"

"Not exactly," Anthony responded. "We were investors. And we were really good at it. We made millions speculating on high-tech stocks, and we also predicted when the bottom was going to fall out of that market, so by the time it crashed, we'd already pulled most of our money out and put it in a much safer portfolio."

Maria was dying to ask her boss about a thousand questions, and she was ashamed that way up on the list was: *Can you teach me how I can hit it big as an investor?* But she forced herself to stay quiet.

Anthony sat down in a chair across from her, inhaled deeply, and began again to speak.

"Joe was a really organized person, and one of his favorite things was to plan"—Anthony cleared his throat. His eyes looked a little wet—"to plan for our future together. What we would do, where we would live, how we could have enough money to travel wherever we wanted when we got older—that kind of thing." He smiled sadly. "We had this plan to go to Australia. Joe had a thing about kangaroos. I told him that all we had to do was go to the zoo to see one, but that didn't count. He had to experience one in the wild. That was one of his life goals. See, he kept this list . . ."

Anthony shook his head and laughed softly. "Sounds like I might not have talked about this stuff enough, huh? Hard to believe. Anyway." He cleared his throat and started again, in a slightly louder voice. "Anyway, Joe did a lot of research on various financial products that would set us up for a comfortable future. We both bought annuities, we set up significant SEP investments. . . ." Maria must have looked as confused as she felt, because Anthony shook his head again and said, "It doesn't really matter. The bottom line is that we were pretty much set for life."

He looked off into the distance for a minute. "Most of Joe's relatives weren't comfortable with the fact that he was gay, but he was one of those guys that just loved the idea of being in a big family. So even though it was sometimes a little awkward, he never missed one of their functions—weddings, christenings, reunions—he went to them all. So naturally, when he found out that his cousin was having his thirtieth-birthday party in Boston, he drove in to be there."

Anthony took another sip of coffee. "But that night, on his way back home, just as he was passing the Newton Corner exit on the Mass Pike, this drunk driver crashed right into him. Head-on. He had actually managed to get on the road going the wrong way. Joe never had a chance."

Once when Maria was driving Felix to Sears to get back-to-school clothes, they'd been rear-ended in the parking lot by a teenager who wasn't paying attention. It was a minor accident, thank the Virgin Mary, and nobody was hurt. But Maria had nightmares about Felix for weeks afterward. She couldn't even imagine what she would have done if something serious had happened to him.

"After that, I just wanted to disappear. I didn't want to talk to anyone, I didn't want to see anyone, I didn't even want to think about anyone. I remembered that my sister's college roommate told me that her honeymoon on Bali was the most isolated experience she'd ever had, so I packed a bag, drove to the airport, and caught the first flight out. First stop, Hawaii. What a mistake that was. Everybody on the plane was going on a vacation—it was like a gigantic party. I plugged myself into the headphones and half hoped that the stupid plane would just crash into the sea.

"When we finally landed, I didn't even leave the airport. I just took a nap in the terminal, and then flew to Bali. Where I rented the most isolated cabin I could find on the island. For about five weeks, I didn't do anything except walk around on the beach and stare out into the ocean."

Maria tried to picture Anthony as a beach bum. She couldn't do it.

"Anyway, when I finally started to feel like myself

again, I realized that thanks to all of Joe's planning, including a ridiculous life insurance policy he had gotten a few years before the accident, I had so much money that I could pretty much do whatever I wanted for the rest of my life." He stood up, returned the picture of his family and Joe to the credenza, then sat back down behind his desk. "And even though I knew I'd never get over Joe's death, I also knew that I didn't want to spend the rest of my life with sand in my shorts. So I came back home."

He took another sip of coffee. "I know it sounds silly, but ever since I saw Humphrey Bogart in *The Maltese Falcon,* I'd always had this secret desire to be a private eye. So I did some research and, long story—well, not exactly short, I guess." He shrugged. "Here I am."

Maria shifted in her seat. He was coming to the money part. She could tell. She held her breath.

"As far as your concern about the business," Anthony said, leaning forward and clearing his throat, "I hope this isn't a problem for you, but whether or not I make money doing this job is completely irrelevant to me."

Maria's heart sank. So it really was only a matter of time before this whole thing crashed. She felt a little queasy.

"I take the cases I want to take, and only the cases that I want to take, but it doesn't have to do with whether the clients can pay me a lot of money, or even if they can pay me anything at all. That's because, well, I have enough income from a lot of other sources to take care of myself, and to take care of any money that I might lose in this business, with plenty to spare." He made a point to look directly into Maria's eyes. "So I hope you believe me when I tell you that you are working here because I want you to work here. And as far as I'm concerned, that's the way it's going to stay. Naturally, I'll understand if your situation changes and you have to leave. But if you like it here, you should feel as secure as you can that you will have a job here. As long as you keep doing the work you've been doing, there's no way I'm going to fire you."

Maria wasn't quite sure, but she thought she was either on the verge of a terrible headache or maybe she was just going to burst into tears. When she exhaled, it felt like she'd been holding her breath for about ten minutes. She tried to take a drink of coffee, and it felt like she hadn't moved her arm for a week.

But before she could even think of something to say, the phone rang. She picked it up, and an obviously disguised male voice said, "Keep fucking around with the Gardiner case, and you and your punk boss will be real sorry."

ATTORNEY ZACK WILSON WAS OPENING THE morning mail.

But what he was really doing was still trying to digest yesterday's meeting with Justin's kindergarten teacher. She wasn't worried about the fact that Justin seemed more interested in drawing than in the alphabet, or that he was terrible at sports, or that he happened to enjoy singing with his eyes closed. In fact, she wasn't worried about much of anything. She thought Justin was doing great, and would enjoy first grade very much.

Was it really going to be that easy?

Without any warning, Terry burst through the door, plopped his large frame down onto the sofa at the opposite end of the office, and announced, "You're not going to believe what happened when I was watching Lovell yesterday at court."

Assistant District Attorney Louis Lovell was the prosecutor in the Babe Gardiner case, and although he had a good reputation, he was relatively new to the area. So

Terry had attended a hearing in one of Lovell's cases to get a feel for the way he worked.

Zack opened a letter from a bank offering him a credit card that displayed a television show's logo. He dropped it into the garbage. "Judge Park throw you in jail for contempt?" Zack asked. A while ago Terry had had a run-in with another judge in a different case that had resulted in Terry spending some time in the courthouse lockup. He loved being reminded of it.

"No," Terry said from the sofa. He was now completely stretched out on his back, eyes closed, probably about fifteen seconds from unconsciousness. "But maybe he will after I come over there and beat you like a Christmas drum."

Zack opened the next envelope. This would wake Terry up. "Hey. Did you know that there's a new foreign-car dealership opening up in Springfield this summer? Could be time for that Ferrari."

Terry got up and came over to the desk. "Porsche, nimrod. Here." He took the mailing from Zack. "Give me that before you hurt yourself." He looked it over, shook his head, wadded it up, and fired it into the garbage. "Andy Inverness already has too many dealerships. He's a crook." Terry returned to the couch. "Speaking of crooks, are we going to talk about that hearing yesterday, or what?"

Zack opened up the next envelope. Judge Harold Baumgartner was hosting a statewide criminal justice ethics seminar. "Just a sec. Harry Baumgartner is doing another ethics thing." He flipped the envelope over to Terry. "It's your turn to go."

Terry grabbed the envelope, opened it, and sighed. "Fine. It'll be a miracle if fifteen people show up. I hate those meetings. And the dinners are always really shitty, too." He lay back down on the couch.

"You want a tissue to wipe away your tears?"

"You want to talk about the hearing, or you want a whupping?"

"A 'whupping,' Elvis?"

"Shut up. And don't call me Elvis."

"Okay," Zack said. "What happened at the hearing?"

Terry opened his eyes and sat up. "Well, I wasn't expecting much. It was just a motion to suppress, right? But two minutes into it, and I was seeing things I'd never seen before in my life." He shook his head and laughed softly. "It started when Lovell was asking this cop about a search where they found all this cocaine in the defendant's apartment. By the way, this was a bad search. They went to this guy's apartment, busted in with no warrant, no emergency, nothing. They didn't even have probable cause—"

"They just broke into the guy's home?" Zack interrupted, starting to tear open the last envelope. He'd heard of dumb cops, but this sounded beyond dumb. "How did they justify that—or maybe I should say, how did they try to justify that—in the police report?"

"They said that they thought they'd find a gun that had been used in a shooting around the corner ten minutes before."

Whoa. Besides being totally wrong, it was a little alarming. *Memo to law enforcement: Please be advised that, effective immediately, the sound of a weapon firing in a neighborhood suspends all constitutional rights in that neighborhood.*

"So what happened?"

Terry got up and began to pace the room. "Well, obviously somebody told this cop that if he didn't make up something good, the judge wasn't going to let the D.A. use the drugs as evidence in the trial. So the cop starts going on and on about how the defendant looked like he was hiding something as he went into his place, and how it sounded like he was doing something sneaky after the cops knocked on the door. You know. 'He was putting his hand in his pocket.' 'He was acting in a furtive manner.' 'He said a bad word.' You name it. And Lovell keeps flipping through the police report like the cop is insane."

"Really?"

By now, Terry had completed a circuit of the room and had returned to the couch. "Yeah. At first I thought he was playing along. I was expecting—you know—'But, Officer, it doesn't reflect that in your report. Can you explain the discrepancy?' And then the cop would go: 'Why, as a matter of fact, I can, Mr. Assistant District Attorney. It just so happens that when I wrote the report, I left out some information which I later discovered in my notes....' But it turns out that Lovell really was caught off-guard by this cop. He's fumbling around, trying to make sense of the whole thing, probably without trying to make the cop look more like an asshole than he already did, when all of a sudden, totally out of nowhere, the cop testifies—get this—that he heard a gunshot *inside* the apartment."

"What?"

"I swear to God. This little cop is like the head conductor on the Bullshit Express." Terry popped up off the couch and started to walk around again. "Under oath, right there in the courtroom, with a straight face, he claims that he broke through the door because he heard a gun fired *in the apartment*."

"Even though there was nothing about that in the report?"

Terry nodded. "Lovell looked like he was about to stick his head in the garbage pail and hurl."

No kidding. One of the worst things a lawyer can go through is questioning a witness whose testimony turns out to be a complete surprise. "So what did he do?"

"This was what was so great. After the cop testifies that there was a gunshot in the defendant's place, Lovell asks Judge Park if he can treat the cop as a hostile witness. Can you believe that? Talk about balls."

Talk about balls indeed.

Normally, an attorney who was questioning his own witness had to refrain from asking leading questions—questions that suggested the answer. So, even if you knew that the answer was going to be "yes," you weren't allowed to ask your own witness: "Isn't true that you were wearing a red shirt that day?" Instead, you had to ask: "What color shirt were you wearing that day?"

But sometimes witnesses turned against the attorneys who called them to the stand and started to testify in a manner which was adverse to the interests that the attorney was representing. And at that point, if the judge allowed it, the attorneys could treat them as hostile witnesses and ask them leading questions.

It usually happened to district attorneys when they called a witness who was a friend or a relative of the defendant, and who started feeding the court a line of garbage in order to protect the defendant. But Lovell had asked to treat the cop as a hostile witness even though the cop was actually testifying in a way that would *help* get a conviction. If the judge bought the cop's story, then the evidence would be admissible against the defendant.

What was so ballsy was that Lovell treated his own witness as hostile because he knew that the cop was lying. Lovell was taking the position that the Commonwealth's interests did not include getting a conviction if lies had to be told to get one. Instead, he was taking the position that the Commonwealth's interests included truthful testimony, regardless of the outcome of the case.

It was pretty damn impressive.

"So now, Lovell starts to ask this cop questions like 'Wouldn't it have been normal police procedure to include in your report that the reason you broke into an apartment was because you heard a weapon fired inside the apartment?' and 'After you went into the apartment, did you begin an investigation into the gunshot?' Damn. But the cop just kept flinging bullshit around like it was confetti. 'I followed what I thought were normal procedures.' 'Although I failed to include it in the original report, I did ask the suspect about the gunshot.'"

Finally, Zack opened the envelope and withdrew the letter. It was funny—in all his years practicing, he couldn't remember getting a letter from the police force.

"Hey. Do you have any idea why a detective named Vera Demopolous is writing to us about Babe Gardiner?"

Terry closed his eyes and sank back into the couch. "I'm sorry. There are too many punch lines to choose from."

Zack looked at the beginning of the letter and then glanced up. "How about this one: To let us know that Babe's getting indicted for first-degree murder."

EIGHT

ASSISTANT DISTRICT ATTORNEY LOVELL: *What did you do after the car was towed to the police compound?*

SERGEANT FRED RAMIREZ: *After the vehicle was retrieved, we attempted to identify the owner of the vehicle.*

Q: *And were you able to identify the owner?*

A: *No, we weren't. The license plate on the car was stolen, and the vehicle identification number had been removed.*

Q: *What did you do next?*

A: *At that point, we proceeded to search the vehicle.*

Q: *And what did you find?*

A: *Well, we first looked though the passenger compartment of the vehicle. It appeared as if the vehicle had been recently vacuumed—*

ATTORNEY WILSON: *Objection, Your Honor. Move to strike.*

THE COURT: *Sustained. The jury will disregard the statement about vacuuming. Just tell us what you found when you searched the car, Sergeant, not what it appeared had been done to the car.*

SERGEANT RAMIREZ: *Oh. Sorry.*

ASSISTANT DISTRICT ATTORNEY LOVELL: *No problem. Let me ask the question a different way. When you searched the passenger compartment of the vehicle, did you find anything in that part of the car that was particularly unusual?*

SERGEANT RAMIREZ: *Uh, no. I didn't find anything unusual.*

Q: *Okay. What did you do after you searched the passenger compartment of the car?*

A: *We popped the trunk.*

Q: *And what did you find there?*

A: *We found the body of the victim, Steven Hirsch, wrapped in plastic garbage bags and duct tape.*

(*Commonwealth v. Gardiner*, Trial Volume IV, Pages 201–204)

INVESTIGATOR NANCY SOLOMON: *Tell us what happened when you got arrested.*

MR. ANDROCHOK: *Okay. I wasn't doing nothing wrong, which is why I couldn't understand what was up. I mean, I was just sitting there—*

Q: *Where were you when this happened?*

A: *Down at my friend's garage.*

Q: *Who's your friend?*

A: *Gary Vincent. He owns a place down on Third Street, behind the hospital, where he works on cars.*

Q: *Do you work there?*

A: *Sometimes. I mean if Gary gets backed up and needs a hand, I help him out sometimes. But my regular job, I drive a cab.*

Q: *So you weren't working when this incident occurred?*

A: No. Like I said. I was just sitting there, eating lunch, reading the paper, when all of a sudden this car rolls up, this big guy gets out, walks right over to me, and shoves my face into the table.

Q: And you had no idea who this was?

A: I never saw the guy before in my life.

Q: And you had no idea that an arrest warrant had been issued out of the West Springfield district court?

A: That bullshit charge my ex-girlfriend was trying to use against me?

Q: I have no idea what the underlying charges were, Mr. Androchok. I was just asking if you were aware that at the time you were arrested, there was an outstanding warrant for your arrest?

A: No. Like I said, that was a game my ex and her lawyer were running up there.

Q: Okay. Let's get back to the arrest itself. Can you describe the car that Detective Morrison was driving that day?

A: I don't know. It was a big, unmarked cop car.

Q: Okay. And what did Detective Morrison say to you during the arrest?

A: You mean after he smashed my head down onto the table?

Q: I mean why don't you tell us exactly what Detective Morrison said to you that day. Whenever he said it.

A: Um, I'm not sure what he said.

Q: Well, what was the first thing Detective Morrison said to you?

A: I don't remember. I can't remember every single thing the guy said.

Q: All right. How about this? What is the first thing that you remember Detective Morrison saying to you that day?

A: Let's see. I think he said, "Okay, punk. Let's go."

Q: And when was that?

A: That was after he cuffed me. My face was smashed down on the table, and he grabbed me by my hair, and pulled my head up, and then he yanked me up off my chair, and he said, "Okay, punk. Let's go."

Q: And those are the first words you remember Detective Morrison saying to you?

A: Yeah. Like I said, I don't remember every single word.

Q: He didn't identify himself to you as a police detective?

A: Not that I remember. I mean everything happened so fast...

Q: So you're saying that Detective Morrison simply walked up to you and, without saying anything, pushed your face down on the table, handcuffed you, and then pulled you up by the hair, saying only, "Okay, punk. Let's go." Nothing else?

A: I don't know. He might have said something else.

Q: Before or after he arrested you?

A: I don't remember. Maybe before, maybe after.

Q: Is it possible that as he approached you, he identified himself as a police detective?

A: Anything's possible, I guess.

(Transcript of Police Investigatory Board Interview of Ulf Androchok, June 11, 2004)

Hostage

SHE WAS GOING TO HAVE TO FIGURE OUT A WAY to move. She couldn't just sit here forever.

She needed the Swiss Army knife that was sitting on the far side of the table to cut herself free. Her arms and hands were going to be completely useless until she managed to get hold of it.

Each of her legs was taped separately to the chair, just above the ankle, but her feet were resting flat on the floor. That meant that if she could rise up on her toes, she might have a chance of being able to somehow get herself across the room.

The chair she was taped to was sitting about five feet from the folding card table. She was going to have to find a way to make it over there, and then work her way around to the far side of the table, where the knife was resting.

She listened to the noises from the television in the outer room. Every so often, the sound changed abruptly, as if the kidnapper was channel surfing, or occasionally changing the volume. But it was still too muffled for her to make out anything useful.

Gingerly, she began to push herself up onto her toes, and a pain immediately shot through her temples. God, everything she did made her head pound like a slow, violent jackhammer. But she couldn't let that matter. She had to get this to work. She took a deep breath, then slowly raised herself up.

And sure enough, as she transferred her weight from her rear end to her toes, the legs of the chair rose slowly. But they were only an inch off the ground before she realized that the transfer of weight included tipping herself forward so the legs of the chair could get farther off the floor—

Whoa. She was on the verge of falling forward, right onto her face. She dropped back down to where she had started, and the very slight impact of the chair legs returning to the floor created an intense shock wave of pain that reverberated through her entire skull.

She sat there for a minute with her eyes closed, dizzy, her head throbbing, fighting the terrible feeling that in a matter of seconds, her stomach was going to begin to spasm. She really wished that she didn't have to worry about vomiting from this awful headache.

She swallowed, took a deep breath, and tried to will the dizziness to pass. Her goal here was simple. She had to make her way over to the table, get hold of the knife, and then get herself back to where she started. She didn't want the ski mask man to know that she had figured out how to move around, and she had no idea when he was going to come back—

He wasn't going to kill her.

The thought was so certain, it was a little unnerving. It wasn't a guess, or a desire. It was a conclusion.

How could she possibly know that? Of course, that's what she was hoping, but to believe something just because she wanted it to be true made no sense. He had kidnapped her, and he had her completely vulnerable. It would take next to nothing to murder her—a gun, a fist, a rope—she couldn't defend herself at all.

Still, she just knew he wasn't going to kill her. How could she possibly be so sure?

And then the answer delivered itself to her as if it were the simplest thing in the world: The reason he wasn't going to kill her was because he was still wearing his mask.

That was it! That was why she'd had that weird feeling of security earlier about the mask. It was completely irrational to hide his face from her if he was just going to kill her anyway. The only way there was a risk that she'd identify him was if she was going to live through this.

So that made her feel a little better. But just a little. If that was a ray of sunshine, it was still a pretty darn cloudy day. Rational thought processes did not always apply to people who kidnapped other people. And she was still bound and gagged with a paralyzing headache and no obvious means of escape.

It was time to get that knife.

Slowly and very carefully, she tipped forward, trying to keep her head absolutely still as she shifted her weight forward onto her toes and as the legs of the chair again rose up from the floor. She was still fighting the dizziness and nausea that always seemed to be ready to pounce at the least little movement. Then she took a tiny step with her left foot. And then another with her right.

You may take six umbrella steps, one giant step, and three baby steps.

Mother, may I?

Yes, you may.

So at one time, she had been a child, and had played Mother May I. One of these days, she was going to figure out why the only memories bright enough to shine through the fog in her mind were so absolutely useless. If her brain was so committed to letting her know how she passed the time in her childhood, would it be too much to ask it to supply her with something that might actually help her out? Like the name of the person who had done this to her? Or, speaking of names, how about her own?

But concentrating on her lack of memory did nothing more than make the headache worse. She squeezed her eyes shut, tried to relax, took a breath, and kept going.

She lifted her left foot and took her third step forward. And then her fourth. She began to sweat. Moving like this was really hard. The muscles in her legs and back were straining. Was she going to be able to keep it up?

She dared to tip her head back the slightest bit to check her progress. It was undeniable. The table was closer. She had probably closed the gap to about three feet. She could do this. She lowered her gaze again and struggled forward another step. And then another.

She was moving painfully slowly, but after about another minute, she finally reached the table. Now it was just a matter of making her way around to the other side, where the knife was—

And then the sound of a click came from the outer room.

The television had been turned off.

He was on his way into the room.

July 14, 2004
Eight weeks before the Babe Gardiner trial

WHEN DETECTIVE JOHN MORRISON ENTERED the room and smiled at her, Vera wished she'd worn something different for the meeting. Dark gray pants and a plain white shirt just seemed so boring.

It wasn't like Morrison was wearing anything special— his normal jacket and tie—but his presence, especially when he was smiling, seemed to make the sparsely furnished interview room just a little bit, well, nicer.

It was silly to think that way. It's not like they were on a date. They were meeting as part of Vera's very unpleasant role as the Springfield Police Department's representative on the citizen review board set up to monitor police misconduct. A complaint had been lodged against Detective Morrison for misconduct in the arrest of someone named Ulf Androchok, a wife-beating thug who'd failed to appear for a court date.

It was only the worst luck in the world for Androchok that he'd gotten nabbed in the first place. After all, it wasn't like Morrison was out trolling the streets of Springfield, looking for fugitives from the district court.

But now that Androchok was complaining about how Morrison arrested him, they had to go through this formal interview. It was pretty stupid to believe that somebody as smart as Morrison was going to jeopardize his career over a punk like Androchok, but rules were rules.

"Hey, Vera," Morrison said as he sat down across from her. Somehow, the smile got a little bigger. It felt like the room actually got warmer. "Listen. I know that we haven't had a chance to get to know each other, but I'm going to go out on a limb here and guess that this isn't exactly the most comfortable situation you've ever been in. I know it isn't for me, anyway."

Talk about understatements. Thank God Morrison had spoken first. Vera had no idea how she was going to do this. A part of her knew that it was actually kind of easy—all she had to do was ask some questions, write down the answers, and that was that. But the other part of her felt like she was in that dream that she'd had when she was in third grade, where she'd scolded her parents for not eating their dinner. She'd awakened with a stomachache that had stayed with her for most of the day. What in the world was she doing, questioning the best detective in the department like he was some suspect, about the arrest of a loser like Ulf Androchok? It was outrageous. "Um," she stammered, stupidly. "Yeah. 'Uncomfortable' about covers it."

"And my union delegate and the lawyer are going nuts that I'm doing this interview without them, but you know what? This whole thing is going to be over in about fifteen seconds, so I told them to relax. I'm happy to answer anything anybody wants to ask, because I didn't do anything wrong."

Vera took a deep breath. In a normal interrogation situation, that's exactly what you wanted to hear if you were a cop. Somehow, it didn't make her feel any better. "You know before we start I've got to give you your rights." This felt absolutely awful. It wasn't exactly like she was on the rat squad—internal affairs—but it felt close enough.

Morrison nodded, the smile still intact, but now it softened a bit. "Okay. Maybe this will make it easier." He stood up and cleared his throat, as if pretending he was about to make a speech, but the smile never left his face. He had nice eyes. And he was really trying to make her comfortable. Talk about mission impossible. "I know that I have the right to be silent, and that anything I say could be used against me. And I also know that I can have an attorney here, and that if I can't afford one, I'll get one appointed to represent me." He spread his hands, as if a crowd were applauding him. "How'd I do?"

No matter what he said, or how he said it, this thing still felt very bad. But Vera smiled, despite herself. "You did fine." She sighed. If only that were the end of it. "In case it wasn't already ridiculously obvious, I haven't done this before...I mean, questioned another cop...and...well, I guess—"

"How about this?" Morrison offered. "I'll tell you what happened, and you jump in anytime you want and ask me anything you want. You know: 'How many times did you shoot him? What weapon did you use? Where did you learn those neat ways to torture suspects?' Whatever."

The best she could muster was a weak smile.

"Okay. Bad joke. Sorry. But is that all right? I'll just tell the story, and then you take it from there? Wherever you want to take it."

That couldn't have been a line, could it? He was just sitting there, waiting for her to give him the go-ahead. He was doing everything he could to make her feel like she was in charge. There was no hidden meaning there—no flirting, no innuendo.

"All right," Vera said, exhaling a little too forcefully. Had she been holding her breath? "I really am sorry about this. I just...I'm just..." She shrugged, and laughed. This was so awkward. "That's fine. Go ahead. Just tell me what happened so I can make a report and be done with it. And if I haven't died of embarrassment by the next time you see me, can you please remind me to get off this committee as soon as I possibly can?"

Morrison nodded. "Fair enough. So, Androchok." He gestured to the pad and pen before her on the table. "Ready to take notes?"

Vera opened her pad and said, "Ready."

"Okay." He sat back in his chair. "To tell you the truth, there wasn't too much about this arrest that was out of the ordinary, I mean except how I learned that there was a warrant out on this guy. I mean Vincent—the guy who owns the garage—is a pretty good guy. He's done some work for my father. But it sounded like he was friends with this 'Ulfie' he was talking to on the phone, so I didn't say anything about coming back. All I needed was for Vincent to jump into the middle of things and make a mess. And of course Androchok had no idea I was coming after him."

Vera took notes, but she knew this was a waste of time. She had a terrific ear for the truth. It was obvious that Morrison was being honest with her.

"So I pulled up to the place. The overhead garage door was open, and before I even park the cruiser, I can see from the mug shot I'd gotten that the guy sitting there, eating a sandwich at the front of the garage, was Androchok. So I get out of the cruiser and walk toward him."

One of the few things in Androchok's story that was slightly worrying was his charge that Morrison didn't identify himself as a police detective before taking him into custody. It was normal procedure to make sure that suspects who were being arrested knew that they were dealing with police, so that they understood the fact that there was authority behind their actions. Otherwise, a suspect would be justified in acting like he was getting grabbed up by some stranger.

"So I waited until I was close enough so that if the guy bolted, I'd be able to catch him," Morrison continued. "I don't know—I was probably about ten feet away—and I said, 'Ulf, my name is John Morrison. I'm a detective with the Springfield Police, and I'm here to take you into custody. Please remain seated and put your hands behind your back so I can cuff you.'"

Hello. That didn't sound right. Vera had arrested plenty of people, and been around plenty of cops that had placed plenty of other people under arrest, and she couldn't remember one of them sounding anything like what Morrison just described. *I'm here to take you into custody.* That sounded more like a doctor talking to a child in the hospital. *I'm here to take a quick look at that infection.*

Morrison must have picked up on her expression, because he added, "I know it sounds a little formal, but sometimes I go that way. It's just a gut feeling, I guess. I try to figure the way that's going to lead to the lowest chance of resistance."

Vera nodded and tried to smile. She didn't know exactly what was going on here, but Morrison was starting to sound less credible. Normal police procedure was to intimidate and dominate in arrest situations to minimize the chance of physical confrontation. Even if Morrison remembered the tone he used as he approached Androchok, would he have remembered the exact words? Sure, Morrison had a good memory, but something wasn't right here.

"Anyway, turns out it was a bad call, because sure enough, he jumps up out of his chair and tries to run. But like I said, I was so close I had him in custody in about— oh, I don't know—five seconds. Maybe ten."

Vera made a few more notes. At least that sounded believable. Now to get to the physical stuff. "So, when you actually laid hands on him, do you remember exactly what happened?"

Morrison hesitated for a second, as if trying to remember something. Shoot. How was it that Morrison could remember the exact words he said, and not remember what he did when Androchok ran?

"I'm just trying to get the sequence right in my mind," Morrison told her.

That didn't ring true, either. Morrison knew they were going to do this interview, and it was about a charge of excessive force. He must have thought about this before now. Why the big show of remembering?

"Okay. When he got up, he shoved his chair back and then sort of pushed it in my direction, kind of as a barrier between us. I mean, it was quick—I'm not even sure he meant to do it. But it sort of worked a little, except that I was already so close that even though the chair was in the way, I still could reach him by leaning over it. The thing was, when I actually got him, I was jackknifed over the chair, and all I grabbed hold of was the sleeve of his shirt with one hand, and his hair with the other."

And suddenly, Morrison was back to telling the truth. So what was with all of the dancing around about what he said as he approached, and pretending to try to remember something that he had obviously been thinking about long before this discussion?

"I kept hold of him and told him to get down on the floor," Morrison said. "And that was it. He laid down, like I told him, and put his hands behind his back. I cuffed him, picked him up, put him in the cruiser, and came back to the house."

"Do you remember how you picked him up after he was cuffed?" Vera asked. "Was there any problem getting him into the car?" Thank God this was almost over.

"Oh. Yeah. Of course." Morrison smiled again. "Sorry about that. I forgot you've got to follow this all the way to the end. But no. No problems. After he was cuffed it was pretty much SOP. I put my hand on his arm at his elbow, lifted him a little, he got up to his knees and then he stood up. I walked him to the car, opened the back door, and he got in. No banging his head on the roof of the car, nothing. Peace and quiet all the way to the station. Except for me giving him his rights on the way."

Vera closed her notebook. Hallelujah. This thing was over. "Thanks, John," she said, standing. "And again, I'm really sorry—"

"Hey, don't even say it." Morrison was smiling again, and shaking his head. "I can't believe they gave you this detail right off the bat. Seems like somebody in command doesn't like you. I know I'd never—"

Just then, there was a knock on the door. A temp who was covering for one of the usual secretaries came into the room and handed Vera a phone message.

They had a possible ID on goatee man, the mysterious companion of fugitive Davy Zwaggert.

NINE

Dear Sharon,

How's Bernie? I was so sorry to hear about the infection, but it sounds like the doctors did a good job with it. It must be so hard watching Bernie fight his way through these things. I'm thinking about you all the time.

It's really different out here in Massachusetts. I knew that Springfield was bigger than Fairbanks, but it's still hard to get used to how many people there are out here. You know how you drive five minutes outside of Fairbanks and all you can see are forests, mountains, and a moose or two, clean and clear as a bell?

Let's just say that the area around Springfield is a little more hazy—almost like the city atmosphere is invading the countryside.

It's a little weird.

Anyway, I wanted to let you know that I met a nice guy out here. He's a detective named John Morrison, and just like Bernie, he's got this huge reputation for being able to do anything.

I'd be lying if I said he wasn't drop-dead gorgeous, too. And I think he's single. Hello.

Of course, none of that matters, because thanks to some crazy assignment, I had to question him about an arrest that happened recently. It went okay, but I could have done without that.

Anyway, I'd better get going. You'll see another e-mail I wrote to Bernie right after this one. Thank you so much for reading them to him for me.

> *Say hi to the girls.*
> *Love, Vera*

(E-mail sent 07/15/04 from Vera Demopolous [vera49@imail.com] to Sharon Washman [sharchar@imail.com], Exhibit 16, *Commonwealth v. Morrison*)

On June 18, 2004, investigators interrogated staff and management at The Burger Barn, in Norton, Massachusetts. Follow-up interviews occurred on July 7, 2004, with those not working on date of original interviews. Individuals questioned included the following: Roberta Ewing, Habib Muhammed, Steven Shey, Dory Kinder...

All interviewed were shown a photograph of Babe Gardiner, and none recognized the photo. Subjects interviewed were not made aware of the legal context of the inquiries. Although no subjects identified Gardiner, impression of investigators was that all were genuine responses.

Possible conclusions:

—One or more subjects lying—unlikely.
—One or more subjects mistaken—possible. The Burger Barn was busy and crowded on both days investigators visited, which were a Friday and a Wednesday. Gardiner states that he was there on a Friday.
—Gardiner was there but not remembered, or Gardiner was never there—likely.

(Investigator's report dated July 9, 2004, *Commonwealth v. Gardiner*, prepared for defense counsel by Maria Gallegos)

July 19, 2004

TERRY TALLACH LOOKED UP AS THE CORREC-
tions officer opened the door to the attorney/client visiting room, stuck his head in, and said, "Your guy should be
here in a few minutes. We were locked down for a little
while after lunch, and that's slowing things down." He
backed out of the room and shut the door.

"Locked down?" Terry's twenty-year-old nephew,
Sean, sounded terrified. "Wasn't everybody already locked
down?"

Sean might have been the skinniest kid Terry had ever
seen in his life. He didn't look unhealthy. Just bony. His
light, painfully thin hair swooped down over his forehead
as if he had time-traveled straight out of the 1970s. And in
case anyone doubted that he was the Grand Duke of
Geekistan, he was wearing his ridiculously out-of-date
teardrop-shaped aviator glasses, a button-down short-
sleeve shirt, and pants that were about an inch and a half
too short, revealing white socks and, naturally, black
shoes. Jesus Christ.

The last Terry had heard, Sean was acting in school
plays. And trying out for the track team. Then, out of
the blue, his sister called to report that the kid was interested in becoming a lawyer. Evidently, insanity ran in the
family.

Sean was the latest in a recent series of things that
Terry couldn't believe. He couldn't believe that his sister
had asked if Sean could work for Zack and him as an in-
tern this summer. He couldn't believe that Zack had said it
was up to him. He couldn't believe that he'd said yes.

And now he couldn't believe that the three of them
were here, in a state prison, waiting to share another
spellbinding hour with Babe Gardiner, the person most
likely to fatally injure himself while putting on a pair of

socks. While Sean got the shit scared out of him every time that somebody said boo.

Not that he could blame the poor kid. Terry's maiden voyage into a state prison to visit a client had left a very serious impression. The first time that big metal door clanged shut behind him, trapping him inside a building filled with hundreds of violent and angry people, he almost crapped his pants.

" 'Locked down' just means that, inside the prison, the inmates are locked into whatever room or area they are in at the time, and they can't move from place to place." Zack was the one who should have been Sean's uncle. He was the one with the abnormally large amounts of patience. "Usually they have some freedom of movement, as long as they have passes, or permission from the COs."

"Kind of like a college campus for sociopaths," Terry said. "Liberally decorated with razor wire."

They sat for a few moments in silence. Prison was a lot about waiting.

"So, what do you think Babe will say when he finds out that the grand jury indicted him for the murder of that convenience store clerk?" Sean asked.

"Well," Zack replied, "it may take a little while to explain it to him. It's hard to know exactly what's going on in Babe's head. Sometimes communication can be—well, challenging."

Sean looked confused. Welcome to the world of Babe. "Let me make it easy for you," Terry said. "Babe is an idiot savant without the savant part. Talk to him for more than sixty seconds and I guarantee your IQ will drop ten points. It will be a miracle if we get out of this meeting today without brain damage."

Just then, the door opened, and Babe shuffled into the room. Somehow, he managed to look both older and younger than the last time they had seen him. His hair was longer and stringier than before and still needed a good washing, but now there were a few strands of gray plainly visible. Babe was evolving from a sorry-assed fool to an aging, sorry-assed fool. It was pretty damn pathetic.

In contrast, their client's body language was headed in the opposite direction, and had regressed from high school back a few years to elementary school. Instead of his normally endearing shifty-eyed, surly slouch, Babe had adopted a more cowering pose, clutching to his chest his omnipresent, raggedy-ass manila file folder as if it were his favorite teddy bear. God only knew what was in there. Every time Terry saw the thing it got bigger, and now it must have been an inch and a half thick. Zack and Terry had only sent Babe a few letters, updating him on the case. The dozens of dog-eared papers threatening at any moment to spill all over the floor were undoubtedly the results of some intensive research that Babe had undertaken. Going through them all would take hours.

They were so screwed.

Babe sat down, Zack introduced Sean, and finally they got down to business.

"So, Babe, we wanted to come out to see you because there's been a change in the case," Zack began.

Babe had prepared himself for the meeting by opening his folder on the table, taking out a pencil, and starting to doodle in the margin of what looked like a copy of the Massachusetts criminal code.

"As you know," Zack continued, "the police found the body of Steve Hirsch, the convenience store clerk who had been robbed, in the trunk of a car a couple of weeks ago. He had been beaten to death."

Zack paused to let Babe respond. But apparently, Babe had not yet composed his thoughts. His work on what appeared to be a rendering of the rings of Saturn continued, unabated.

"Anyway," Zack continued, "the police did some more investigating, and then the Commonwealth went back to the grand jury with the evidence that the police found, and they have indicted you for the murder of the clerk."

Babe kept cruising along at full doodle ahead. If you hadn't heard the conversation, you might have guessed that Zack was giving him yesterday's baseball scores, for all it seemed to matter. Sean was looking at their client like he was a rare animal at the zoo.

"Hey, Babe, you getting all this?" Terry asked. "Zack's talking about some very important shit. They aren't just saying you robbed this guy. They're saying you killed him, too. Is there anything you can help us with? Here? On earth?"

The doodling slowed, and then stopped. Babe took a breath and then said, to no one in particular, "But the grand jury is wrong. I didn't kill that man."

Well, that was something. Of course, it wasn't a particularly useful something, but hey. This was Babe. Utility was a little much to ask for. It was, however, a start.

"Okay. You didn't kill him," Terry said. "But did something else happen with him that night? Did you go to the store at all? Do you know anything about the robbery, or how he might have gotten killed? Do you have any idea why they would be saying you did these things?"

This particular horse was already quite thoroughly beaten, dead, and buried, but shit—if Babe was going down for first-degree murder, it wasn't going to be because Terry didn't push a little. At least he was keeping his voice down.

But then, instead of answering any of the questions, Babe started to flip through the papers in the folder. Swell. Why deliver a simple answer, when you could pull some obscure document out of your ass and confuse the only people in the world trying to help you?

Sean sat back, as if Babe were on the verge of producing some frightening weapon. Zack simply asked, "What are you looking for in there, Babe?"

But Babe just kept digging until he finally, triumphantly, extracted a small group of papers. "There," he said, thrusting them at Zack. "This is an important case you can use."

Legal research was a favorite pastime of inmates. No matter what their level of education, all criminal defendants seemed moronically fixated on spending countless hours in the prison library, poring over the endless number of criminal cases decided over the past two centuries, looking for that one undiscovered detail that would unlock the door to their cell.

Zack took the papers, glanced at them, and then spread them out on the table so that Sean and Terry could see them, too. It was a photocopy of a three-page opinion, written by the Eleventh Circuit Court of Appeals, entitled *United States v. Wayne Rinaldi.*

Terry scanned the decision quickly. It was a 1982 case appealed from a decision of the District Court of Alabama, involving a guy charged with racketeering. Apparently, the government's evidence had featured some irrelevant and highly inflammatory information involving the defendant's personal life—something about the guy or his roommate being a drag queen—that the trial judge never should have let the jury hear about. So the appellate court determined that the trial was unfair, threw out the conviction, and ordered that the defendant be retried or set free.

And in a concurring opinion, one of the judges also determined that the sentence that had been imposed was improperly calculated.

If Terry had spent hours looking, he might have been able to find a case that was less related to Babe's than this one.

But it would have been tough.

"Jesus Christ, Babe," Terry began. So much for keeping his voice down. "Would you mind telling me exactly what the fu—"

But before he could finish his question, Zack pointed to the opinion and Terry looked down. His partner's finger was resting next to the last paragraph of the second page, where the court had spelled out the facts against Rinaldi. *The defendant, who was also known as "Babe," had returned from his trip earlier than expected....*

God Almighty. Babe thought this case was relevant because he and the defendant had the same nickname. And, naturally, since the Eleventh Circuit had decided that female impersonator Babe Rinaldi had been unfairly tried by some clown judge in Alabama more than twenty years ago on a gambling scheme, it was obvious that Babe Gardiner was innocent of the murder of Steve Hirsch.

Babe had recommended his interplanetary artwork. He was probably wondering why the COs weren't planning his going-away party. Sean swallowed loudly and wiped his glasses on his shirttail. It looked like there was a little sweat on his top lip.

Terry began to feel ill.

But Zack hung in there. He picked up Babe's precious research and said, "Listen, Babe, this is a very interesting case, but we're still going to have to decide what we're going to do at the trial when the government introduces, uh, tries to tell the jury that you robbed this man and killed him. Remember how we were talking about that the last time? I wonder if you remembered where you were that night, so we can tell the jury that you couldn't have robbed or killed this man, because you were doing something else."

And once again, Babe underwent his incredible transformation from idiot to lying idiot. One minute, he was just a clueless schlub, dumber than dirt, barely able to wrap his head around the concept of the difference between an accusation and proof.

And the next, he was a lying sack of shit, a festival of unmistakable nonverbal cues announcing his complete lack of veracity. He averted his eyes, he cleared his throat, he stammered, his hands shook, and he all but broadcast the following message: *Don't believe anything I'm saying.*

And what he actually said was "I, uh, I was, uh, I'm pretty sure that I was at The Burger Barn that night for dinner, but I'm not sure, exactly."

"You know what, Babe?" Terry stood up. His voice must have been a little loud, because poor Sean looked like he was about to dive under the table. Whatever. They had been trying for weeks to talk to this cretin in a calm, reasonable, Zack-like way, looking for some kind of direction in creating a defense. And yet here they were, with their heads still firmly up their asses, still stumbling around in the dark, waiting for somebody to open a map or light a candle.

Well, fuck candles. It was time to light a fire.

"Here's what I think. I think you know exactly what you did that night, and you're afraid to tell us. Maybe you went to The Burger Barn, maybe you didn't. But this 'I don't remember' story is a bunch of bullshit."

Zack was watching Babe intently. Babe was still looking down at his papers, but he had stopped doodling, which was something. Sean looked like he had come to the conclusion that the only things safe for him to move were his eyes, which were rapidly flickering back and forth between Terry and Babe.

"And you know what else I think?" By now, Terry was in full voice. Finally letting himself get into it with this guy was kind of freeing. It wasn't exactly fun, but it sure didn't suck. "I think that when the jury hears the evidence against you, they're going to wonder what you have to say for yourself. And if you get up on that witness stand and say, 'I went to The Burger Barn, but I don't remember anything else,' I swear to God they're going to convict you. Because they're going to think you're lying, and you're trying to hide something." He paused for a minute. "And you know what else I think?" Terry said. "I think they'd be right."

For a minute, no one spoke. In fact, no one moved. Which was good, because if they had, they probably wouldn't have heard Babe whisper, "Maybe they would be right."

TEN

ASSISTANT DISTRICT ATTORNEY LOVELL: *Can you describe the condition of the victim's body?*

DR. TRAHN: *Yes. The body was in a state of advanced decomposition....*

Q: *And as a result of your investigation, Doctor, what were you able to conclude with respect to the cause of death?*

A: *Because of the condition of the body, certain tests and observations were not possible, so I couldn't rule out several possible causes of death. For example, if the victim had suffered injuries to the skin, muscle, or internal organs—soft-tissue injuries, if you will—they were, for the most part, not able to be detected, because those tissues had deteriorated in the normal course of decomposition. Even with those limitations, though, I was able to observe that the victim's skull had been fractured—actually severely crushed—and the presence of dried blood on the collar and upper portion of the victim's shirt, as well as on that portion of the plastic bag that had been covering the victim's head, strongly suggest that the victim died as a result of a severe cranial injury.*

Q: *The victim died merely as a result of a broken skull bone?*

A: *No. As I said, I can't be 100 percent certain how the victim died, but when a skull is fractured as this one is, the brain suffers injuries, too. There is swelling and hemorrhaging at the site of the skull fracture, and occasionally, if the injury is severe enough, a situation develops called contrecoup contusion hemorrhaging.*

MR. WILSON: *Objection.*

THE COURT: *Overruled.*

Q: *And what is contrecoup contusion hemorrhaging?*

A: *That is bleeding in the cortex of the brain at the opposite side of the skull from where the contact injury occurred.*

Q: *Can you be sure that contrecoup contusion hemorrhaging—or any hemorrhaging—took place in this case?*

A: *No. As I said, by the time that I examined the body, the brain had decomposed too severely to make that determination.*

Q: *But is it likely that there was hemorrhaging in this case?*

A: *I would say that it is overwhelmingly likely that the brain swelled, and hemorrhaged, both at the site of the skull injury as well as on the opposite side of the brain.*

Q: *And what would the likely result of such swelling and bleeding be?*

MR. WILSON: *Objection.*

THE COURT: *Overruled.*

A: *The likely result would be what is called herniation.*

Q: *And what is that?*

A: *The brain swells to such a degree that it strangles itself against the skull, cutting off the blood supply to itself. Brain cells die. And ultimately, the entire body dies.*

(Commonwealth v. Gardiner, Trial Volume V, Pages 66–69)

* * *

AS THEY PULLED INTO THE PARKING LOT, MARIA wondered, for about the fiftieth time that day, whether they were crazy for doing this.

According to Anthony, getting a threatening phone call was a sure sign that they were doing something right.

But to Maria, getting a threatening phone call was a sure sign that she wasn't going to sleep for about six years.

They were back at The Burger Barn, the restaurant where Babe swore he'd eaten dinner on the night of the robbery. They were there to meet with the owner.

It wasn't that Maria was stupid—she knew that it was the job of private investigators to get involved in other people's business, and she also knew that there were going to be times when those people weren't going to like that very much.

But there was a huge difference between a vague understanding that her work might upset some unknown stranger at some random point in the future and a phone call in which a very real and very angry person took the time and the trouble to actually call her up on the phone and scare her to death.

"You sure you're okay?" Anthony asked as they got out of the car. Unlike the Volvo that Anthony had rented for that time they were working undercover, he was driving the vehicle he actually owned—a hot green Audi.

Every time she got into and out of the sports car, Maria felt a tiny sting of envy. One of these days she was going to be able to buy a new ride for herself.

"I'm fine," she lied, closing the door and following her boss across the parking lot and into the restaurant. The truth was that she wasn't really going to be fine until the Gardiner case was over and done with. Anthony had decided that until they finished the case, or until they found out and dealt with the person who had made the threat, whenever Maria was working, he would be with her. Thank the good Lord and Saint Francis for that, anyway.

On the way to the restaurant, Anthony had told Maria that they were now officially investigating a murder case. This high school girl had found the body of the clerk that had been robbed, and the cops had found evidence that linked Babe to the murder.

Now it was more important than ever for them to establish Babe's comings and goings on the night of the robbery. Anthony said it didn't matter if what they found confirmed that Babe spent the whole night at the convenience store, or whether they found him an airtight alibi. Their job was to find out what happened. Period.

So he had arranged a meeting with Fred French, the owner of The Burger Barn. They arrived after the place had opened for lunch, and had to be ushered back through the kitchen to Mr. French's office. "I was hoping that you might be able to look through this list of employees that Maria and I spoke to over the past couple of weeks," Anthony told the short, skinny man with the thick glasses as they entered the small, dimly lit room. "We're hoping to confirm that these are all the people that were working on Friday, March 19. We're trying to verify the story of a client who says he had dinner here that night, but your place is so busy, we haven't found anyone who specifically remembers whether he was here then." They sat down in a couple of folding chairs that were so close to the desk that their knees almost touched it.

Mr. French was old—probably sixty at least. And he looked about as brittle as a bread stick. The little hair he had left was white, and his skin was leathery and tan. His glasses were big, and tinted yellowish, and his voice was kind of rough, like he was a heavy smoker.

The thin old man coughed, took the list that Anthony

handed him, sat down at his desk, and hoisted a huge, three-ring notebook off the floor. Then he took off his glasses, flipped through the binder until he found the page he was looking for, and began to read.

Fred French's tiny desk was covered by messy mountains of paper, a telephone, and an ancient-looking Rolodex. There was also a skinny bookshelf in the corner of the room behind the desk that was overflowing with papers. There were a few old pictures sitting up on the shelves, including a black-and-white one of some soldiers standing in front of an old airplane. Next to it was a framed patch of something that looked like an angry hawk or eagle.

"I'm not on the dining room floor much anymore," Mr. French said, squinting at the paper and then back at the open binder. "But I keep the books. . . ." He left the sentence unended. As he read down the list, he reached for a pencil. "I can tell you that Shirley, and Max, and Alberto . . ." His voice trailed off again as he began to make a series of check marks on the sheet.

A minute later he put the pencil down, put his glasses back on, and handed the sheet over to Anthony. "The ones I checked off were working that night," he said. "And the only one that was working that night that you didn't talk to was Bruce Flowers, who was washing dishes. So as far as him remembering anybody specific who came in for dinner . . ." He shrugged and made a face that managed to say "You can ask him, but there's no chance."

Of course, by now, Anthony had seen the stuff on the bookshelf, too. He motioned to it and asked, "You served in World War II?"

World War II. Jesus, Mary, and Joseph. Mr. French was a lot more than sixty.

The old guy looked over his shoulder at the photo and then back to Anthony with a small smile. "Yep. Airborne."

"Wow," said Anthony. "Hundred and first?"

"Able Company. Dropped in on D-Day, liked it so much I stayed for the whole war." The smile faded. "But then again..."

Anthony was quiet for a moment, then leaned over the desk with his hand outstretched. "Thank you, sir," he said.

Mr. French was taken aback, but just for a second. He took Anthony's hand and shook it. "You're welcome," he said gruffly. Then he cleared his throat and asked in a rough voice, "Did you bring a picture of your client? Has he been coming to the restaurant for a long time?"

Whatever confusing men's moment had just happened seemed to have disappeared as quickly as it had arisen, and Anthony reached into the breast pocket of the blazer he was wearing and held out the picture they had been showing around. "His name is Rufus Gardiner, but his nickname is Babe. The other reason we came was to check and see if you recognize him at all."

That's not exactly what Anthony had told Maria. The *real* other reason that they had returned to The Burger Barn was because Anthony figured that if their prior visits had shaken somebody up, they'd visit some more, this time while the lunch staff was on duty. He planned to keep shaking until something came loose.

Maria was just hoping that whatever came loose didn't land on her head.

Mr. French coughed, took his glasses off again, and peered at the picture. "Oh him!" he said with a laugh. "I know this fellow. What did you say his name was?"

"Babe Gardiner," Anthony said.

"Yeah. That's right. Babe." He put his glasses back on and handed the picture back to Anthony. "I've seen him here a lot. A while ago he started talking to me about getting a job here, which wasn't exactly..." The restaurant owner shook his head and laughed, which started a fit of coughing. He took a handkerchief out of his back pocket and covered his mouth.

Maria stole a quick look at Anthony, who remained focused intently on Mr. French. As soon as the coughing stopped, Anthony asked, "So Babe never worked here, right?"

"I don't do much of the hiring anymore," Mr. French replied. He put the handkerchief back, then closed the three-ring binder and replaced it on the floor. "I leave most of that to the managers now, because they've got much more..." He waved his left hand vaguely. "But when you've been in business for as long as I have..." He looked down and shook his head back and forth.

It was weird, but even though the man never seemed to actually finish a sentence, Maria was always pretty sure she knew what he meant. And in this case, he meant there was no way in the world he would ever hire Babe Gardiner.

Of course, that was not exactly a great surprise. From the way the lawyers talked about him, it was a miracle Babe had any job at all.

"Can you be more specific?" Anthony asked, sitting back. "I really don't know Babe that well. Was there something about him—" He hesitated. "I guess I'm wondering how you could tell that he wouldn't have been a good worker?"

"It's funny," Mr. French said, "but after a while, you learn to go with your gut. It was a few years ago when your client was looking for a job. And even though he seemed like a nice enough kid, he always seemed to be hanging around with these other fellas..." He pursed his lips and shook his head again. Disapproval.

Anthony was still sitting back in his seat, but if he had been a dog, his ears would have been standing at attention. "Really. You know, Babe said that he was here alone that night, but I wonder if he might have forgotten that he came with somebody else."

"Well, like I said, I don't spend too much time in the dining room anymore, but come to think of it, I saw your man fairly recently, and he was here with a friend I hadn't ever seen before." He paused for a minute. "That other one—I don't know."

"You don't happen to remember the other guy's name, do you?" Anthony asked.

"I didn't speak to them—I just saw them for a few minutes. But I had this feeling that the other man was watching me..." The old man shook his head again. "I don't like to say things about other people, but there was something, I don't know, something not right...." What kind of guy was this Babe person hanging around with?

"Not exactly at the top of your party invitation list, huh?" Anthony said with a smile. "I've run into a few of those myself over the years. The kind of job I have..." And taking a page from Mr. French's conversation stylebook, he just let the phrase dangle there.

The older man smiled back and nodded. "I can imagine."

"You don't happen to remember what he looked like, do you?" Anthony continued. "I'm wondering if we can check and see if he might have been with Babe that night."

Mr. French considered that for a moment, took a breath, coughed a little, and then said, "He was a white guy, with dark hair and dark eyes, but what I really remember was that he had this pointy little beard. You know the kind. They used to call it a Vandyke."

"A goatee?"

"That's it. Exactly. A goatee."

* * *

VERA OPENED THE FILE FOLDER ONCE MORE AS she waited for the parole officer to get off the phone. The mug shot of a thick-necked, dark-haired, scowling young man with a goatee stared up at her. Roger Tedesco. Age twenty-six. Made parole about a year ago after doing four years on a conviction for robbery. Before that, he'd been on probation a few times—twice for assault and once for violating a 209A order. Apparently he had ignored the court's directive to stop calling his ex-girlfriend's new husband.

Vera had already checked with Irene Quarrels, and sure enough, the man that Irene had seen with Davy Zwaggert on the night that he'd disappeared was Roger Tedesco. Irene's description had been remarkably accurate. Right down to the barbed-wire tattoo on Tedesco's left arm.

So Vera had made an appointment to meet with Oscar Welansky, Tedesco's parole officer, hoping to find out what she could about the man who might have been the last person to see Davy Zwaggert before he disappeared.

Now she sat in a little waiting room outside Welansky's office. The phone must have rung two dozen times in the past twenty minutes. Nobody was at the receptionist's desk, so Welansky was frantically juggling calls and taking messages.

The sound of a phone being hung up was followed by a pause. Silence. Amazing. A short man in his fifties poked his head out of his door and said, "Detective Demopolous? I'm Oscar Welansky. Sorry about that. Our administrative assistant is out sick. C'mon in."

Vera sat down across from Welansky's desk as he opened a file drawer. "I set the phone to take messages for the next few minutes," he said, sifting through tons of folders, some several inches thick, and pulling out a modest-sized one. He put it on top of two stacks of file folders that sat side by side in front of him, like a little makeshift lectern.

"Tedesco, right? Let's see. He's only been out for a little while, so I don't have a heck of a lot on him." He opened the folder and began to scan through it. "Okay. Here we go. Living in a studio at Cedar Crest Apartments down on Fifth Street." He flipped over more pages. "Got two part-time jobs. Night janitor at a place called Ibis Industries on Saturday and Sunday nights, and medical supply runner—mostly blood, that kind of thing—for St. Elizabeth's Hospital, Mondays, Wednesdays, and Fridays."

He shuffled further through the file. "So far, no problems at work, AA meetings all okay, weekly drug and alcohol scans, so far so good. In fact, he's due—wait a sec." He flipped over another page, scanned it, and then turned it over and read a chart that had been made on the opposite side. A look of concern crossed his face. Then he put the paper down, flipped back through the folder, and removed a single sheet of paper. He picked up the phone and began to dial a number from the sheet.

"Excuse me, Detective," he said to Vera as he held the phone up to his ear, waiting for a connection. "It looks like we might have a little problem."

ELEVEN

ASSISTANT DISTRICT ATTORNEY LOVELL: *And what observations did you make with respect to the victim's clothing?*

DR. TRAHN: *As I mentioned, the upper portion of the victim's shirt was discolored and encrusted with dried blood. The shirt itself was a green and black T-shirt....*

Q: *Did you make any observations with respect to the pants that the victim was wearing?*

A: *Yes. The victim was wearing blue jeans and a black belt. I observed two light brown strands of hair, which appeared to be human, in the area of the victim's belt buckle.*

Q: *Did you perform any tests on the hairs?*

A: *Yes. I first made microscopic examination of the hairs and confirmed that they were, in fact, human head hairs. I then compared them to the victim's head hair, to determine if they were from him.*

Q: *And what did you find?*

A: *The victim's head hair was relatively short—about one inch in length, wiry, curly, and very dark brown. The hair found on the victim's body was longer—approximately four inches long—and as I mentioned, it was light brown. It was clearly not the victim's head hair.*

Q: *Were you able to make any other determinations regarding the hair?*

A: *Yes. At my supervisor's request, I submitted the hair for DNA analysis, along with a hair sample taken from the defendant.*

(*Commonwealth v. Gardiner,* Trial Volume V, Pages 100–102)

Hostage

AS SOON AS SHE HEARD THE TELEVISION GET turned off, she froze. And then, as quickly as she could, she began to work her way backward across the floor. She had to get her chair back to its original position, or he'd figure out what she was up to and take away the knife.

"Pain in the fucking balls. Don't tell me."

The man's voice came through from the other room loud and clear. Then there was movement, a rustling of some kind.

"Fuck! Where are you?"

He was walking around in there, looking for something. If he didn't find it, it was only a matter of time before he came through the door.

She was sweating freely now, trying hard to maintain her balance as she shifted her weight from foot to foot, moving backward slowly. She had to get back to the place in the room where he'd left her tied up. But slowly. If she moved too quickly, she'd drop the chair to the floor. And if it made too much noise when it fell, the kidnapper would come in to see what was going on, figure out what she was doing, and that would be the end of her escape plans.

Her head was killing her, and she was getting dizzy. And then a sharp pain shot through her stomach, like a quick cramp. It didn't matter. She just had to keep moving.

She took another step back with her left foot. And then one with her right. She was going to make it. Another minute, maybe two—

"Goddammit!" And then there was the sound of a bottle breaking. "Fuck!"

And then another bottle shattered. "Where *are* you?"

The sudden violence startled her, and she accidentally dropped the chair back down to the floor. Luckily, the sound of the chair hitting the floor was masked by another oath from the kidnapper. Pain tore through her skull and neck like she'd just been hit in the head with a sledgehammer.

There was a crowbar. Oh my God. The ski mask man had hit her in the head with a crowbar.

As the realization flashed into her mind, a new level of fear surged through her, and for a moment, tears welled in her eyes. And then the voice of an older man came into her mind.

Fear is like an alarm clock. Once it wakes you up, turn it off or it'll drive you crazy.

Easy for you to say, whoever you were. You weren't tied up to a chair, with some raging maniac smashing bottles in the other room with a crowbar.

She leaned forward in the chair, rose up on her toes, and started to move backward again. But then the voice from the other room resumed his crazy talking. "I know you're in here, goddammit. Where the fuck are you?"

But this time his voice was louder. He was very close. And then there was the sound of the doorknob turning.

She hadn't gotten back to where she had started, but she was out of time. She had to hope that he didn't realize that she had moved her chair since he had first taped her up. If he figured out what she had been doing, everything would be lost.

She froze as the door squeaked open, and gingerly lowered herself back down so that the legs of the chair were again resting on the floor. She closed her eyes and tried to make every muscle in her body relax, as if she were still unconscious.

The doorway he was entering was behind her, so she had no idea whether the man with the ski mask had seen her as she was trying to make her way back from the table. She realized that she was holding her breath, and slowly exhaled, desperately trying to imitate how a person would breathe if they didn't know that their angry kidnapper who had lost something had just walked into the room.

When the door stopped squeaking there was a moment of silence, followed by "Ha!"

And then he was walking toward her.

Had he seen her trying to move around? Would he realize that the chair was a few feet from where it had been when he first tied her up? Was he going to hit her in the head again with the crowbar? She fought the tears that threatened to leak out of her closed eyes.

In three steps he had reached her, and in his fourth step, he walked right past her. Yuk. He smelled like he'd just taken a bath in beer. And then splashed on a little body odor cologne.

She stayed absolutely still, but dared to open her eyes a slit.

Through her eyelashes and unshed tears she could just make out that he was at the table. Then he was leaning across it, reaching for something. A beer can fell to the floor.

"Fuck," he said absently. Then he said, "Here we are. Yeah. This'll work." He moved a little to his left, leaning on the table to steady himself. He looked totally drunk. And something else was wrong, but before she could figure it out, he turned back around, and she closed her eyes again, terrified that somehow he'd know she was looking at him.

Her head throbbed so badly it felt like her skull was vibrating. Would this headache ever go away? And then there was another stab of pain in her stomach. God. Stomach cramps. Could anything else go wrong?

There was the sound of a paper bag rattling, and then the sound of the top being twisted off a glass bottle. Then he was drinking something.

Of course. He had been looking for alcohol. And that little brown bag on the table must have been holding a small bottle of whiskey or something.

"Yeah," he said in what sounded like relief, exhaling loudly. And then he was walking past her again, and the door squeaked, and then it closed.

She just sat there. She had to remember to keep breathing. In and out. In and out. Slowly. Listen. Was he still there?

The man seemed so drunk she couldn't believe that he had the presence of mind to try to catch her in some kind of trap, but she didn't want to take any chances.

And then, from the other side of the door, she heard the television come on again. Hallelujah. He was gone from the room.

She opened her eyes fully and took a deep breath. She had to get over to that table as soon as possible. With him as drunk as he was, there was no predicting what might happen. He could barely stand up straight. God help her if he decided to move her, or anything else.

She steadied herself, preparing to tip forward and make her way over to the table. And then she saw what he had done.

He hadn't just taken the bottle with the alcohol in it.

He had also taken the Swiss Army knife.

July 20, 2004

ZACK PUSHED HIS CHAIR BACK FROM HIS DESK and looked over at Terry as the burly lawyer paced back and forth in the office. Sean was sitting on the couch, reading through a book on criminal procedure. He had been immersing himself in the Gardiner case, reading old files, the transcripts of Babe's old guilty pleas, and running to the law library every time he came upon a subject he didn't understand. He learned at a terrific pace, but lately, he looked a little nervous. Or maybe that's just the way he always looked.

" 'Maybe they'll be right'?" Terry spat out, pausing for a minute to sit down. Then he got right up again and headed back across the room. "I tell him that the jury is going to think he's a liar, and he says, 'Maybe they'll be right'?" Terry had reached the far wall, and turned back. "Who does he think he is? Fucking Confucius? This guy used to piss me off because he was so goddamn stupid. Now he's just pissing me off." He made his voice sound like Babe's. " 'I'm lying; I'm not lying. I was at the restaurant, I wasn't at the restaurant. I did it, I didn't do it.' " He threw his hands up in exasperation. "You know what? Fuck it. I say screw pretrial preparation. Screw cross-examination. Screw everything. Let's show up at the trial, sit there, let the prosecution witnesses say whatever they want, and then just stick Babe up there on the stand and see what happens."

Whenever Terry and Zack had a criminal client like Babe Gardiner, there came a time in the case when Terry's peanut-sized reserve of patience just disappeared.

Usually it arrived fairly late in the game. Sometimes he would blow up when a client resisted a particular trial strategy they suggested. Other times he just exploded when the ever-present realization that they were probably going to lose reasserted itself.

It was funny how criminal defense work sometimes appealed to very competitive people. Talk about a death wish. You're the kind of person who loves winning, and you get into a field where if you win a few cases, you're a big hero. Win close to as many as you lose and you're a force of nature.

But in Babe's case, Zack understood Terry's frustration. For whatever reason, Babe seemed unusually committed to his plan of self-destruction. Step One: Withhold from his attorneys any useful information about his actions on the night of the robbery. Step Two: Repeat Step One.

Terry's instincts were right on—it was obvious that Babe was hiding something from them. What was so frustrating, though, was that Zack's instincts were screaming that whatever Babe did that night, it wasn't rob and murder that store clerk.

Sean watched as his very large uncle finally came in for a landing on the chair across from the couch. "Okay," Terry said, closing his eyes and squeezing his forehead with one hand. "I've got three quick questions. What? The? *Fuck?*" He opened his eyes and looked over at Zack. "I mean really. He admits that he's hiding something, you ask him to explain himself, and he says to forget it—it doesn't mean anything. I swear to God, I was about five seconds away from dumping the case. Or beating the shit out of him. That would have worked for me." He turned to Sean. "'Course, then I'd have been stuck explaining to your mother how I managed to put you in the middle of a prison riot."

Terry's nephew forced a smile. The poor kid looked like he could use about a week of relaxation therapy. Sean seemed to be one of those people who adopted the stress levels of whoever was around him. Which meant that since he was planning on spending the next few months working with his uncle Terry, he was going to have a pretty exhausting summer.

Especially since they were going to be involved with the Babe Gardiner case, which promised to drive Terry crazier than normal.

Thankfully, the big man had settled back in the chair and had started to read the newspaper. Although these days, even that was a mixed blessing. It would distract him from how angry he was at Babe, but it was only a matter of time before some political thing would set him off.

Babe's behavior was weird, to put it mildly, but when you worked with people who got accused of crimes, you ran into weird a lot. And Babe's unwillingness to trust them was also something that Zack and Terry had experienced plenty of times before. In fact, it had become a kind of running joke.

Despite the fact that it was a complete falsehood, more than half of Zack's criminal clients had at one time or another told him that they feared he would "sell them out" because, among other things, he ate lunch all the time with the prosecutors and judges.

Terry made a sound of disgust and then said, "Goddamned Nazis," as he dropped one section of the paper onto the floor and picked up another. Sean glanced over at his uncle, then looked at Zack, before he returned his attention to his book.

By this time in the case, usually Zack and Terry had managed to convince their clients that they were, in fact, actually fighting for them, and not against them. Clearly, they had not yet managed to get that message through to Babe.

But Zack wasn't ready to give up on the case. There was something driving their client to be so ridiculously closemouthed. It was up to them to find out what was going on, because the last thing they needed was for there to be a surprise at the trial.

And thanks to the new indictment charging Babe with the murder of the store clerk, there was absolutely no chance that they could plead this case out. It had been bad enough when Babe had just been facing the robbery charge—the best they could have done with a plea to his third felony was agreeing to the minimum sentence, fifteen years.

But pleading out this murder charge was going to be next to impossible. First of all, murder carried with it an automatic life sentence. Their only hope was to talk the D.A. into reducing the charge to manslaughter, which had a twenty-year maximum. And given what Zack knew of the evidence so far, there wasn't a chance in hell that they were going to be able to talk the D.A. into anything. If Zack were the D.A., he wouldn't touch a plea bargain with a ten-foot pole.

And then Zack got an idea. Oh boy, was Terry going to hate this.

"Hey. Remember that cop that sent the letter asking if she could talk to Babe about the murder charge?"

Babe's case had already established itself as a pretty strange one by the time that Zack and Terry had received that bizarre letter from the female detective—Vera something—asking if they would permit her to ask their client some questions about the murder.

"No," Terry said absently. He had put the paper down and was flipping through the latest issue of *Sports Illustrated*. He'd probably found the ads in there for the special reissue of the swimsuit edition. It looked like it was going to be a good one. "Didn't we ignore her, or tell her to go away or something?"

The detective's request itself wasn't that bizarre—cops were always happy to talk to defendants whenever they could. Zack had once lost a case because a client he had been defending at a trial went to the bathroom during a recess and got into a conversation with the guy standing next to him at the sink.

Who just happened to be an out-of-uniform state trooper taking a break from testifying in another trial, and who was only too happy to listen to the defendant say some smug and foolishly incriminating things about himself, and then report them to the prosecutor. Next thing you know, the state trooper is a witness in Zack's case.

"Trooper Browning, can you tell the jury what the defendant said to you as you were in the bathroom this afternoon?"

"He said, 'I'm not saying I did it, but I'm not saying I didn't do it, either. All I'm saying is that there's no way this jury's gonna convict me. My lawyer is way too good, and the cops have no idea what happened. They got it all wrong.'"

About an hour and a half later, the defendant got the guilty verdict he so richly deserved.

Now Zack stood up and walked over to a file cabinet. "Yeah, but then the detective wrote again about a different case she was working on." He began to look through the correspondence folder in Babe's case. "Here it is," he said, pulling out the letter. "She's trying to track down some fugitive. This guy had a part-time job at the same place Babe worked. He disappeared around the same time as the robbery."

Terry put the magazine down. "What?" Zack could almost see his friend wrestling his attention away from the bathing suits and back to what Zack was saying. "Wait a minute. How does talking to a cop help Babe? I mean, good luck to the police finding their fugitive, but I'm sorry—please do it without interrogating our so-much-of-a-loser client."

Normally, Zack would agree with Terry. But this was an unusual case.

"Yeah, I know what you mean, but I was wondering." Zack sat back down in his chair and reached over for the Nerf football that was resting on his desk. Justin loved playing catch with Zack, but even for a six-year-old, he was amazingly bad at it. So far, the Nerf football had caused no injuries to the little guy, and had proven relatively easy for him to catch.

"Wondering what?"

Zack tossed the ball to Terry, who caught it with one hand. "I was just thinking that the way things stand right now, if we go to trial, we have basically nothing. We have no alibi, we have no explanation for how or why Babe might have been misidentified by the clerk, we have no explanation for how Babe's hair was found with the victim's body."

Terry snorted. "Yeah, and that's before our secret weapon starts testifying. As soon as the Babinator opens his mouth, it's a lock that the jury will hook him for murder."

"That's why I was wondering if we should let him talk to this detective. The guy she's looking for disappeared around the same time as the robbery. So far we haven't been able—"

"You cannot be serious," Terry interrupted, throwing the ball back to Zack. "Let this asshole talk to a cop? That's all we need. This is Babe Gardiner here. The facts can only hurt us. Besides, how do you think this detective is going to handle it when Babe starts in with his 'Maybe they'll think I'm a liar' routine? I'll tell you one thing. I'm not going to be the one trying to cross-examine her."

"I'm not saying we let him talk about this case," Zack said. "I'm just thinking that we let him talk to her about the missing persons thing. Especially since it's around the same time as the robbery. I don't know." Maybe Terry was right. Letting any client talk to the cops was pretty crazy. And letting Babe talk to the cops...

"Of course, we've got absolutely nothing to lose," Terry said. "For all we know, Babe knows this guy did something and is protecting him. But still, letting that idiot start to babble—"

"That's the thing," Zack interrupted. "I'm not sure, but I thought maybe if Babe actually started talking about things around that time that he was confident wouldn't get him in trouble, maybe he'd say something, or remember something, or, shit." He shrugged and turned to Terry's nephew. "I don't know. This is all so crazy. What do you think, Sean?"

The young man had been following the conversation like a tennis match, doing little more than pivoting his head back and forth to watch whoever was talking. The question startled him, and he lost hold of the book he had been reading. It snapped shut abruptly in his lap, which startled him again.

"I, uh—" He cleared his throat. "It's not a trap, is it? I mean, the cops. They aren't trying to trick Babe into saying something they could use in the trial, are they?"

"I suppose they could be," Zack responded.

"No freakin' way." Terry got up to pace. "I mean, don't get me wrong. I wouldn't put it past them to try anything to nail a defendant. But remember. This is Babe." He shook his head as he reached up and straightened a row of books on the highest shelf in the bookcase opposite the chair he normally occupied. "The case they've got against him is so solid, I can't see them wasting their time. And besides, that moron O'Neill has the whole county buying into his 'Case Closed' bullshit. They think they've got our guy cold. They are so done with this thing."

Hampshire County District Attorney Francis X.

O'Neill had made headlines several months ago with the announcement of his "Case Closed" program. It was a new philosophy of law enforcement purportedly designed to ensure that prosecutors and police were rededicated— whatever that meant—to getting quick and final resolution to all criminal cases. According to F.X., the public deserved such a system, because it gave them "the most efficient and effective criminal justice system that their tax dollars could buy."

O'Neill was only a district attorney, so he had no official authority over anyone but assistant district attorneys, but the local cops had all bought into the plan anyway because what was good for F.X. was probably good for them, too. The cops knew that, in theory, the "Case Closed" program was supposed to be a revolutionary way to bring criminals to justice; but, in reality, it was nothing more than a publicity stunt to get O'Neill on the front pages so he had more momentum behind him when he announced that he was running for governor.

In practice, all it meant was that as soon as the police thought they had enough evidence to convict someone of a crime they were investigating, they passed the case on to the prosecutor's office and moved on to another investigation. That was fine with the police. And as soon as the assistant district attorney handling the case got a conviction—either through a trial or a guilty plea—he or she was directed to never look at the case or the facts around it again. "Let convicted dogs lie," declared F.X. He'd probably worked on that line for a long time.

"Case Closed" wasn't so much about getting the guilty man. It was about getting any man. Quickly. And forever.

"So what do you think?" Zack asked his partner. Letting Babe talk to anyone was a gamble, but going forward

with what they had was a sure bet—that he'd get convicted.

"I guess so," Terry said, dropping himself back into
his chair. "It can't get much worse, can it? And maybe Detective—what's her name?"

Zack picked up the letter again. "Demopolous."

"Right. You never know. Maybe Detective Demopolous
will make a scary face, Babe will confess, and we can all go
home."

TWELVE

MCI–WAKEFIELD INMATE DISCIPLINARY REPORT

Date:	*June 1, 2004*
Reporting Person:	*Sergeant Femau*
Inmate Charged:	*Rufus Gardiner*
Rules Violated:	*3, 4, 16*
Charges:	*Fighting, refusal to obey direct order, conduct dangerous to institution*

Report: On May 31, 2004, while monitoring inmates at the basketball court, I and C.O. Yellen observed Inmate Roderick Rolle approach Inmate Gardiner and begin to speak to him. Gardiner began to walk away, and Rolle grabbed him by the front of the shirt.

Gardiner tried to pull away from Rolle, but while still speaking to Gardiner, Rolle began to slap Gardiner in the face. Gardiner began to struggle with Rolle, and slap back.

At that time, I reported the fight on my radio, called for backup at the basketball court, and initiated a lockdown. At that time C.O. Nucci was already responding, and I approached the inmates with him and C.O. Yellen, instructing them both to stand down. Rolle and Gardiner ignored our orders and continued to fight.

We then pulled the two apart. Gardiner was escorted to health services pending treatment for injuries received in the fight. Rolle was placed in segregation pending a hearing on this matter.

Recommendations: Rolle—major infraction—instigating a fight, refusal to obey orders, conduct dangerous to the safe operation of the institution. Gardiner—minor infraction—fighting, refusal to obey orders, conduct dangerous to the safe operation of the institution.

MEMORANDUM AND ORDER ON DEFENDANT'S MOTION TO SUPPRESS

This matter came before the court on defendant's Motion to Suppress evidence on grounds that it was obtained by police as the result of an unconstitutional search of the defendant's premises....

The testimony of the police officers was not fully credible. Recognizing this, the Commonwealth advances a novel argument: the volume of drugs seized by the police establishes the severity and the extent of the criminal activity of the defendant, and public policy demands that this case establish an exception to the exclusionary rule, such that the evidence may be used at trial against the defendant.

The Commonwealth's argument, however, ignores the fact that the exclusionary rule was established by the United States Supreme Court with full recognition that, occasionally, defendants who committed serious crimes would not suffer successful prosecution....

Accordingly, it is the order of this court that the defendant's Motion to Suppress evidence is ALLOWED, and in accordance with the representations of the Commonwealth, the case against the defendant is to be dismissed....

By order of the Court,
Robert K. Park, Justice of the Superior Court

(Commonwealth v. Tippett, Trial Paper Number 12)

August 2, 2004
Five weeks before the Babe Gardiner trial

ASSISTANT DISTRICT ATTORNEY LOUIS LOVELL
had just logged on to do some research at the exact moment that his boss, District Attorney Francis "F.X."
O'Neill, learned of the outcome of the Tippett case.

"Goddammit!" bellowed F.X. from down the hall. "Is
he in his office? I told him this is exactly what I did *not*
want to happen. Where is he?"

Warren Tippett was a drug dealer who had been
caught with a huge stash of cocaine in his apartment. But
the cops who had found the drugs had been about as bad
as cops could be, and that virtually guaranteed the drugs
couldn't be used as evidence in a trial.

Knowing that the case was likely to be thrown out because of the bad search, Tippett's attorney had told Louis
that she'd accept a guilty plea, but only to a reduced charge—
straight possession, instead of possession with intent to distribute—and with a ludicrously inappropriate sentence.

So Louis was faced with a dilemma. He could accept
a deal that was a mockery of justice. Or he could push
forward and try to make some argument that even though
the cops had probably violated the Constitution, the nature of the crime was so serious that the drugs should be
admitted as evidence anyway.

Against what he knew his boss would want, Louis rejected the plea bargain. Because bargains like that were
just *wrong*.

But at the suppression hearing, where Louis hoped to
convince the judge that the case should go forward, it became clear that the cops not only violated the federal and
state constitutions in ridiculously blatant ways when they
searched the place for the drugs, but they were shame-
lessly lying about what they did.

It was beyond embarrassing.

Thank goodness Judge Park had seen through their baloney. It would have been awful if one of Louis's witnesses had fooled a judge into getting a totally false picture of what had happened.

But predictably, Judge Park had also recognized that what the cops had done had effectively guaranteed that the Commonwealth would be unable to use the drugs as evidence against Tippett. He rejected all of Louis's arguments to the contrary.

Good-bye drugs, good-bye case.

Hello screaming F.X. O'Neill.

Even when he was calm, F.X.'s natural skin tone and prematurely gray hair made him look a little red in the face. But when he was angry, he looked like a human fire truck.

And he was angry now.

"Didn't we talk about this?" F.X. raged as he barged into the crowded office. "Didn't I tell you that it would be much better if you took a plea than if this case got kicked because of some stupid suppression motion?" He was holding a copy of Judge Park's decision in his hand. Crushing it, actually. "This is really going to screw me in the press, you know. I can't wait until I start to see the headlines." He shut his eyes. "They're going to say 'Case Closed.' I just know they are."

F.X. was probably right.

Of course, any mocking in the newspapers that he got, he probably deserved.

It was hard not to be cynical about a boss who was obviously more interested in convicting anyone of any crime than in convicting the right person of the appropriate crime.

It wasn't that F.X. was out to put innocent people in

jail. Far from it. He wanted to lock up the bad guys just as much as the rest of them.

It's just that convictions were so important to the politically motivated district attorney that he didn't seem particularly worried when, during the course of a case, doubt arose as to the guilt of a defendant. Nor did he seem overly concerned with things like the Canons of Ethics that supposedly governed all lawyers' actions, or even ethics in general. For F.X., the ends pretty much always justified the means. And in the world of district attorneys, the ends were convictions.

"I like you, Louis, I really do. But if this is the way you're going to handle your files, I think you and I might begin to have a problem. In fact, we already do have a problem with the Gardiner case."

Louis should have realized that he was going to run into such problems right from the start of his employment with the District Attorney's Office. His very first meeting with his new boss had been highlighted by a strange mix of small talk—gossip about judges and lawyers whom Louis had never heard of—and a fatherly recitation of F.X. O'Neill's twin philosophies of criminal law:

—In the language of prosecutors, the word "guilty" has only one translation: job well done. So you can guess what "not guilty" means.
—An assistant district attorney's job is simple: do whatever it takes to convict the defendant. Leave the rest to somebody else.

It wasn't that Louis had ignored F.X. It was just impossible to accept that the man really believed exactly what he had said. That kind of language only made sense if you looked at criminal trials like high school football games. Because if you truly understood criminal justice, what F.X. had said to Louis in that first meeting was flat-out wrong.

A prosecutor's duty was not simply to get convictions. Some of the most eloquent words ever uttered by American judges dealt with the vital role that prosecutors played in ensuring juries and judges learn the truth—whatever it might be—surrounding an alleged crime. In fact, Louis's favorite quote of all time was from former Supreme Court Justice Felix Frankfurter, which had been inscribed into a beautiful curved wall on the first floor of the new federal courthouse in Boston: *Justice is but truth in action.*

Not exactly one of the foundations of the F.X. O'Neill school of criminal law.

Instead, with the "Case Closed" program now in full swing, it was almost like F.X. had taken a major step toward institutionalizing a complete disregard for the truth in the criminal justice system. What difference did it make what *really* happened? The cops did what they were supposed to do—they arrested somebody. Now it was time for the District Attorney's Office to finish the job and get that somebody behind bars.

Louis was extremely proud of his role as an assistant district attorney. But he was not just a hired gun hoping to notch his belt with a gaudy number of guilty verdicts. He was a part of a great system that was, in turn, a part of the greatest country in the world. And if the system produced a certain number of acquittals, that did not necessarily mean that prosecutors were failing to do their jobs.

In some cases, it might mean that the police failed to do theirs—say, when they completely trampled someone's constitutional rights when they searched his apartment without a warrant.

"I understand, F.X., but the best plea deal I could make was eighteen months for simple possession under twenty-eight grams. The guy had over thirty pounds of cocaine in his place. I just couldn't in good conscience put your office in the position of accepting that kind of a deal. It would have made you look terrible." It would have made the whole system look terrible, in fact, but F.X. was pretty exclusively worried about how he would look, so Louis decided to focus on that, and see what happened.

"Look *terrible*? Are you kidding? How do you think I'm going to look when this decision is pasted all over the front pages?" F.X.'s volume knob was still up to ten, and his face still looked like he had spent the last week and a half on a sunny beach in Florida. "Do you think they're going to blame the *cops* for this? Absolutely not. This is going to land right on *me.* . . ." His voice trailed off, and his eyes narrowed a bit. "Who was the judge on this one again?"

"Judge Park."

F.X. pursed his lips, looked over at the framed diplomas that Louis had on his wall, and took a noisy breath. "Where's he from? Korea, right? Didn't he hand out that three-to-five for that rape thing last year? Maybe we can drop this on him," he said, in a much more controlled voice. "I'll call Denny Garrity over at the *Post* and see what he thinks."

Then he walked over to the office door, closed it, and turned back to Louis, meeting his gaze directly. "I'm going to tell you something now, Louis, that you had better remember." Although the district attorney had lowered his voice, a vein in his florid forehead was frighteningly visible. He was still extremely angry.

"When I heard that you rejected that guilty plea and went ahead with the suppression hearing, I thought that you were going to lose. So I decided to take the Gardiner case away from you."

Louis inhaled deeply. He had been afraid that it was going to come down to this.

He had worked on misdemeanors and low-level crimes for five years and had just started to take on the most serious felony cases. He was good at his job, and he loved the fact that by being a part of the criminal justice system, he was helping make his society safe and fair, and his country strong.

But there was no way he was going to be able to keep working, at least in this office, if he was going to be demoted for refusing to accept a plea bargain that served nobody's purposes except his boss's personal political one. But before he got a chance to respond, F.X. kept talking.

"And then I learned that Stacy Ruben had to go out on emergency maternity leave or some kind of nonsense, Blaine and Jesse already have way too much on their plates, and you're the only one with enough experience left to do it."

Of course F.X. wouldn't get his own hands dirty on a case like this. There was nothing to gain. The last case he actually tried was a high-profile death penalty case, and the only reason he did that one was to get in front of the television cameras.

"So I've got no choice but to leave this file with you. But I'm warning you. If you have any doubt—and I mean *any* doubt at all—that you're not going to get a conviction, you'd better get a plea bargain out of this thing, or I swear to God, I will fire you so fast, Louis, your head will spin."

IT DIDN'T MATTER HOW MANY TIMES HE WENT into one of these places—Elmo still hated them.

MCI–Wakefield was a medium-security prison, and that meant that you had to go through the whole damned search process every time you went for a visit. Elmo signed in at the outer control room desk, and then sat down in the waiting room with all the pathetic wives and girlfriends and mothers and fathers who were waiting to get in.

Elmo hated all of it, and would never have been here if he could have used the mail. But they read everything that comes into the prison, and there was no way he could risk having this information getting into the wrong hands.

A gigantic colored woman—damn, there were a lot of female guards here—came out from behind a desk and shouted, "Numbers one through five line up over by the lockers on the left side of the table. Take off your shoes and belts and make sure you have everything out of your pockets."

Elmo hated taking off his shoes and his belt and walking through the X-ray machine. He hated standing there with his arms outstretched while they waved that electronic wand around. It made him feel like the prison guards thought he was some kind of loser.

The truth was, anyone who worked inside a prison was a loser. The clowns that signed up as correction officers couldn't carry the jockstrap of a real cop. Most of them were alcoholic high-school dropouts that beat their wives. Or husbands. Jesus, that colored woman was *huge*.

He'd timed his visit to begin in the middle of the afternoon, just after the shift change, so he didn't have to share the visiting room with a huge crowd. Most of the regulars had come right after lunch and were already heading home. That was best—he could say what he had to say without other people sitting so close that they could hear him.

MCI–Wakefield's visiting room, like all Massachusetts prison visiting rooms, was full of security cameras. The cameras were supposed to prevent visitors from trying to slip things into the hands of inmates, or vice versa. And that was a good thing, because these assholes would try anything. He'd heard one time that a woman smuggled drugs into the prison in a condom shoved up into her sex. Then, after she passed through security, she went into the bathroom, took the condom out, washed it off, stuck it in her mouth, and then passed it to her boyfriend when she kissed him in the visiting room.

But as far as Elmo knew, they hadn't started bugging rooms. Guards walked around a little, but they were mostly lazy, and as long as you didn't raise your voice, they didn't know and really didn't care what you were saying.

That was good, because what he had to say today was very important.

THIRTEEN

ASSISTANT DISTRICT ATTORNEY LOVELL: *Can you describe DNA?*

MS. WARDLAW: *DNA stands for deoxyribonucleic acid. It's a very long molecule found in the nucleus of cells, which are the building blocks of living things.*

Q: *And how is DNA used in the tests that your company was asked to perform in this case?*

A: *DNA is basically a chain made up of links, and each link is one of four different amino acids—adenine, cytosine, guanine, and thymine. Every person's DNA has a unique sequence of these four amino acids, making their DNA different from everyone else's in the world.*

In this case, our company examined and compared DNA samples we were provided, to determine whether the samples came from the same individual.

Q: *Can you describe the techniques used to perform your tests?*

A: *There are a variety of techniques available for DNA testing, such as Restriction Fragment Length Polymorphism, and Polymerase Chain Reaction....*

Q: *At the end of the testing, were you able to come to any conclusions?*

A: *Yes. We were able to determine that there was a 99.9969 percent probability that the two hair samples provided to us came from the same individual.*

(*Commonwealth v. Gardiner*, Trial Volume V, Pages 111–183)

August 10, 2004

BEFORE DETECTIVE VERA DEMOPOLOUS EVEN said a word, Terry knew that her interview with Babe was going to be a disaster. An irritating disaster.

First of all, the woman was too damn good-looking. The moment she walked into the room where he, Zack, and Sean were waiting for Babe to arrive, it was like somebody turned up the lights. And then, when she smiled and introduced herself, Jesus Christ.

She was in her late twenties or early thirties, and probably a little shorter than normal. Maybe not. She had shiny, wavy dark brown hair that didn't quite reach her shoulders, dark eyes, a surprisingly fair complexion, and a slightly exotic look to her.

The woman didn't belong in a police department. She belonged on a billboard for Hooters.

Actually, that wasn't fair to Detective Demopolous. She was dressed in a totally professional manner that made it impossible to tell much about her body—black pants and a black and gray shirt thing with a gray jacket. She looked all business, but somehow, she seemed to radiate something...extra.

The thing was, whether Vera Demopolous was hot or just good-looking, or whatever the heck she was, it was a pain in the ass that Terry found her so attractive. First of all, he was a defense attorney. Falling for a cop made about as much sense as taking mambo lessons in a minefield.

And second, Terry had plenty of other things to worry about, like his dumb-ass client, who just at that moment chose to join them by opening the door and showcasing his spill-every-legal-paper-he-had-all-over-the-place routine.

It wasn't clear whether it was Babe's nervousness at the idea of speaking to the police, his refusal to leave that moronic file folder in his cell, or the dark cloud of dim-wittedness that perpetually enveloped him, but something about Babe's stupidity today was really pissing Terry off.

He really shouldn't have been expecting anything good from this meeting. The detective had given them written confirmation that the only people she was going to ask Babe about were his coworker, Roger Tedesco, and the fugitive she was looking for, a guy named Davy Zwaggert. But even so, Babe Gardiner was such a guilty-looking shit-for-brains that it would be a miracle if they got out of this interview without him racking up another five or six felony charges.

Right now, Babe seemed desperately committed to misunderstanding every single thing that anyone said to him. He had just answered a perfectly obvious question like the utter idiot he was.

Zack was looking at their client in a weird way. Probably forgot about Babe's superhuman powers of incomprehension. The Astounding Mr. Rockhead.

"I'm sorry, I should have been more clear," the cop was saying. "When I said how did you meet him, I meant to ask, when you started working at Ibis Industries, was Roger—did Roger Tedesco already have a job there at that time? At the time you started working there?"

Terry had to give this detective credit. No matter what foolish thing Babe said, she managed to work with him until they all understood what he meant. No lunging across the table to murder him, no collapsing into a sobbing, suicidal heap on the floor.

Babe turned to a blank sheet in the middle of the morass of his invaluable research and was now penciling away at some geometric mess on the side of the page. "Um, no. Roger didn't start working there until later."

"Do you remember the first time you realized that he was missing?"

As Babe went on about how much he didn't know, Detective Vera's voice seemed to relax him, at least a little. Babe was now able to answer about every other question without donning his trademark mask of concentration—a disturbing facial contortion achieved by shutting his eyes so tightly that he looked like he was either taking a crap in his pants or trying to keep his brain from blasting through his skull.

But whatever was going on in Babe's head, enough of him had grown comfortable with Detective Demopolous that although he still was ridiculously unable to make eye contact with her, at least it looked like he wanted to.

Maybe the fact that Vera's voice was sexy was somehow getting through to him. Or wait. Sexy and something else. Reassuring? Whatever it was, it was starting to look like the man without a brain was crushing on the detective.

And wasn't that just dandy. All they needed was for this guy to start drooling over some female cop. As if Babe didn't have enough to worry about.

"I never worked the same shift as Roger except one night," Babe explained. "The regular night janitor was named Pedro. He was Roger's partner, but he got sick or something, and my boss asked me to stay for the night shift. So I did."

Detective Vera shifted a little in her seat, which was

nice to look at. How did women do that? "When did you work together?"

Babe stopped doodling and licked his lips. His Neanderthal brow furrowed. "The night shift. Six to two in the morning."

Could this guy be any dumber?

"Not what time of day, Babe," Zack said. "When you worked together with Roger, was it close to the time he disappeared? Was it months before? What time of year was it? Do you remember?"

Vera smiled at Zack's futile attempt to un-confuse Babe. She was one of those women that looked better when she smiled. She probably knew it, too.

Terry began to feel uncomfortable. He felt stupid enough letting a cop interrogate their client. Getting attracted to the cop while she was doing it was making him feel extra stupid.

And what if she knew what kind of an effect she was having on him? Jesus Christ. What if she was some kind of manipulative—

"I think that's all I have, Babe, unless you can think of something else that might help us find Roger."

Good luck with that.

Babe kept doodling. "I don't think so."

Vera stood up. "Well, thank you very much, Babe, and Sean, Zack, Terry. It was nice meeting you."

She shook hands with all of them. Her grip was firm and dry. Her hand was smooth. He regretted when she broke contact with him and signaled to the guard. Swell. Now *he* was crushing on her.

Babe was escorted out, and then Vera followed. Damn. She looked good leaving a room. He was *so* fucked.

And then Zack's voice broke the silence. "So," he said. "Now we've got something to work with."

* * *

"WAIT A MINUTE," MARIA SAID. "HOW DO YOU already know the name of the guy that Mr. French told us about?"

She and Anthony were driving out to Laurelton to check into a lead. They were hoping to find the creepy man with the goatee that Mr. French had said was hanging around with Babe at The Burger Barn. She watched as Anthony passed a slow-moving tractor-trailer. Then he moved into the lane in front of the truck, shifted into high gear, and answered, "I got a call from Babe's lawyers last night. They wanted me to look into some guy on parole named Roger Tedesco. I guess the cops were questioning Babe about him because he was on parole and now he's missing."

Uh oh.

Maria did not believe in coincidences. Where there was smoke, there was fire.

And right now, Babe Gardiner seemed like he was fully ablaze.

First he gets ID'd by a clerk as the guy who robbed him. Then the clerk ends up dead, with Babe's DNA on the corpse in the trunk of some car.

And now the cops were looking for a missing fugitive who just happened to have worked at the same place as Babe.

Uh oh for sure. This Babe was starting to sound like a pretty dangerous guy.

"Anyway," Anthony continued, "they sent over a picture of Tedesco, and guess what? He's got a goatee."

Another coincidence. As if this case wasn't already freaky enough, with the threatening phone call and the disappearing people and the dangerous-sounding client.

"So I thought I'd take a chance, and earlier this

morning, I faxed a picture of Tedesco over to Mr. French. Sure enough, he confirmed that Tedesco was the guy he saw with Babe that night at The Burger Barn." He reached over and adjusted the air conditioner. The little car already felt great just as it was. Anthony was always tinkering with things to make them a little bit better.

"So I figured we could head out to the place they worked—Ibis Industries. I want to talk to their boss, see if I can pick up a lead on this Tedesco guy."

Anthony turned into the parking lot of the facility and drove toward the entrance. It was impossible to know what anyone did at Ibis Industries from the outside. It was just a big, flat brick building on a road with a lot of other big, flat brick buildings.

"But what difference does it make about Roger Tedesco?" she asked as they walked through the parking lot toward the front door. "Babe said that he was alone the night he went to The Burger Barn. The night that clerk got robbed. Or killed."

"The coroner's office is saying it's possible that he died on the same day as the robbery."

"So if Babe was alone that night, why do we care about Roger Tedesco?"

Anthony opened the entrance door for her as they stepped into the lobby. The ugly waiting room was empty, and the receptionist's desk had a little sign on it that read *Back in 5 Minutes*. Anthony and Maria sat and waited in the uncomfortable plastic chairs.

"Zack said that they're getting kind of desperate," Anthony said. "Trial's supposed to start in a couple of weeks. If we don't turn up something soon, Babe's hardly going to have any defense."

Maria looked up at her boss and said, "I'm sorry, but from what everybody's telling me, it's starting to look like there might not *be* any defense."

* * *

RIGHT AFTER THE MEETING IN THE PRISON, Zack and Terry dropped Sean off and headed for dinner at The Sun Spot. As soon as Sean closed the door and they drove off, Zack asked, "So, what do you make of Detective Demopolous?"

Terry made a face and passed a minivan. "I think we might have a problem."

Zack was instantly transported back six years into the past.

He was sure that Terry didn't remember, but those were the exact words he had used when he came to tell Zack that Justin's mother had gone into labor almost six weeks early.

Zack hadn't been nearly ready. And obviously, neither was the mother. But suddenly, regardless of anyone else's timetables, the baby was coming. And there were complications.

Every time Zack recalled the experience it played back in his mind more like a dream than a memory—probably because he didn't sleep for two straight days during the worst of the ordeal. But in the swirl of images of doctors and nurses and occasional glimpses of a tiny, angry-looking baby surrounded by people with masks, the only clear memory Zack had was of Terry sitting in the waiting room, saying that everything was going to be okay.

And occasionally standing up and saying, to no one in particular, "Goddammit, everything had *better* be okay."

Now Zack said to his friend, "Don't worry. I'm an expert in criminal law. She can't bust you for checking out her ass."

"Yeah, well, here's what I don't need. I don't need a good-looking cop distracting me right in the middle of…" His voice drifted off. He had clearly lost his train of thought. "Fuck," he said absently.

What this situation needed was a shift in focus. Zack popped open the glove compartment and pulled out the car's owner's manual.

"Hey, careful with that," Terry said as Zack began to flip through it. Terry was extremely overprotective of his stuff.

"So how come you bought this car?" Zack asked. "I thought you hated BMWs." Terry loved BMWs. Nothing made him happier than to get mad about it.

"That was you that hated BMWs, for no good reason, I might add."

"Yeah. I just don't like the way they look, I guess."

"What?" Terry was incredulous. "They look great. Especially this M5. Are you telling me that you don't like the way this car looks? Are you blind?"

The car really wasn't anything special, but whatever. "I like the color." The car was an unusual shade of blue. Terry had gone on and on about it for weeks.

"Damn right you like the color. It's very rare. They only offer it with this particular extra package. You're probably driving in one of a very few models like it in all of western Massachusetts."

The conversation about why anyone in their right mind would give a shit about that would have to wait for another day. They had more important things to talk about.

"So, I saw something in that meeting that I wanted to run past you."

Terry was instantly alert. "What?"

"Babe was hiding something—well, maybe not exactly hiding something, but there was something a little unusual when that detective asked him about Tedesco."

"Babe? 'Something a little unusual'? Why, I'm shocked

and appalled that you would say such a thing about our client."

"Yeah, but this was different. That cop was pretty good at picking up when he needed a little coaxing, but I think something might have gotten past her."

"You mean when they were talking about when Tedesco started work?" Terry asked.

"Right around then. I think Babe was worried that she was going to bring up something else. That's when he really started to hunker down over that little paper he was working on. Remember how she asked him whether Tedesco started work before he did?"

"Yeah. I thought he answered that amazingly clearly. Well, amazingly clearly for Babe."

"Exactly. But did you notice that when she asked how they met, he gave her some stupid answer? And then she changed the question, and asked him whether Tedesco started working there before he did. I think she assumed that they first met each other at work, but I think she's wrong. I get the feeling that Babe was afraid of answering how he met Tedesco."

"So what do you think?" asked Terry. "Babe knew Tedesco beforehand, and got him the job? So what?"

"I don't know," Zack answered. "But if you were Babe, and you were constantly worried that anything you might say could get you in trouble, why would you hide the origins of your friendship with somebody?"

Terry shrugged. "What's there in Babe's past to be ashamed of? I mean, besides being Babe."

Zack nodded. "Exactly. Which is why I think we need to talk to Mrs. Gardiner."

FOURTEEN

Ketoacidosis is a condition that arises when the body's normal mechanism for obtaining glucose in order to produce energy fails. In the case of diabetes, this occurs when a patient, for example, fails to take his insulin....

Early warning signs of ketoacidosis include extreme fatigue and weakness, dry tongue, leg cramps, abdominal pain, nausea...

Ketoacidosis is a very serious condition that can quickly become life-threatening. Although early symptoms can be slow in developing, late symptoms, often initiated by vomiting and/or difficulty in breathing, indicate a severe chemical imbalance that can rapidly lead to coma, and then death.

(*Everything You Never Wanted to Know About Diabetes,* pages 34–35)

Hostage

SHE WOKE UP CONFUSED, WITH A SERIOUS PAIN in her stomach. Woke up? How could she possibly have fallen asleep tied to a chair?

And then, the memory of her kidnapper coming into the room hit her like a cold slap in the face.

He hadn't been wearing the ski mask. He wasn't afraid

of her identifying him, because he was going to kill her before she'd get the chance.

She had to escape. Right now.

God, her eyelids felt so heavy. Her headache was no better. And was she ever thirsty. On top of that, her bladder was about to burst. Her tongue felt like it was twice its normal size. And talk about dry. She swallowed, hoping that would help.

She really needed her shot.

Wait a minute. Her shot. She needed her insulin shot. *She was a diabetic.*

The realization shot through her fuzzy brain like a laser beam through a fog.

She had no idea what time it was, or how long it had been since she'd given herself her last shot. In fact, she still couldn't remember anything except these annoying little voices that occasionally delivered snippets of information, and the image of that crowbar swinging toward her. But she knew that she had been through enough close calls to recognize the early symptoms of ketoacidosis.

Stomachache. Dry mouth. Fatigue.

Oh my God. If she didn't find a way out of here in a matter of hours, she'd go into a coma from the lack of insulin, and die. The ketoacidosis was already serious enough to have knocked her out after only a few minutes of trying to move her chair around to get the knife off the card table across the room. How was she going to do this?

Another pain ripped through her stomach.

She had to move. She struggled against her bonds, then stopped abruptly. She was being poisoned by the ketones in her bloodstream, and she was going to run out of energy soon. It was going to do no good to uselessly struggle against the tape that held her to the chair. She had to *think*.

Her kidnapper had taken her only means of escape out of her reach. He had then returned to the other room to watch television and get drunk. Or drunker.

The last thing she remembered was trying to listen to the television. That's when she must have fallen asleep. Which was awfully scary. The fatigue must have come upon her in a real hurry.

She listened again for the television. But instead of the drone of music and laugh tracks and intense voices trying to sell useless things to people, the noises from the other room were rhythmic. And rumbling. As if there were some kind of machine in there.

And the sound—whatever it was—was not nearly as muffled as when the TV was on. It was as if the door were open, or at least ajar.

She listened again, and suddenly, she knew.

He was snoring.

Snoring. Her captor was asleep! Or passed out.

It was her chance.

She was still for a moment, just to be sure, and the snoring continued, steady. There was no doubt about it— he was in a deep sleep.

She wanted to see behind her, where the sound was coming from. She wanted to know if the door was open. To turn around, she would have to move her chair. So she tipped forward a bit, and then, as she did earlier, she lifted herself up onto her toes.

But she pushed too hard, and the upper part of her body moved too quickly. A sudden wave of vertigo hit her, and she was immediately in danger of falling right on her face. Her ankles were taped to the legs of the chair, and she couldn't regain her balance. She was tilting forward too fast. She was going to fall.

In a desperate effort to keep herself upright, she tried

to shuffle her feet and propel her body and chair ahead, to pull her center of gravity back where it belonged.

But the table was in her path, and she was still tipping and stumbling forward. She was either going to hit the table with her face or land on the floor nose-first, unless she caught her balance with one last surge ahead.

With all of her remaining energy she pushed forward, but it wasn't enough to right herself. She merely smashed loudly right into the card table with her chest and the front of her right shoulder, shoving it with all of her un-controlled momentum against the opposite wall, creating yet another brain-shaking and ear-ringing crash.

There was an eternity of silence, and then, as if her in-credible clumsiness hadn't generated quite enough noise already, an empty beer can lazily rolled off the table and landed right on a couple of others already lying on the floor, with a final, hollow clatter.

For a second, she was frozen there on her toes, taped to a chair, pinning the card table to the wall. But then the chair tipped somewhat pathetically back so that all four legs landed on the floor with a *thump,* sending another blast of pain shooting through her head.

She steeled herself for her captor's return. There was no way he didn't hear that racket. He was going to come in here, and then he was going to do something that would make it impossible for her to escape. Or maybe he'd just kill her. She was going to have to hope he wanted to keep her alive and find a way to tell him she needed insulin, or else she was just going to pass out and never...

But wait a minute. Something didn't make sense. Where was he? She hadn't heard him come into the room. Was he behind her, standing there, crowbar raised, silently approaching?

It was hard to hear anything but her own ragged breathing. She tried to control herself so she could listen.

And there it was.

The sound of snoring.

He hadn't awakened. She had all but set off a bomb twelve feet from his head, and he hadn't even flickered to the dimmest form of consciousness. He was still breathing in and out, in and out, steady as a good clock, completely oblivious to what was going on in the next room.

She swallowed as best she could—God, her mouth was dry—and tried to take stock of her situation. Her head was killing her. Her lack of memory might well have been caused by the injury from the crowbar. But she was thinking a little more clearly now.

It's good to focus on the positive. The picture always comes out better that way.

Thanks, mystery voices, whoever you are. Not the most useful memories, but at least she recalled that she had diabetes.

She was still short of breath, and her pulse was racing. It was hard to know if that was her blood chemistry, or the fact that ten seconds ago she thought she had lost her last chance to escape.

Unfortunately, no matter how positive her focus, the only real change in her personal picture was that the impact with the table had bruised her badly across the top of her chest and on her right bicep near the shoulder. What was depressingly constant was that her hands were still tied behind her and her ankles were still tightly bound to the legs of the chair.

The empty beer cans and other garbage that had been lying on the table were now mostly spilled all over the floor. But there had been nothing on the table worth trying to grab, anyway. She sighed, and as she exhaled, she looked up.

Then she looked over her right shoulder.

And suddenly, she knew how she was going to escape.

August 17, 2004
Three weeks before the Babe Gardiner trial

WHEN VERA RETURNED TO THE STATION HOUSE, she picked up her messages from the front desk. The only interesting one was a call from Detective John Morrison.

Nothing had come of the investigation into Morrison's alleged mistreatment of that guy Ulf who had beat up his girlfriend. Vera had filed her report, and just yesterday she'd received notice that the file was being closed without any further action.

It was the best anybody could expect. And Vera was happy to learn of it. The whole thing had made her pretty uncomfortable, and—

"Hey! Vera! You got a minute?" Wow. Speak of the devil. The very handsome devil. Morrison was coming out of the coffee room, holding a couple of mugs and looking as good as ever. "You want a cup? Black, right? Guaranteed fresh brewed only five and a half hours ago."

He motioned her toward the conference room. His smile was warm and, as always, Hollywood gorgeous. He had loosened his tie and rolled up the sleeves on his blue-and-white striped shirt. It was a look that tended to make other men look sloppy, but on John Morrison, it just emphasized his aura of casual confidence.

Whatever awkwardness Vera had felt when she was dealing with Morrison as a result of that investigation seemed to melt away into something entirely different as she stood there, probably looking like an idiot, smiling back.

"Sure," she said, following him in.

They sat down across from each other at the utilitarian table and sipped their coffees.

"So," Morrison said, "I don't know if you got the

word, but the review board is going to let that complaint against me drop."

Vera took another sip of the hot liquid. It had been a long day, and even the burned flavor of the brew tasted good. "I got a copy of the decision. You must be really happy that's over. I know I am. Congratulations."

"Yeah, thanks," Morrison said, turning on the thousand-watt smile again. "It wasn't that big a deal, but I hate those kind of things hanging over me, you know what I mean? They just leave a bad taste in my mouth."

No kidding. Vera was all for doing her duty, but it had been real tough being a part of the investigation of a hero cop, however relaxed he had been about the whole thing. She had already asked Lieutenant Carasquillo to be removed from that detail. She'd really love to avoid another one of those interrogations if she could.

"So, there's another reason I'm glad that decision came out so soon," Morrison said, "because there's something I'd been hoping to ask you, and it wouldn't have been right while the case against me was still, you know, open."

It was funny, but right before her eyes, Morrison underwent a very subtle shift in attitude. Gone was the friendly self-assurance, and in its place there appeared something a little more vulnerable, a little less certain. It was like the little boy in him was peering out at her through those dark brown eyes.

"I don't like to beat around the bush, if you know what I mean." He fiddled with his cup and then looked up at her. His eyelashes were really something else. "So I just wanted you to know that if you aren't seeing somebody right now, I'd like to ask you out sometime. You know, for a bite to eat or something. I didn't see a ring, so I figured you weren't married or engaged, but you never know with these things, and I guess I just wanted to find out if the, you know, if the field is clear." He took a breath. "And if you're up for dating somebody on the job." The smile reappeared. "I think I'll stop babbling now, if that's okay with you."

Vera was stunned. The tiny note of doubt that had crept into his voice just added to an already extremely charming package. Was going out with John Morrison okay with Vera? Oh yeah. "Sure," she said, hoping she sounded as cool as she didn't feel. "I'd love to have dinner with you. That would be nice."

TERRY WAS DRIVING AGAIN. GOOD THING HE liked spending time in his awesome car, or he'd be pissed. To do the kind of criminal defense work he and Zack did required a shitload of investigating.

Since Sean was riding along with them, it actually made sense to take the BMW. Zack's car, a pathetic little Honda, wouldn't have been nearly big enough for all three of them. Right now, Zack was looking at some notes that Sean had made of their meeting with that detective and Babe.

Damn, he had to admit it. That woman was smokin' hot. Something about her smile, or her eyes—he didn't even know what it was. She wasn't tall, she didn't have red hair, and he didn't even have a good handle on her body yet.

The whole thing was irritating. He really didn't need to be thinking about her all the time. He was going to have to do something about this. It was starting to feel like he needed a girlfriend. And that never went well. Crap.

"These are really good," Zack said, handing the papers back to Sean. For some reason, the kid had become fascinated with the Gardiner case. Not only had he helped them prepare the pretrial memorandum, which officially notified the Commonwealth that they might raise an alibi defense—good luck to all of them on that hopeless waste of time—but he was spending an incredible amount of energy reading old transcripts and police reports, going over witness statements, and doing the tons of other things normally necessary to prepare for a trial.

Terry and Zack were doing the same things, but with a lot less enthusiasm. Babe was 100 percent screwed. If he didn't rob and kill that guy, the inevitable guilty verdict he was facing was just going to add a layer of tragedy onto this mess that really shouldn't have excited anyone. There was no reason at all to be enthusiastic.

In their continuing quest to uncover and exhaust last-ditch efforts, they were on their way to meet Babe's mother. She worked at the mall, and had a break for dinner from six-thirty to seven. They were going to join her at the food court, God help them.

Zack had it in his head that in the interview with Detective Hottie, Babe had been hiding some kind of connection that he had with Roger Tedesco, the guy with the goatee. Naturally, asking Babe had been an exercise in futility, so they decided to approach the one person who actually seemed to have Babe's best interests at heart.

In the very unlikely event that Babe's mom would shed any light on this missing Tedesco guy at all, there remained the very real possibility that none of it mattered. So what if Babe knew Tedesco before he worked there? Swell. Now Babe knew *two* people who didn't show up for work after that weekend.

Somehow, that didn't seem like it was going to help the cause.

But when Zack was on last-ditch-effort patrol, he was relentless. No lead was too small, or too speculative, if there was time. And there was still time. Not much—trial started in about twenty days. But when that gavel hit that bench, Zack and Terry would know that they had done absolutely everything they could for their client. If they were going down, there would be no bullets left in their guns.

Terry turned left and headed for the mall parking lot. But just as he got to the entrance, he noticed a crowd of people surrounding a pair of police cars and an ambulance parked there, emergency lights flashing.

"What the heck is going on here?" Zack asked as they pulled up.

"Got me," Terry replied as a cop directed him down a parking lane before he got close enough to the entrance to see.

He pulled to the right, and stopped the car as a couple of paramedics emerged from the mall entrance with a woman strapped to a stretcher. The EMTs made their way to the back of the ambulance, and as they positioned themselves to lift the stretcher into the car, the woman turned her head, giving them a clear look at her face.

It was Katerina Gardiner. Babe's mom.

They lifted her into the ambulance, closed the door, and drove away.

"Guess the meeting's off," Terry said.

FIFTEEN

The *Commonwealth points to Commonwealth v. Tippett as an example of how recent decisions on this issue have, instead of setting out a manageable, predictable set of procedures for ensuring constitutionally valid guilty pleas, distorted the holdings of prior cases into a confusing judicial directive to employ an entirely unnecessary and cumbersome litany now followed, with mixed results, by lower courts.*

Accordingly, it is the ruling of this court that from this time forward, a guilty plea shall be seen as constitutionally valid if the following takes place at the guilty plea hearing:

1. *the defendant states that he is mentally competent and understands the rights he is waiving by pleading guilty;*
2. *the defendant states that his attorney has explained the charges and allegations against him;*
3. *the defendant states that he is guilty of the charges and allegations; and*
4. *the judge states that he believes the defendant.*

(Excerpt of *Commonwealth v. Wilkerson*, 445 Mass. 2d, Pages 304–305 [2004])

August 31, 2004
One week before the Babe Gardiner trial

WELL, AT LEAST F.X. WOULD BE HAPPY ABOUT this.

Louis finished reading the new decision from the Supreme Judicial Court on guilty pleas, and sighed. The Tippett case had everyone so upset that the highest court in Massachusetts had gone out of its way to dumb down the requirements for constitutionally valid guilty pleas. They figured that if Tippett hadn't been able to overturn his original guilty plea in the first place, he never would have gotten off. So the courts decided to make it much easier for defendants to plead guilty, and much harder for them to later undo their decision.

It was understandable. It was ridiculous how many defendants would make a deal with the prosecutor, plead guilty, go to jail, and, within six months, charge right back into court with a motion to withdraw their guilty plea.

Most of them were guys who'd agreed to plead guilty in exchange for a sentence that was shorter than they might expect if they lost at trial. And usually these defendants would enter the prison system honestly figuring they'd just do their time and get on with their lives. But sooner or later—and it was amazing how it was almost always sooner—they'd meet an inmate who'd gain their confidence and tell them about a lifer they should really talk to, because he knew everything there was to know about flipping guilty pleas and getting people out of jail.

It never seemed to matter that this knowledge came about not from any formal training, but as a result of spending a lifetime behind bars for some horrible felony, reading law books in a prison library.

The jailhouse lawyer was always an expert salesman. He'd go on and on about how the inmate had gotten screwed by his lawyer and the system. You pleaded to unarmed robbery and Judge So-and-so gave you five to seven? Outrageous. There was a guy in the next cell block who was doing a three to five for rape. Tell me how that's fair. You got a transcript of your guilty plea hearing? Let me take a look at it. Judge So-and-so is a terrible judge. I bet I can flip the plea.

The huckster would promise the new inmate whatever he needed to promise—it would all be reinterpreted or flat-out denied later—and then, despite the prison system's strict prohibition, the inmate would pay for the jailhouse lawyer to draft a motion to withdraw the guilty plea. Payment methods were infinitely diverse and ingenious. Cigarettes—formerly the currency of choice for guests of the governor—were no longer available, as smoking had been prohibited in prisons.

But there was still the canteen. A motion to withdraw a guilty plea could buy months of snacks, coffee, and soda. And if the new inmate happened to be that golden combination of unusually stupid and rich, arrangements would be made between the inmate's family and someone outside the prison who would take a ludicrous sum—sometimes in the thousands of dollars—and hold the money for the lifer.

Because, of course, the lifer was saving up to hire a real lawyer to try to get his own conviction overturned. There was no way he'd ever handle his own case.

Louis finished making a note sheet summarizing the holding of *Wilkerson,* so that at his next guilty plea hearing he would make sure that the necessary steps were followed. Then he put his copy of the court's opinion into the correct file drawer and opened up the Rufus Gardiner case file.

He certainly wasn't going to have to worry about a guilty plea on this one.

There was a surveillance tape from the convenience store, which was far too fuzzy to identify anyone, but which clearly showed that on the night in question, a man armed with a knife came into the Nite & Day Convenience Store and robbed it. That same night, the clerk who had been on duty at the store when it was robbed identified the defendant as the perpetrator. The clerk vanished soon thereafter, and was never seen alive again.

Months later, he was found dead in an abandoned car, with the defendant's hair on his clothes.

Gardiner hadn't made any statements to the police, so Louis would get no help there, and it was obvious that the defense attorneys—Zack Wilson and Terry Tallach, a pair that Louis had never faced before—would make some headway because skin cells found underneath the victim's fingernails did not match Gardiner's DNA. But if Gardiner testified—and it was hard to believe he wouldn't—the jury would also get to hear about his two previous felony convictions for larceny and possession with intent to distribute marijuana.

And if Louis got lucky, he'd be able to get into the trial the fact that ever since he'd been arrested, Mr. Gardiner had been racking up quite a prison disciplinary record.

In the five months since he first went into the system, Gardiner had already managed to be ticketed eight times, all for fighting. Twice with an inmate named Rolle, until they finally figured out to keep those two away from each other, and then twice more with another inmate whose name was Mestone, or possibly Mistoni. It was hard to read the shift commander's handwriting.

Anyway, when the trial began next week, it was going to be pretty straightforward. Louis would call the cop who had spoken to the clerk on the night of the robbery, an excellent detective named John Morrison who always made a good impression on juries, and establish the defendant as the bad guy. Then he'd just follow the timeline—first the girl who found the car, then the cop who recovered the car and the body, the medical examiner, the DNA expert— and that would probably be that.

The defense had indicated that they intended to raise an alibi, consisting of the defendant and his mother. Apparently, Babe intended to claim that he was home at the time of the robbery.

That was going to be interesting, because Detective Morrison had gone off to arrest Gardiner as soon as the identification was made, but didn't find him at home until hours later. In a credibility contest between the defendant and Detective Morrison, it was not going to be close.

Although you could never be sure with trials, it really did look like this one was going to be a smooth ride to an easy conviction.

His very strained relationship with his boss could use it.

MARIA WAS JUST PUTTING HER JACKET ON WHEN the window behind her exploded, and then Anthony was tackling her, and they were rolling around in the broken glass.

Before she could even breathe he was talking. "Are you all right? Were you hit?"

"What are you doing? Of course I'm all right. Get off of me. What happened?" The words were out of her mouth before Anthony's questions fully sank in.

"What?" she demanded, feeling stupid. She was still getting over the shock of the window breaking and being wrestled to the floor. She just needed a second. What was Anthony talking about? Was she hit? Hit with what? The only thing that had hit her was her crazy, flying-across-the-room boss who was a little too heavy to be squashing her like this.

And then the realization went through her like an electric shock.

Sweet Saint Jude and the Apostles. Someone had just fired a gun at them.

"Yes, this is Anthony LoPresti," Maria heard Anthony say. He had already called someone on his cell phone. Probably 911. "I'm in my office at 220 Fifth Street near Lakeland, and someone just fired a bullet through my window from the street." He listened, then said, "I don't think so, but I'll check." He looked at Maria and asked, "Are you sure you're all right?"

"Yes, I'm sure that I'm fine," Maria answered. If fine meant angry, and scared.

And her elbow hurt a little. She had banged it when she fell.

This wasn't supposed to be the way it was. She was supposed to be able to have a real job, and make real money, and take care of her mother and her brother, and not have anybody shooting at her. That just wasn't the way it was supposed to be.

Maria had lost her cousin Ricky to street violence nearly ten years ago. He had been hanging around with those gangbanger fools, and they got him started doing drugs. Next thing you know, his mother, Aunt Rose, throws him out of the house, and he moves in with his stupid friends. Then he buys himself a gun, and all of a sudden he's a big shot, doing robberies, getting high, getting girls pregnant.

One night he was messing around in a club, drunk, stoned, whatever, when all of a sudden a fight broke out.

Like an idiot, Ricky pulled his gun. Well, tried to pull his gun. Instead, he was so wasted that what happened was he shot the gun while he was trying to pull it out of his jacket, and hit himself in an artery in his leg.

He bled to death before they even got him to the hospital.

And that was it. Little Ricky, with the funny-colored eyes, and the lisp, and the terrible weakness for Hershey's Kisses, who Maria used to play with on the swings when they were kids, was gone.

Maria was sixteen when Ricky died, and by that time she had already pretty much made up her mind that she wanted nothing to do with the kind of life Ricky had chosen. But if there was any doubt about her decision, it was firmly and completely eliminated when she saw Aunt Rose at the funeral.

Maria's mother was a crier. When she was happy, when she was sad, when she was angry—anytime her emotions got going, the waterfall would start.

But when Aunt Rose lost her Ricky, she wept for days. She couldn't stop sobbing. For the whole funeral, she just kept saying "no" over and over and over, quietly. Like she couldn't believe it.

And then, at the cemetery, she started screaming "No!" Like she wouldn't accept it.

And yet her only son—her baby boy—was in that coffin. And no amount of crying or screaming was ever going to bring him back.

Maria was a little surprised at how mad she was at Ricky. Oh, she was sad, too. She cried at the wake, and at the funeral, and again at the burial.

But she left the cemetery that day absolutely determined that whatever it took, she was going to get her mother and Felix out of that neighborhood before anything could happen to him.

And after all her hard work, and saving money, and sacrificing, here she was, on the floor of an office, with her boss lying on top of her, because some fool took a potshot at her through a window.

She couldn't quit. She needed this job. She needed the money.

But something was definitely going to have to change.

Fast.

SIXTEEN

THE COURT: *The record will reflect that the defendant, Mr. Gardiner, has taken the witness stand, and has been sworn. Mr. Gardiner's attorneys are present, as is Assistant District Attorney Lovell. The jury is not present.*

Now, Mr. Gardiner, as you know, as I'm sure your very capable attorneys have advised you, you have the right to testify in your own defense. And you have the right not to testify. As I'm sure you remember, we went over that decision before you took the stand yesterday.

However, after you began to testify, it became clear that some of your testimony was, well, I think it's fair to say that some of us in the courtroom were surprised by your testimony.

THE DEFENDANT: *Yes, sir.*

THE COURT: *Yes. So what I've decided to do is to interrupt your testimony to hold what we call a competency hearing, just to make sure that you have a sufficient understanding of the proceedings here today, and to make sure that you are fully able to participate and assist your attorneys in your defense. All right?*

THE DEFENDANT: *I guess so.*

THE COURT: *Fine.*

(Commonwealth v. Gardiner, Volume VI, Pages 10–11)

Hostage

IF SHE WAS EVER GOING TO ESCAPE, IT WAS GO-
ing to have to be now. Her kidnapper was virtually unconscious in the other room. His snoring was loud, and
constant. He was obviously in a very deep sleep.

And he was going to have to stay in one, if she was going to get away with this.

She had to stay focused.

Forget about focused. She'd be happy if she stayed
awake.

Ironically, the throbbing in her head and the stabbing
pains in her stomach—and shoot, her sore shoulders and
wrists, too—were helping her fight the fatigue that seemed
to be draping itself all over her like a smothering, leaded
blanket. It was hard to doze off when you hurt as bad as
she did.

*You play the hand you're dealt. Sooner or later you'll get
new cards.*

She really wished the voices in her head would take a
break.

Happy freakin' birthday.

It wouldn't be so bad if she could remember anything
from before the time that crowbar was swinging at her. It
was like her identity was hidden behind a thick haze, and
all she could hear were these annoying messages and
floating words of wisdom.

A pain ripped through her stomach, jolting her back
to the business at hand. She was going to have to get some
insulin soon, or her identity wasn't going to matter.

The last time she tried to move while tied to the chair,
she almost fell right on her face, which would have been
the end of her. With her hands tied behind her back, she
wouldn't have been able to protect herself. The way she

was feeling, a serious blow like that might have put her out cold.

And in her condition, if she lost consciousness, she might never regain it.

She was going to have to be very careful. She looked over her right shoulder at her target and, slowly, tipped forward so that the legs of the chair rose up from the floor. Then she shifted her weight onto the toes of her right foot, swung her left shoulder and hip slightly to the left, and then dropped her weight back down onto her left foot. The impact hurt her head, but she couldn't let that matter now.

One step down. Fifteen, maybe twenty, more to go.

She shifted forward again, and took another step. And then another. Each step was a little easier than the last, and soon she found herself in a kind of a clunky rhythm, shifting left and right, bent over at the waist, chair on her back, shuffling forward agonizingly slowly.

It was a big risk using up all this energy, when her body was now burning fat at a dangerous rate just to keep her breathing. But she really had no choice. If she didn't get out of here, she was going to die.

She could feel a buzzing in her body—maybe it was adrenaline—but so far, she was successfully fighting the fatigue. The headache was there, the stomach cramps were getting more frequent, but, at least for now, she was able to ignore them. Well, most of them. What else could she do? Sit there and cry?

What really scared her was that she had no idea how much time she had until whatever reserve of energy she was tapping ran out, and she just collapsed from exhaustion. She had to keep moving. Only a few more steps before she was ready to stop.

And then she was there, finally, sitting directly in front of the long floor lamp that stood so completely uselessly beside the sofa.

Now came tricky part number one. Two, actually, since walking while tied to a chair had to count as tricky.

First, she listened for the sound of snoring, which came steady and strong from the next room.

And then she shifted the chair around so that the lamp was directly behind her.

This was going to be it. If she could grab hold of the lamp, and then move with it back to where she had fallen against the table, she was going to be able to do this.

But sometimes these kinds of lamps were so heavy at the base that it wasn't easy to pick them up even if you weren't tied to a chair while on the verge of going into diabetic shock.

She opened her hands and wrapped her fingers tightly around the slim shaft of the lamp. Then she tipped forward, rising once again onto her toes, clasping the lamp as firmly as she could. She could feel the weight of the lamp tug against her hands, but it was so cheap that the base wasn't as heavy as she thought, and thanks to the laws of physics, and the terror of knowing that within hours she might be dead, she lifted the lamp off the ground. As she leaned forward, preparing to walk again across her prison, it slowly fell forward, so that it was resting on her back.

But now that she was in position, and ready to move, she realized that her legs were feeling even more heavy than usual. She took a deep breath. She had to make it across the room again. One more time.

She was so tired. It was entirely possible that she didn't have it in her to get all the way across. She really needed to rest. Find some more energy.

But she was afraid to close her eyes, fearing vertigo. If she lost her balance and fell, that would be it. There was no way she'd have enough strength to get herself back up.

And now that she was up on her toes, she was also afraid to tip back down again with the lamp in her hands.

She was just going to have to fight this nearly overwhelming feeling of exhaustion.

When you can't do it all, just do a piece of it. Then the next piece. After a while, who knows?

Good idea, voices. Just a piece. Just a step. One step at a time. Just take one step. Then worry about the next one.

She inhaled fully and, for what seemed like the thousandth time, shifted her weight onto her right leg and swung her left shoulder and hip forward.

And then back to the right.

One step at a time.

As she moved forward, at the top of her field of vision, barely in sight through her eyebrows, she could make out the top of the lamp, about three or four feet ahead of her as she lumbered forward. What must she look like? A hunchbacked knight making the slowest charge in the world. On a chair instead of a horse. With a floor lamp for a lance.

The vision thing was going to be a problem, because the next maneuver was going to require aim.

One piece at a time. Just reach the table. Then worry about aiming.

With each step, she saw the distance between her and the table shrinking. A few more lurches forward, and she would be there. Three more. Two.

One more step.

Finally, she had returned to the position she had been in minutes ago, essentially pinned up against the table, which itself was pinned up against the wall.

By now, the headache and the shooting pains in her stomach were old hat. It was the muscles in her hands, fingers, and shoulders that were demanding her attention.

And oh yeah. She was feeling sicker by the minute. She had to get this tape off her mouth for tons of reasons, but vomiting was high on the list.

And yet, there were other things to worry about before that. That tape wasn't going anywhere unless she could finish this job.

It was the moment of truth. Or the first of many moments.

One moment at a time.

She checked the rhythm of the snoring, which stayed steady as ever. If he was still in a deep sleep, this might work. If he wasn't...

Thinking like that wasn't going to do her any good. She paused to catch her breath, looked up at the wall above the table, and sighted her target. The cheap glass wall sconce just hung there, ugly as ever.

She swallowed, inhaled deeply, twisted slowly to the left, took her best guess, and then sharply twisted back to the right.

And as if she had been breaking wall sconces with the ends of floor lamps that she was holding while her hands were tied behind her back forever, the glass light fixture smashed into a million pieces, crashing down onto the table and the floor below.

Her heart was pounding so loud that if the sound of the glass breaking hadn't been so deafening, she was sure that the snoring man would have burst through the door to find out what the thumping was.

She was dead still, listening for the sounds of snoring.

But there was only silence.

September 2, 2004
Five days before the Babe Gardiner trial

ZACK WAS WAITING WITH TERRY AND SEAN IN
the attorney/client room for their last meeting with Babe
before the trial. They'd visited with Babe's mother at the
hospital, but she'd never heard of Roger Tedesco, so this
would be their final shot at finding a connection between
the fugitive and Babe.

Terry was pretty pissed at their client, and was now
sitting at the table with a blank pad in front of him, clicking his pen and staring off into space, probably daydreaming about Detective Vera. But Sean was poring through
the police reports in the case file, and was full of questions
about evidence that he thought shouldn't be allowed into
the trial.

"If that detective—Morrison—tries to testify about
what the convenience store clerk told him, isn't that
hearsay?"

Terry blew out an exasperated sigh and turned to face
his nephew. "You'd think so, wouldn't you? But don't
worry—we're still screwed. There's an exception to the
hearsay doctrine."

"It's called the excited utterance or spontaneous ex-
clamation rule," Zack explained. "You can't testify to
something that another person said, unless what they said
was said in the heat of the moment, with no time to make
up a lie."

Sean pushed his huge glasses back up the bridge of his
nose. He was puzzled. "So who decides whether something was said spontaneously?"

"The judge," Zack continued. "It's usually allowed in
if there's enough evidence—"

"It's usually allowed in if it's the prosecution that
wants it in," Terry interrupted, clicking his pen furiously.

Terry was right. Over the past several years, the courts had distorted the definition of "excited utterance" pretty badly to make sure that damaging evidence got admitted against defendants.

"Technically, the court is supposed to allow the evidence in only if the person who made the statement is really upset," Zack said. "So they look for whether the person was nervous, or frightened—you know, were they stammering, were their hands shaking—that kind of thing."

"Gee, that's funny," Terry said in mock surprise. "I seem to remember something that sounded like that in Detective Morrison's police report. Why don't you read it to us, Sean?"

The young man flipped over a couple of pages in the file and began to read. " 'The victim was upset. He seemed nervous and scared. His hands were shaking as he described the incident to me.' "

Terry shook his head. " 'Upset,' 'nervous,' 'scared,' 'hands shaking.' Amazing coincidence, isn't it?"

Terry's skepticism was well grounded. Morrison was slick. He knew the evidentiary rule. He'd made sure that his report left no doubt that the clerk's statements would be admissible.

Sean still looked confused. "I'm not sure I understand. . . ."

Just then, Babe entered the room. He sat down next to Zack. Even for Babe, he didn't look very good. He seemed unusually pale. "We're discussing an evidentiary rule that might come up in your trial, Babe." Except for a slight nod, there was no response.

Zack turned to Sean. "Think of it as the 'Oh my God!' exception. If you can add the phrase 'Oh my God!' to the beginning of the statement and have it make sense, then it will probably be admissible at trial."

Babe opened his folder and started to doodle.

" 'Fuck me!' works, too," Terry noted, "instead of 'Oh my God!' " He looked from Sean to Zack, but no one responded. "I'm just saying."

Babe had begun work on an airplane in the margin of a disciplinary report. It looked like he was sweating. Zack focused again on Sean. "For example, if someone wanted to testify that they heard another person shout, 'That car just ran a red light!' the statement would be admissible, because if you put 'Oh my God!' in front of it, it really wouldn't change the meaning or spirit of the statement."

"So, 'I just shot somebody!' would work, but 'I'm going to the store' wouldn't," Sean said.

Babe looked up from his doodling. He looked worse than when he first came in.

"Exactly," Terry replied. "Because 'Fuck me! I'm going to the store' doesn't make any sense. But 'Fuck me! I just shot somebody!' makes total sense."

Babe stood up and closed his folder. "I'm sorry," he mumbled, heading for the door, "but I think I'm going to throw up." He opened the door and called out to the guard. "Hey, Red, I've got to get back to the unit because I'm sick." And with that, he left the three of them alone in the conference room.

There was a moment of silence as Terry watched the door close behind their client. Then he turned back to Sean and Zack and said, "So, I don't know about you, but now I'm ready for the trial."

But Zack didn't bother to respond. He had just figured out how Babe was connected to Roger Tedesco.

SEVENTEEN

Dear Bernie,

I know how much Sharon reads to you every day, so I won't make this too long so she can save her voice (Hi Sharon!), but I wanted to let you know that I met a detective out here that I think you'd like.

At least I think so.

His name is John Morrison, and he's a very good cop. Just like you, he had this huge reputation when I joined the squad, which was pretty intimidating, but he seems really down-to-earth, which is another thing that reminded me of you.

But then, thanks to a stupid assignment, I had to take his statement in an investigation into an excessive force charge made by this wife-beater.

Anyway, that whole thing blew over (thank goodness!), so now things are basically back to normal. It's still a little strange out here, but I think I'm getting used to it. Trying to, anyway.

Take care. I'll write again soon.
Vera
P.S. I found a softball team. Finally.

Hey Sharon,

This part of the e-mail is just for you.

That cop I was telling you about before asked me out. He seems nice enough, but my instinct tells me there's a little more to him than nice guy/good detective. After I get to know him better I'll know whether that's a good thing.

Anyway, I just wanted to let you know I'm actually seeing somebody—or at least starting to see somebody—and he seems nice. I'll write soon to tell you how it's going.

And I hope you and Bernie are doing well. The bedsores sound just awful. Bernie's tough, but God!

I'm thinking of you both all the time.
Love, Vera

(E-mail sent 08/16/04 from Vera Demopolous [vera49@imail.com] to Sharon Washman [sharchar@imail.com], Exhibit 16, *Commonwealth v. Morrison*)

September 3, 2004
Four days before the Babe Gardiner trial

ELMO DIDN'T PARTICULARLY LIKE WALLY, BUT Wally had already proven that he could get things done. And Elmo needed some important things done.

Elmo had picked up the ex-con in the parking lot at Biggie's, and they were driving around, sharing a bottle of Jack and a case.

"Did you handle the private investigator?" Elmo asked. "I need him sniffing around this thing like a hole in the head."

Wally finished off a can of Bud and opened another. "I don't know what the big deal is with him, but it's your money." He took a swallow from the can. "I threw a shot into his window the other day. And there's a new message on his answering machine. I told him to get off the case, or the next bullet would hit somebody."

This whole thing was taking too long. If they'd just

get the trial over with, things could go back to normal. But the courts were dragging their asses. The more time that passed before the trial, the bigger the chance somebody would find out something Elmo didn't want them to find out.

"What about the mother?" Wally asked. "She's in the hospital now. You still want to do something with her?"

Elmo pulled up to a red light, took a swig of Jack, and chased it with a swallow of beer. "Yeah, but we gotta wait until she gets home." The light turned green and he drove on. "You checked her out before, right? She's the one that takes walks at night."

"She's the one."

Elmo nodded. "Okay. The trial's supposed to start in a couple of days. If she's home from the hospital before then, we gotta go after her. We might need to use my van."

"Whatever, man." Wally took a long pull from the bottle of whiskey. "You know where to find me."

MARIA WAS JUST ABOUT TO PUT A FORKFUL OF scrambled eggs into her mouth, when Anthony blurted out, "I'm starting to wonder whether it's a good idea for you to keep working for me."

And just like that, her appetite disappeared.

They were in a diner, having breakfast. The office window was going to take a few days to repair, so they were working mostly on the road, which was probably what they would have been doing anyway, because there was so little time to find Roger Tedesco. Maria and Anthony were at it full-time, calling every Tedesco in the local phone books, and driving all over the place, running down hopeless leads.

"Um, have I been doing something wrong?" Maria asked. She couldn't believe that Anthony was going to fire her, especially after that conversation they had a few months ago. She had been working as hard as ever. In fact, everything seemed to be going so well.

Except, of course, when they were getting shot at.

Anthony took a sip of coffee and wiped his mouth with a napkin. "No, it's got nothing to do with you. I just don't know if this job is safe enough. That guy on the phone was basically threatening to shoot one of us if we stayed on the case. I'm not sure that I'm going to be able to protect you. We called the cops, but I really don't know what they can do."

The night of the shooting, they had spent a long time talking to a female detective with a long Greek name—Demopoli, or something like that—who was really nice, but also really blunt with them.

In situations like this, they could increase police patrols in the neighborhood, but there was no way they could ensure that Anthony or Maria wouldn't be followed, or attacked.

For some reason, that information scared Maria more than anything that had happened over the past crazy months. It didn't matter, though. She had already made up her mind.

There was no job Maria could imagine that was as good for her and for her family as this one. Anthony was extremely flexible about her schedule. He understood that there were times when Maria needed to take her mother to the doctor or go to some school meeting for Felix. And Anthony was always respectful to Maria, treating her like an equal in almost every aspect of their work.

And the job paid almost twice as much as any other that Maria was qualified for.

She took a drink of water and then put the glass down. "This is probably crazy," she said, "but I have to ask anyway." Why couldn't things just happen like they did on TV sitcoms? Why did everything have to be such a drama?

"I can't lose this job—" she began, only to have Anthony break in.

"Maria, there are lots of other jobs out there—"

"Not like this one, Anthony. Wait," she said, taking another sip of water and holding her hand up to prevent him from interrupting her again. "You know my situation," she said, putting the glass down. "My mother is sick with I don't know what, and my little brother is going to be eleven next month. I'm the only thing they have. And I know there are other jobs out there, but none like this one. Believe me. I've looked."

"I bet you have," Anthony said.

"Anyway, I decided that I want to keep working for you, even if there is some crazy person out there who wants to shoot me. Or you. But if I die, then my family . . ." Her voice broke, and she took another sip of water. Why did everything always have to be so hard? She took a shaky breath and let it out slowly. "If I die," she began again, "then my family will have nothing. So I was wondering if you thought, instead of firing me, whether it would be possible for you to buy life insurance for me."

Anthony looked surprised. He probably thought she was trying to scam him.

"I would have gotten it myself—" she began to explain, but he cut her off.

"You don't have life insurance?" he asked, incredulous. "Maria. That's crazy."

She looked at him for a moment, shook her head and laughed softly, although nothing was funny. "You really have no idea, do you?"

He just sat there for a second. "I guess not," he said. "Tell me."

She nodded. "Even after we moved to the new

apartment, when my mother was working, we had enough money coming in to pay the bills and still put away a little every month for my brother Felix's college account. It got all the way up to seven hundred dollars." She laughed again. "At the rate we were going, when he started school, he'd be able to afford to buy his books. And maybe lunch for about three weeks."

"You know there's financial aid available at most schools, right?"

"Oh yes, I know all about financial aid. But ever since Mama got sick and stopped working, we can barely afford to pay the electric bill. Forget about saving for college. And life insurance? I called yesterday, when I first thought of this, and they told me that I could get a half million dollars of insurance for about thirty dollars per month. That was more than we were saving every month when things were going well. Right now, thirty dollars a month is ridiculous."

"But life insurance isn't going to make this job any safer, at least right now."

There was a part of Maria—a small part, but it was growing—that not only understood it but resented it. There was something really wrong about the fact that she needed to risk her life for her family's welfare. But there was absolutely no way she was going to let her mother and her brother down. They were not moving back into the old neighborhood. And Felix was not going to find a life on the streets.

"I know," she said, trying to sound more confident than she felt. "But that's the way it is. If I have to be brave to keep my job, it's worth it. I mean as long as if something happens to me, my family is going to be taken care of."

Anthony looked at her for a long time before saying anything. "You have health insurance?"

"We're covered under my mother's plan. She's in the teachers' union."

He nodded. "Okay. We'll get you life insurance. On one condition."

"What's that?"

"That you keep looking for another job. I appreciate how much you're willing to sacrifice to keep working for me, but if something happens to you, life insurance isn't going to begin to replace what your family will have lost."

Before Maria could answer, Anthony's phone rang. It was Babe Gardiner's lawyers. They had a lead on Roger Tedesco.

SO WHAT IF VERA HAD BEEN KEPT UP ALL LAST night by bad dreams again? Being out on a date at a nice restaurant with a good-looking man was just the kind of change of pace she needed.

If the good-looking man would ever get off the phone and come finish his steak.

This last version of Vera's nightmare was the worst yet. Because it was exactly how she imagined the real catastrophe had happened.

In the dream, she had been assigned to work with Bernie for the entire day. That was ridiculous, of course, but that's the way dreams worked. In reality, Vera was on the other side of the continent when everything went bad.

So when the call came in requesting backup in her dream, Vera was standing right there with Bernie in the station house. The dispatcher said the words "Possible Code Red," and Bernie was out the door and into the parking lot so fast Vera almost didn't make it into the cruiser before he drove off.

Again, like in every version of the nightmare, as they were driving toward Bernie's terrible fate, he calmly invited

Vera to join him for dinner that night with Sharon and the girls. And then, as if it were the most normal thing in the world for him, he pulled up alongside the squad car already parked at the end of the driveway of the home on the outskirts of town and jumped out, drawing his weapon as he ran across the front of the property to join his fellow cops at the doorway to the house.

But he didn't even make it halfway. The first bullet hit him in the shoulder, spinning him around, so that when the second one hit him, it got him right at the top of the neck, at the base of the skull. Bernie went down instantaneously. Blood was everywhere.

A busboy startled Vera as he poured some more water into her glass. She forced herself back to the present. She had to leave Alaska behind. She was supposed to be having a nice dinner out.

Unlike most people she knew, Vera kind of liked first dates. She genuinely enjoyed getting to know people. And as she glanced across the Italian restaurant and stole a quick look at John Morrison as he returned from the lobby outside the men's room, well, she had to admit that it really didn't hurt that the particular person she was getting to know happened to have such a nice smile.

Although tonight, for some reason, the smile seemed to be just a little bit forced. Maybe John was feeling awkward. It was definitely strange getting together outside of the squad.

Vera took another bite of her salad with grilled chicken. It was a boring dinner, she knew, but she had never been to this restaurant, and she liked playing it safe with new places. No need to add any extra excitement to a first date by having some silly food issue.

"So," John said as he sat back down. "Sorry about that. Where were we? Somebody took a shot at a private eye?

First time I've heard that one. Seems like something you'd run into on a bad television series."

Another weird thing was that John seemed a whole lot more interested in work than in anything personal. Of course, he might just have been feeling like they should spend their time on common ground until they got more comfortable with each other. But even though that was a reasonable explanation for why he seemed to be driving the conversation in that direction, it just didn't feel like the real one.

He seemed particularly interested in the Babe Gardiner case. Maybe it was because John was the first cop on the scene, and was going to have to testify at the trial. Whatever. But he honed in on the fact that one of Gardiner's lawyers, the big one named Terry, had sent Vera a letter, asking her to look into Gardiner's disciplinary record at prison. Apparently, no matter what institution he was transferred to, he always seemed to get beaten up.

But whatever the reason for Mr. Gardiner's problems, Vera was hoping that she and John might talk about something else before their evening was over. Maybe favorite musicians. Or movies.

"Yeah," she replied. "It was strange. This private detective named LoPresti—you ever hear of him?"

"Office over on Fifth?"

"That's the one. Anyway, a few months after LoPresti starts working on the Babe Gardiner case for Gardiner's lawyers, his secretary gets a threatening phone call, telling LoPresti to back off. Then, a few weeks later, somebody fires a bullet through his office window and then makes another threatening call, saying the next bullet was going to hit somebody."

The shooter obviously had no intention of hitting anyone with that first shot. The trajectory from the street guaranteed that the bullet would end up hitting the office ceiling, which is exactly where they found it.

"And you're sure this guy specifically wanted them off the Gardiner case?"

"Yup."

"You don't think there's any connection, do you?" John asked. "I mean between the threatening phone calls and the fact that Gardiner keeps getting stepped on in prison?"

Vera had thought of it, and looked into it, but couldn't find anything to tie it together. Babe Gardiner was a really skeevy guy. Some inmates just got picked on more than others. "No. He just seems like, well, like a kind of a punching bag."

John nodded, then swallowed a piece of steak and took a sip of beer. "Nobody's been bothering you, though, have they?"

Vera laughed. "Threaten a cop? No way. Besides, who'd bother me? The people getting intimidated are working for Gardiner. Which is why this is kind of puzzling. I mean, who cares? The guy's going to go down for murder. So let him go."

"Yeah, I hear you," John replied. "I mean, what's been happening with that case, anyway? I thought it was pretty cut and dried."

It looked like the conversation about movies was going to have to wait.

EIGHTEEN

THE COURT: *Next is the Commonwealth's motion to allow television cameras into the courtroom to televise the trial. Mr. Lovell, has your office been approached by news media with respect to this case?*

ASSISTANT DISTRICT ATTORNEY LOVELL: *Actually, Your Honor, it is the policy of the District Attorney's Office to make this motion before every trial of a serious felony.*

THE COURT: *I see. And that's not your personal policy?*

ASSISTANT DISTRICT ATTORNEY LOVELL: *I, um, I guess I don't have a personal policy on this issue, Judge. But to answer the court's prior question, the local cable news station has informed my office that if the court allows the motion, they will be broadcasting the trial.*

THE COURT: *Very well. Mr. Tallach. Or Mr. Wilson?*

ATTORNEY WILSON: *We would oppose the motion, Your Honor. My feeling is that television coverage does not add to, and sometimes detracts from, the ability of the defendant to get a fair trial. Also, because of the size of this courtroom, I'm not sure that there's enough room to have television cameras and crews everywhere.*

THE COURT: *I'm going to allow the motion, but Mr. Wilson is right. The courtroom is small, so only one camera will*

*be allowed. My normal practice is for the attorneys to ask
questions from the podium set up here in the middle—between their tables—and I think that if the camera is set up
in the center aisle, toward the back of the room, it will be
able to see about half of the attorney's tables and the
podium from the back, as well as the bench and the witness stand. I don't want anything else on camera anyway,
so that will work out well.*

(*Commonwealth v. Gardiner*, Volume I, Pages 13–14)

JUROR QUESTIONNAIRE

JUROR 1-15

*Name: Raymond Scollari
Address: 44 West Pine Street, Springfield, MA
Age: 49
Occupation: Retired
List involvement in any prior court proceedings (other
than as a juror): Witness at two civil cases brought by dis-
gruntled prison inmates
Have you or any family members been employed by
any law enforcement, court, or government agency? If yes,
explain: I was a corrections officer in Massachusetts for
twenty-two years before I retired as a sergeant.*

(*Juror ID Card #15, Commonwealth v. Gardiner*)

Hostage

SHE WAS SOAKED WITH SWEAT, HER TONGUE
felt like it was wearing a thick woolen sock, her headache
was so bad that every blink felt like a slap in the face, and
the cramps in her stomach were so severe that they were
making her double over. And they were getting more and
more frequent.

Not to mention the rising tide of nausea and fatigue that threatened to wash over her with every passing moment. And the pain in her bladder was so bad that if she didn't get to the bathroom soon, she was going to wet herself.

She tore off the piece of tape that had been gagging her for the past several hours, burning the skin on and around her lips raw. She took the deepest breath she'd ever taken and, for the first time in hours, felt a little better.

She never would have guessed how hard it was to cut through duct tape with a piece of broken glass.

To start with, finding a good one among all the shattered shards on the tabletop wasn't the easiest thing in the world. A ton of the glass had fallen to the floor. The piece she needed had to be thick enough so that it didn't just break apart as soon as she started pressing it into service.

And it had to be long enough for her to be able to grasp it with her fingers and still drag it back and forth across the edge of the tape.

But there were a couple of candidates lying on the table, and with a little shifting around, and only one cut on her left thumb—jeez, did that ever hurt—she got hold of one and started, agonizingly slowly, to cut herself loose.

It took a ridiculous amount of concentration to fight the fatigue that made it hard to just hold the stupid piece of glass tight enough, but finally, the tape began to fray. And once it did, it was only a short time before she was able to cut and rip through the rest of it.

She listened again for the sweet sound of her captor's snoring. Steady and strong. Exactly like she didn't feel herself. Soon though, that was going to change.

She bent over to untape her left ankle from the leg of the chair, and instantly lost her balance. All the blood in her body immediately rushed into her head, threatening to burst it wide open. She sat back up slightly, hugged her knee, closed her eyes, and prayed that she stayed conscious.

An involuntary spasm contracted her stomach, and she almost vomited.

After vomiting, an individual suffering from ketoacidosis can lapse into a coma at any moment. The situation should be considered a grave emergency.

No kidding.

At least she was remembering some useful things now, and not these stupid disembodied pearls of wisdom.

You will always have what you need. You just need to know where to look.

Fine.

The moment of nausea passed, the throbbing in her head returned to merely half-blinding, and she freed first her left leg and then her right.

She lifted herself stiffly off the chair and suddenly pins and needles raced up and down her arms and legs. Then a brutal pain shot through her stomach, and before she could even make it into the bathroom, she lurched to the corner of the room and vomited.

The coma might be only minutes away.

September 7, 2004
Day 1 of the Babe Gardiner trial
10:34 A.M.

TERRY TURNED TO HIS RIGHT AND WATCHED Babe watch the prospective jurors as they filed past him and Zack and entered the jury box. It would be a real kick if Captain Not Credible had some kind of sixth sense about who would be a good juror.

Zack leaned over and whispered to Babe, "Have you

got any feeling for how these fourteen shape up?" Terry had the same thought.

Babe swallowed, and made a big show of looking the candidates over carefully as the last of the group, a thin, elderly black man, took his seat.

The top row of seven was unremarkable except for a stern-looking woman who had an amazingly stiff hairdo, and a U. Mass student who looked like he was really hung-over.

The bottom row, though, was chock full of rejects, including a couple of guys whose questionnaires revealed one to be a cop and the other an ex–prison guard. The first looked like a bulldog with a beer belly. The other one just looked scary. Anybody with half a clue wouldn't want them anywhere near a jury deciding their fate.

Babe finished his inspection, then leaned over to whisper to Zack. "Uh, not really."

Maybe his sixth sense was busy working on the unified field theory.

Babe's latest knucklehead move was to steadfastly refuse to attend the trial in anything other than the Day-Glo-orange jumpsuit he wore in the prison, with the stylish "MCI–Whitemarsh" stenciled in white letters across the back.

No matter what Zack or Terry said, the young man could not be convinced that it was a better idea for him to appear at the trial in a regular suit. His mother was still in the hospital, so Zack even volunteered to buy one for him.

But the slouching, greasy-haired, mouth-breathing defendant was not to be swayed. The orange jumpsuit stayed.

Babe Gardiner—what a dreamboat. The jury was going to fall in love with him.

The fourteen people already in the box, plus the fifty or so who were still seated in the gallery, had all acceptably answered the standard questions that Judge Park had asked: Could they be unbiased? Did they know any of the lawyers or the defendant or the judge? Could they serve without hardship for the week or two that the trial would take? Did they understand and accept the fact that, believe it or not, people in this country were still supposed to be presumed innocent until proven guilty?

So now it was time for one of the most bizarre rituals the Massachusetts criminal justice system had to offer. The automatic challenges of jurors by the parties in order to ensure that the defendant was tried by a jury of his peers.

A jury of Babe Gardiner's peers. What would that look like? Twelve eight-year-olds who refused eye contact? A dozen stringy-haired mannequins?

Zack handed Terry a sheet of paper with two rows of seven boxes drawn on it, the appropriate juror numbers written in each box, and the fourteen questionnaires that corresponded with the people currently sitting in the jury box.

They'd pick a jury of fourteen, so that if anyone got sick or had to leave for another reason, when it came down to deliberations, they'd have at least twelve.

"Can I see counsel at sidebar?"

There was something obnoxious about the whole sidebar business. It made sense that there were some things that the jury shouldn't see or hear. But somehow, the idea that at various times in the trial, the lawyers and the judge would all huddle at the side of the judge's bench opposite the jury box and whisper—well, it just seemed rude.

Terry looked over at the prospective jurors and shrugged a silent apology as he headed to sidebar with Zack and the A.D.A. The cute high school teacher in the bottom row with the short blond hair smiled at him.

Zack and Terry hadn't been sure about her when they first went over the juror questionnaires. Now it was clear. She was a keeper.

When the lawyers had all joined the judge, the court reporter, and the clerk at the far side of his bench, Judge Park leaned in and whispered, "Have you told your client that he has the right to attend these meetings at sidebar?"

Zack answered, "Yes, Your Honor. The defendant has waived his right to be present at sidebar."

That was a damn good call. All they needed was for Babe to be trotting up here every fifteen minutes, annoying the shit out of everybody. As the defendant in a criminal trial, he was already the guy in the big, muddy hole. No need to volunteer to dig it deeper.

"Very well. The defendant has fourteen peremptory challenges. And both parties please make note of the fact that I am extremely conscious of anyone attempting to exclude jurors from the pool on the basis of race alone." The judge turned to Zack. "Does the defendant wish to exercise any challenges at this time?"

"Yes, Your Honor. The defendant would like to excuse Juror 1–3 in seat 2, Juror 1–10 in seat 7, 1–12 in seat 8, 1–19 in seat 10, and 2–2 in seat 13."

And away they went. No one had ever satisfactorily explained to Terry why prospective jurors had two-part numbers, why some judges went through this process fourteen people at a time and why some did it one person at a time, or, for that matter, much of anything about this crazy business. But the bottom line was that Ms. Helmet Head on the top row, and four others in the bottom row, including the two tough guys, were going home. The clerk read out loud the numbers of the five jurors who were let go, and then the numbers of the five others who rose from the gallery to take their places in the jury box.

Zack and Terry checked out the questionnaires of the

new five, and only one was a problem—his brother-in-law was a cop. So they challenged him, got a satisfactory replacement, and had a jury they could live with. With eight challenges left. With any luck, they might be able to keep one or two of the better candidates in the box for the trial.

Now it was the A.D.A.'s turn. He had fourteen automatic challenges, too.

This was the part where, despite what the judge had said, every black, gay, Asian, low-income, Hispanic, and any other kind of person you could name that might possibly be sympathetic to someone in the underdog's shoes would disappear from the jury. Because prosecutors didn't really want a cross section of the community represented in the jury box.

They wanted twelve bloodthirsty, vengeance-seeking hotheads, because they wanted a conviction.

"Judge, since the prospective jurors already seated in the box have all made it clear that they can try this case fairly and without prejudice, the Commonwealth is quite content with the jury as currently constituted. I see no need to exercise any peremptory challenges."

There was a moment of silence as everyone paused to absorb that one. In the dozens of trials for murder and every other serious felony you could think of that Terry had been in, he had never seen a prosecutor decline to exercise his peremptory challenges. This lawyer wasn't going to throw *anyone* off the jury. The skinny old black guy in seat 14, the young Asian dance instructor next to him who was either gay or the gayest-looking straight guy Terry had ever seen, the Hispanic telephone installer, the truck driver with the hearing aid, sweet grandma number one and sweet grandma number two, the cute high school teacher—damn. This wasn't one of the best juries Terry had ever seen.

It was *the* best jury he'd ever seen.

"Ladies and gentlemen," the judge said with a surprised smile as he straightened up and moved his high-backed leather, swivel desk chair to its normal place behind his bench. "Thank you for your patience. We have a jury."

As the court officers escorted the unused members of the jury pool back downstairs to the holding room, Terry sat down next to Sean, who was writing furiously in his notebook.

Jury selected at 11:22 A.M.—consists of five men and nine women—two African-Americans, one Asian-American, three Hispanics, and eight whites, one under 20, three 20–30 yrs old...

Terry sneaked a look across at A.D.A. Lowell, who was looking over his notes, probably preparing to make his opening statement. It was true that all the Commonwealth was supposed to want in a criminal trial was for an honest presentation of the facts before a fair jury.

But Terry had to admit that it took balls for that guy to actually act like it.

If somebody didn't watch out, with this judge, and this prosecutor, and this jury, Zack and Terry's guilty-looking, always-lying-about-something, good-for-nothing, orange-jumpsuit-wearing, probably-did-it client was going to get a fair trial.

Damn.

NINETEEN

**Massachusetts Correctional Institution Inmate
Status Report as of September 8, 2004**

> GARDINER, RUFUS. aka Babe, Babe Gardiner.
> DOB: April 2, 1976
> Height: 72 inches
> Weight: 160 lbs
> Dist. Marks: None
> Inmate #: W–84440
> Incarceration Status: MCI–Whitemarsh,
>   08/24/04–present (CH3)
>   MCI–Wakefield,
>   07/30/04–08/23/04 (CH3)
>   MCI–Bayview,
>   06/22/04–07/29/04 (CH3)
>   MCI–Wakefield,
>   03/20/04–06/21/04 (CH3)
>   MCI–Bayview,
>   08/15/00–10/02/00
>   (CH1–2)
>   MCI–Wakefield,
>   07/11/99–07/12/99 (CH1)
> Criminal History (convictions/open cases only):
> 1. DATE: 07/11/99. Possession Class A with Intent to
> Distrib.

2. DATE: 08/15/00. Larceny, night; intentional destruction of property over $250.
3. DATE: 03/19/04. Armed robbery, night; murder.
   Note: Multiple enemy issues, multiple disciplinary report issues. See disciplinary file for details.

Massachusetts Correctional Institution Inmate Status Report as of September 8, 2004

TEDESCO, ROGER. aka Robert Tedesco,
    Robert Rogers, Ted Rogers.
DOB: March 30, 1971
Height: 74 inches
Weight: 200 lbs
Dist. Marks: Barbed-wire tattoo, left bicep; scar, left
                eyebrow
Inmate #: W-79032
Incarceration Status: Parole Fugitive
                    05/24/04–Present (CH 9)
                    Parole 01/05/04–05/23/04
                    (CH9)
                    MCI–Bayview,
                    07/31/00–01/04/04 (CH9)
                    MCI–Wakefield,
                    02/22/00–07/30/00 (CH9)
                    Probation,
                    10/13/99–02/21/00 (CH8)
                    MCI–Wakefield,
                    01/01/98–10/12/99 (CH8)
                    Probation,
                    11/28/97–12/31/97
                    (CH3–7)
                    MCI–Whitemarsh,
                    09/19/95–11/27/97
                    (CH3–7)
                    Probation,
                    08/23/95–08/23/96 (CH2)

> MCI–Whitemarsh,
> > 08/23/94–08/22/95
> > (CH1–2)
> Probation,
> > 04/04/93–07/05/93 (CH1)
> MCI–Bayview,
> > 01/15/93–04/03/93 (CH1)

Criminal History (convictions only):

1. DATE: 01/15/93. Assault and battery.
2. DATE: 08/23/94. Possession Class B with intent to distrib.
3. DATE: 09/19/95. Armed robbery.
4. DATE: 09/19/95. Violation 209A Order.
5. DATE: 09/19/95. Assault and Battery with Dangerous Weapon.
6. DATE: 09/19/95. Kidnapping.
7. DATE: 09/19/95. Illegal possession firearm.
8. DATE: 01/01/98. Larceny.
9. DATE: 02/22/00. Possession Class B less than 28 g.

September 8, 2004
Day 2 of the Babe Gardiner trial

MARIA LOOKED AT THE TWO CRIMINAL HISTORY sheets, and there it was, clear as day. Babe Gardiner and Roger Tedesco had been incarcerated in MCI–Bayview at exactly the same time, for about two months, back in 2000. The lawyer was right. There was a connection other than their employer.

She was sitting with Anthony in the office of Ward Tyson, the associate commissioner of the Department of Corrections—the man with the worst haircut Maria had seen since her uncle Ernesto went to that overpriced thief barber in Worcester. Apparently, Tyson, Anthony, and Anthony's boyfriend, Joe, had been good friends back when they were in grad school together, and they had remained in touch.

Although what Anthony and this man—with his Julius Caesar short bangs and his nasty brown checked polyester blazer—ever had in common was hard to imagine.

Regardless of how lame they might look, Maria sure wished she had some big-shot government friends like Ward Tyson. Although if she'd had a choice, she probably would have picked someone working for a different agency than the Department of Corrections.

But thanks to Anthony, even though she didn't have friends in high places, she had a big fat half-million-dollar life insurance policy, already in effect.

It was amazing how much better that made her feel. Oh, she was still plenty scared working for Anthony on this case. Every time somebody slammed a door shut, Maria jumped about ten feet into the air. But now, she didn't feel quite so foolish when she pushed her way through the fear.

"And I can get you some more detailed stuff, but it's going to take me a minute." Tyson moved his mouse around, then clicked it a couple of times. "Okay, here we go. Some of these records aren't the greatest, because they're just the officers' handwritten logs that we scanned in over the past few years. But the police have found them to be very helpful. In fact, a detective out of Springfield was here the other day. She was looking for Tedesco, too."

He hit a button, and a printer hummed to life. When the last of several pages emerged from the machine, he gathered them up and passed them over to Anthony. "I hope this helps," he said.

Anthony took the sheets of paper, glanced at them, handed them to Maria, and then looked back up at Tyson. "Thanks, Ward," he replied. "You know how it goes—head down, legs moving." Anthony used that phrase a lot. It had something to do with football. Basically, it just meant working hard.

Tyson smiled and nodded. "Even when they're shooting at you?"

"Especially then."

Maria studied the papers while the two friends started to share some memories of the old days.

Even though Tedesco had had a prison record, nobody had thought to look into that as a possible connection with Babe Gardiner because Babe had never gotten any jail time for his prior offenses. He'd pleaded guilty both times and had gotten probation.

But what they had all forgotten was that when Babe was arrested for stealing that car radio, not only had he committed a crime—he'd also violated his probation on the drug charge. So he'd been thrown in jail, pending the resolution of the larceny charge, with a pretty high bail. His mother hadn't been able to come up with the bail money because she was sick and out of work at the time.

So for about six weeks, between the time that Babe got arrested and the time he pleaded guilty, he was locked up at MCI–Bayview, in the same cell as Roger Tedesco. In fact, thanks to a temporary overcrowding situation at the prison, a third inmate had shared the cell with them for about a month during that time. Some guy named David Zwaggert.

Tyson was handing a copy of another form to Anthony. "Here's the only contact information I have on Tedesco, but I doubt it's going to do any good. First of all, it's about four years old, and second, I'm sure that Tedesco's parole officer already gave this to the detective who's looking for him. Warrants have been issued, the state cops have been notified, the whole nine yards. I doubt you'll be able to track him down before they do, but you're welcome to try."

"And how about the visitor logs?" Anthony asked.

"Oh yeah." Tyson moved his mouse around, and clicked again, saying, "This is going to be a little bulky." When the final page emerged from the printer, Tyson handed them all to Anthony.

"Thanks, Ward," he said, as they all stood and shook hands.

"Stay safe," Tyson said. "They're saying this Tedesco guy could well be armed and dangerous. They have no idea why he bolted."

Good thing that life insurance policy was in place.

A LIGHT MIST WAS FALLING WHEN VERA PULLED up to the Regal Estates Apartments, home of Roger Tedesco's mother. The lofty name of the place merely emphasized the dilapidated condition of the building. It looked terrible.

Vera hurried into the lobby through the main door, and the broken lock allowed her entrance into the core of the building. She found Apartment 16 at the end of the hall on the second floor, and rang the bell.

A little dog started barking. Then a woman's voice screamed, "Shut up, Barnaby! Get in the damned bathroom!" The barking stopped, and an interior door slammed shut. Then footsteps approached, and the entry door swung open. A thin, gray-haired, wrinkled woman smoking a cigarette asked, "Are you the detective?" as Vera presented her identification and badge.

According to the parole officer, who had spoken to her some weeks ago, Mrs. Tedesco had been about as useful as a blizzard in May. But Vera really didn't have anywhere else to turn.

The fugitive's mother looked much older and frailer than Vera had expected. Of course, having a son like Roger probably aged a mother pretty quickly. When they had spoken on the phone earlier today, for some reason, Vera had imagined a more robust-looking woman. Maybe that was because of her no-nonsense attitude toward her son's disappearance. There was no question that Mrs. Tedesco would cooperate in trying to find Roger. She wanted absolutely no part of her son's criminal behavior, and was only too happy to help the police or anybody else find him and try to straighten him out.

"Yes, ma'am. I'm Detective Demopolous. May I come in?"

The dog started yapping again. "Shut up, Barnaby!" screeched Mrs. Tedesco. Then she turned back to Vera. "Sure. Come on back and have a seat." As they headed into the apartment, she continued, "But like I already told that parole officer, I have no idea where Roger is. He called me exactly once after he got out of jail, and that was more than a month ago, asking for money." She looked down and sniffed, then shook her head and laughed softly, but without any humor. "Said he would pay me back."

The living room in Mrs. Tedesco's apartment was no smaller than Irene Quarrels's, but somehow it managed to be a whole lot more depressing. And not just because Barnaby was whining from the bathroom.

The entire place smelled like wet dog. The paint was peeling on the ceiling over the small television in the corner, which was tuned to a rerun of some game show. Mercifully, it was muted. There was a single chair in front of the TV with a small book of crossword puzzles sitting on the frayed upholstery of the arm. Several stains on the carpet attested to Barnaby's toilet habits, and the sole window looked out upon the Dumpster stationed in the apartment's parking lot.

Mrs. Tedesco led Vera into the kitchen, where a card table and a couple of chairs were set up in a corner, under a small crucifix hanging on the wall. A nearly full ashtray, a pack of cigarettes, a glass of soda, a badly worn deck of playing cards, and a small book sat on the table in front of the seat that Mrs. Tedesco went for. Vera sat in the other.

"I'm sure the parole officer went over this," Vera said apologetically, "but we're also looking to find Roger. Right now we have no idea what's happened to him, so if you don't mind..." Her voice trailed off as she opened her notebook.

"I don't mind at all," replied Mrs. Tedesco. "I just don't think there's anything I can help you with."

"Well, my grandmother always says, 'When you got nothing, sometimes a little looks like a lot.' And right now, I got nothing. So whatever you can tell me is going to look pretty good."

Mrs. Tedesco flicked the ash off her cigarette and smiled. "Your grandmother sounds like a pretty smart lady." She took a sip of soda, put the glass down, and looked up at Vera. "Why don't we put our heads together and see if we can find this lost soul before he does something we all really regret?"

ELMO WAS SWEATING, AND NOT JUST BECAUSE IT was hot. He took a hit of beer.

He was watching the trial on TV, and the A.D.A., this kid named Lovell, was giving his opening statement.

There wasn't actually too much to see. The way they had the camera set up, it faced the judge, who was in the center of the shot, and the witness stand, which was to the right of the judge on the screen. In the center of the foreground, directly in front of the judge, you could see the podium and the back of Lovell's head and shoulders as he made his opening remarks.

The jury was off to the far right, out of the view of the

camera. But just to the right of the podium you could see where Lovell sat during the trial, and just to the left of the podium you could see one of the defendant's lawyers at their table, and to the left of him was Babe Gardiner, the defendant, in his prison-issue orange jumpsuit.

The problem was that Lovell sounded so matter-of-fact. He was telling the jury what the Commonwealth's case was against Gardiner. It should have sounded good—Christ, they had the victim's ID and a DNA match—but the prosecutor wasn't putting anything extra into it. He didn't sound angry, or upset, or much of anything. Just kind of straightforward.

Elmo took another swig of beer. He didn't have any margin of error in this case. He would have been a whole lot more comfortable if the A.D.A. sounded like one of those guys on television, banging on the table and screaming, like his life depended on whether the defendant was convicted.

Because Elmo's life depended on whether the defendant was convicted.

If Gardiner went down for this murder, like he was supposed to, everything was going to be fine. But if the stringy-haired idiot somehow beat this thing, then shit was going to fly all over the place, and Elmo had no desire to see that happen.

He had done a lot of work to make sure this played out right. Messages had been sent, people had been talked to, things were already in place. It really didn't make sense for Elmo to get any more directly involved.

But just in case, he was going to be having dinner over the next few nights with Wally.

Because if this kid Lovell didn't wake up and start lighting a fire under somebody's ass, and if the trial started to head south, there was no question that Elmo was going to get directly involved.

Seriously directly involved.

TWENTY

ASSISTANT DISTRICT ATTORNEY LOVELL: *We will present evidence that on the night of March 19, 2004, a young man named Steve Hirsch was working alone at the Nite & Day Convenience Store on Route 15 in New Wilton. And we will present evidence that at about 11:45 P.M. that night, the defendant entered that store, threatened Mr. Hirsch, overpowered him at knifepoint, and then robbed the cash register of approximately one hundred dollars and some lottery tickets. He also told Mr. Hirsch that he would kill him if he reported the robbery, and then he ran off.*

We will also present evidence that on the following day, Mr. Hirsch did not show up for work. And later, on July 6, nearly three months after the robbery, Mr. Hirsch's body was found, locked in the trunk of an abandoned car, in the woods in the town of Overton. His skull had been crushed.

The evidence will also show that DNA tests done on certain strands of hair found on the victim's body revealed that the hairs were, almost certainly, the defendant's hairs.

And then, after all of the evidence has been heard, at the end of the trial, I will address you again. And at that time, I will ask you to return a verdict of guilty.

Thank you.

THE COURT: *Ladies and gentlemen, as you know, our system of criminal justice here in the United States puts the* entire burden of proof on the Commonwealth. In other words, the defendant has no obligation to say anything, and the defense attorneys are under no obligation to make a single statement, or ask a single question. If the Commonwealth fails to prove to you beyond a reasonable doubt that the defendant committed a crime, then you are obliged to return a verdict of not guilty, whether he has raised a defense or not.

And that extends to the opening statement. There is no obligation on the defense to make such a statement, and I have been advised that defense counsel wishes to defer making an opening statement. Later on in the case, after the prosecution has presented its evidence, if the defense wishes to do so, it may make an opening statement at that time. Of course, it may also choose to decline to make such a statement....

(*Commonwealth v. Gardiner*, Volume II, pages 18–21)

Hostage

SHE WAS GOING TO HAVE TO MOVE FAST TO GET help in time.

She crept to the open door to see how to get past her kidnapper, and froze.

The flood of information that washed over her at that moment was so intense, she actually blinked and staggered back, as if she had been physically hit by everything she suddenly knew.

First, her captor, probably knowing that he was in danger of falling asleep, was sitting in a big easy chair which he had moved directly into the doorway. He was still asleep, but there were only two ways she could leave the room—move the chair, which was going to be impossible with him in it, or climb over it, which would be sure to wake him up.

And second, just a few feet in front of the chair a television set was on with the volume turned down, tuned to the local news channel. A reporter was standing outside a courthouse, speaking into a microphone she held. Then the picture changed, and the screen was filled with the mug shot of a thin young man with very stringy hair.

And suddenly, she remembered everything.

Including who she was.

BY THE TIME LOUIS LOVELL STEPPED ONTO THE bus, just about everyone else—all fourteen jurors, the court reporter, the clerk, and the defense attorneys—were already on board. Louis took his seat across the aisle from the other lawyers, just as Judge Park and his court officer joined them. Everybody but the judge sat down, and he began to speak as the bus pulled away from the curb and started down past the expensive clothing stores on State Street.

"Ladies and gentlemen, as I mentioned to you yesterday, today we are going to interrupt the testimony portion of the trial to travel together to certain locations that the attorneys have decided would be best for you to see in order to assist you in performing your duties in the trial.

"First, we will be visiting the Nite & Day Convenience Store, in New Wilton. The way we will proceed is that when we reach the location, we will all exit the bus together, and we will stay together, because the lawyers will have some brief remarks...."

Judge Park was a good judge. He knew the law, and he managed to put a great deal of energy and effort into all of his criminal trials—at least the ones Louis had done—without attempting to influence the outcome. He seemed to accept the notion that justice was served if a criminal defendant received a fair trial, period. Regardless of the verdict.

That was impressive. Sometimes it was really tempting for judges to try to tip the scales in favor of the prosecution. Especially for those judges who had worked as prosecutors before they were on the bench. But that was not only a perversion of the system, it often backfired, distorting the trial so badly that the defendant ended up winning a new trial on appeal.

The bus turned down Spring Street, passing the sandwich place where Louis ate lunch when the weather was nice enough to walk from the courthouse. Then it turned at the corner past the Parade Theatre, where the local community group still put on musicals twice a year, the costume shop next door, and lastly Freddie's Pizza Shop, before finally merging onto the ramp for the interstate.

So far, the Gardiner trial was going fine. The scheduling was a little odd—the judge had some other cases he had to handle, so he couldn't work a full day on the first two days of the trial. That meant they only could do jury selection on day one, and on day two, they were only able to do opening statements and a few of the shorter witnesses, like the victim's employer. Today they'd spend the whole day traveling to the convenience store and to the site where the body was found. Tomorrow began the really important witnesses, starting with the one who was probably most important, Detective John Morrison.

In some ways, Louis had a tremendous amount of respect for the detective. Morrison had a terrific reputation, and was obviously a great cop. And in most of the cases that Louis had handled in which Morrison testified, he was a good, and sometimes great, witness. Maybe a little bit of a showman, but that was his personality.

What was troubling was that in this case, Morrison seemed agitated in some way. He just wasn't quite himself.

The facts were a little unusual—Morrison knew that since the victim couldn't testify, he was going to have to spend a lot of time describing exactly what went on between them—and maybe that was what was upsetting him.

Or maybe Morrison was freaked out because Hirsch disappeared only hours after he'd told the detective that Babe Gardiner had threatened him. Maybe Morrison was feeling embarrassed, or guilty about the victim's death.

Whatever it was, the conversations that Morrison and Louis had in preparation for the trial left Louis with an uneasy feeling. Maybe it was nothing.

Or maybe there was more to this case than anybody expected.

"SO, WHAT KINDS OF THINGS DO YOU LIKE TO DO away from the job?" Vera asked John as they sat down for their second date. They were back at Stella's—the same restaurant they'd gone to their first night out. Not the greatest sign. But if all that came of going out with John Morrison was that Vera got a chance to have dinner out with a nice guy, then that would be fine.

"I don't know," John answered. He was wearing a dark blue suit today, with a black-and-silver striped tie and a white shirt. He looked good. Maybe a little more corporate than usual, but there was nothing wrong with that. "I had to be ready to testify in that Gardiner case today, you know, but they didn't get to me. So I'm on for tomorrow. Lou Lovell, the A.D.A. that's doing the case, says I'm going to be fine. But I don't know. I don't like those defense attorneys—Zack Wilson and Terry Tallach. I've run into them a few times on some old cases. Something about them rubs me the wrong way. I don't know." He flashed the big smile and shrugged. "I'm just gonna be glad when it's over."

That was a little strange. Vera had heard from the other detectives in the squad that John liked being a witness, and that he was really good at it, too. Maybe he just put up a good front when he was around them.

John's cell phone rang; he checked the caller ID and excused himself. Just like on their first date.

That was kind of disappointing.

It was also a little disappointing that he didn't answer the question about what he liked to do when he wasn't being a cop. And, to be honest, it was a little disappointing that Zack Wilson and Terry Tallach rubbed him the wrong way.

Vera had to admit that when she had met the two attorneys, back when she was questioning their client, she had been impressed with Wilson. He seemed like he was a straight shooter. Unlike a lot of defense attorneys Vera had met since she'd first joined the force, he didn't seem afraid of learning the truth about things.

And his partner, Terry Tallach, boy, he was some piece of work. A living, breathing supernova of passion. About everything from the subject matter of her questions to where to eat lunch. He looked like he'd be a lot of fun to spend some time with.

As long as his hair didn't burst into flame every five minutes.

John made it back over to the table just in time to ogle the pretty waitress's tight red tank top. They ordered drinks, and then they looked at each other and smiled. Here was another chance to see what John Morrison was really like. "So, about those things you like to do outside the squad..." she said. Anybody home behind the Super-Cop costume?

"Yeah, I don't know, you know. My dad was a cop—I guess it's kind of hard thinking about not being a cop." He leaned forward, grabbed a piece of bread from the basket on the table, took a bite, and sat back. "So, how are your cases going? I heard that DOA they dragged out of the lake turned out to be that Zwaggert guy you were looking for."

Ah well. So it was just going to be dinner out with a fellow cop who had no boyfriend potential. So what if John Morrison wasn't turning out to be the dream date kind of guy? He was still nice to look at. And everybody needed to eat dinner. At least this one wasn't going to be lonely. And who knows? Maybe John had a brother or a friend he could introduce her to. "Yeah. He was easy to ID. Whoever dumped him left his wallet in his pants. He'd been shot right in the chest. He was dead before he made it into the water."

"Hey—we're on a roll. First my armed robbery turns into a homicide, then your missing person turns into one, too. We better be careful if we ever work a case together, huh?" He laughed hard at his own joke as the drinks arrived.

Vera smiled. She wanted to laugh, but it just wasn't that funny. Maybe she was wrong. Maybe it was going to be a lonely dinner.

TWENTY-ONE

BODY DISCOVERED IN NEIGHBORHOOD LAKE

The decomposing corpse of what police believe was a man somewhere between twenty and forty years old was discovered in Glass Lake early this morning by area fishermen.

Brothers Frank and Peter Maretti and William Skyler were fishing from their boat at the north end of the lake, when Skyler unintentionally hooked a piece of the victim's clothing and reeled the body to the surface. The three men then called the police, who immediately restricted access to the lake and cordoned off the surrounding area, pending their investigation.

Authorities have not yet determined a cause of death, nor have they released the identity of the victim.

(Boston Post, September 9, 2004)

September 10, 2004
Day 4 of the Babe Gardiner trial

"MR. WILSON," JUDGE PARK SAID AS THE A.D.A. sat down. "Cross-examination?"

Zack was going to have to be very careful with Detective Morrison. He was the prosecution's most important witness, and it was through him that A.D.A. Lovell had introduced the video of the robbery and gotten into evidence the statement of the clerk that Babe was the robber.

Terry had objected to that testimony as hearsay, but the judge properly overruled the objection, on grounds that it was an excited utterance.

At the exchange between Terry and the judge, Zack had to work hard to keep from smiling. It was always funny when his friend got involved in those kinds of discussions, since it seemed that every third thing out of Terry's mouth was itself an excited utterance.

Oh my God, look at that waitress!

Oh my God, this traffic sucks!

Oh my God, our client is such a fucking asshole!

But when it came to deciding who was going to do the questioning of the good-looking hero-cop, it was a no-brainer. It would have been impossible for Terry to cross-examine Morrison without letting everyone know that he really thought the detective was a grandstanding windbag. And that would have sent a very bad message to the jury. The people deciding this case needed to know that the defense appreciated and respected the hard work of all police, including this handsome detective. After all, he was just doing his job, right?

But there were enough little things in the case that Zack could raise in his cross-examination—most respectfully, of course—which might just give the jury something to think about.

Unfortunately, thanks to their client's pathetic inability to trust them, that was pretty much the entire strategy of the case. Besides Babe's testimony, which was going to be a catastrophe, they didn't have a hell of a lot else. They were going to have to try to raise a reasonable doubt in the jury's minds with the small but curious and unanswered questions that ran through the case. And it was going to have to start here, with Detective Morrison.

Zack stepped up to the podium, carrying his three-ring trial notebook. To his right, A.D.A. Lovell sat at his table, preparing to make notes on a legal pad. To Zack's left was the defense table, where Babe, then Terry, then Sean sat. Although Babe had brought his legal file to court, remarkably, he was watching Morrison and not doodling. Sean, however, was writing notes furiously.

It was as if the two young men with the slouched shoulders had some kind of pact. No matter what, one must be scribbling at all times.

"Good afternoon, Detective. My name is Zack Wilson, and I've just got a few questions about that night you went to the convenience store, and later arrested the defendant."

"Great, Counselor."

Oh man, good thing Terry wasn't asking the questions. Morrison was already breaking out the swell-guy persona, and they hadn't even gotten started yet.

"Without telling us your address, it's safe to say that this convenience store and the defendant's home are both located fairly close to where you live, isn't it?"

"Oh yeah. Pretty close. Like I said, I go to that convenience store a couple times a week."

"Good. Now, when you first went into the store and the clerk told you that he had been robbed, did he tell you what had been taken?"

Zack expected the A.D.A. to object to that question, since it was technically hearsay—the cop would be reporting what the clerk had told him. The judge was sure to let it in, though, since he'd already ruled that the clerk's statements were excited utterances, but the typical A.D.A. would object anyway. They'd take a chance, figuring, what the heck? Maybe they'd get lucky, and the judge would sustain the objection and make the defendant's attorney look bad.

But not A.D.A. Lovell. No objection.

"Yes. He said the guy ran off with money and lottery tickets."

"I see. Did he say how much money was taken?"

"No. He said the robber just grabbed what was in the cash drawer. He didn't think it was too much. Maybe a hundred bucks."

"The exact amount was determined by the owner of the store sometime later, correct?"

"Correct."

"You're just telling us now what Mr. Hirsch, the clerk, told you that night."

"Right."

If there was one thing that Zack hated, it was when lawyers confused juries. It was tempting, sometimes, to try it as a defense attorney, especially if your guy looked like he did it. But in the end, it almost always blew up in your face. Juries weren't stupid. If they got confused because a defense lawyer misled them or a witness, they usually took it out on the defendant.

There was also just something about it that didn't sit well with him. So he usually went out of his way to make sure everybody was on the same page.

"Now, about what time did you come into the convenience store?"

"It was a little before midnight. I had just finished watching the news, and I wanted to grab some milk before I went to bed."

"But you didn't get to bed for some time that night, did you?"

"No." The detective flashed the Hollywood smile. "That was a late night."

OH BROTHER. TERRY KNEW THAT ZACK WAS SET-ting the cop up for a couple of shots in a few minutes, but oh brother. That phony smile really set Terry's teeth on edge.

The jury was loving everybody so far. The movie-star detective, the golden-boy lawyer, both smiling, pleasant, friendly, respectful. That was also just the way Zack wanted it.

It was early in the day, and everyone on the jury was fresh, and paying close attention. That was good. Because it was going to get fun soon, when that detective's fake smile disappeared.

"So, what time again was it when you arrested the defendant, Mr. Gardiner?"

"According to my report, it was 2:30 A.M."

"I'm glad you mentioned the report, Detective, because I'd like to come back to that in a minute. But before I do, let me just ask you about the arrest. The store was robbed at 11:45, and the arrest took place at 2:30. So, there was approximately three hours between the time of the robbery and the time of the arrest, correct?"

"Let's see. Yep. Three hours."

"Okay. Now, you said you were familiar with the area of the robbery, correct?"

"Yes."

"And can you tell me how many businesses in that area are open after 11:45 at night?"

The detective wasn't expecting that one. He wasn't exactly sure where Zack was going, but the expression on his face looked a little less cocky.

"Uh, gee, I never really, um, I guess I'd have to say

everything in the neighborhood is closed. There's an all-night gas station about fifteen minutes away...."

"The one in Clear Springs?"

Zack's question made it sound like he was very familiar with the area. It unnerved the detective a little.

"Yeah."

"And that's credit card sales only, after midnight, correct?"

And then a look of understanding passed over the detective's face. He knew he was in for some trouble. "Yes. That's right."

The good thing about Zack was that his cross-examination style was just him being his earnest self. Just a guy trying to put the whole picture together. "But aside from the gas station in Clear Springs, which does only credit card sales after midnight, where is the business nearest to the convenience store that is open late at night? That is, after 11:45?"

"I suppose that would be in downtown Springfield," Morrison answered. "There are a couple of restaurants open 'til two in the morning, and the bars are all open until then, too."

"I see. And how long would it take to drive to Springfield from the convenience store?"

"About forty, forty-five minutes or so."

"Okay. Thank you." Zack turned a page in the notebook he always used at trials. "Now, turning to the arrest itself, that took place at 2:30 A.M., correct?"

"That's right."

"And you were the arresting officer?"

"Yes. I had backup from a uniform patrol car, but I arrested the defendant." The message to the jury was that he was such a humble guy, he'd never make it look like he did all the work. They loved it.

"And did you search the defendant at that time?"

"Yes, I did. He was unarmed."

"Right. But how much money did he have on him at the time?"

Even a witness as good as Detective Morrison couldn't hide his frustration. He exhaled and said, "I don't remember exactly, but it wasn't much. Less than five dollars."

Zack made a little show of checking the police report. "Would it refresh your memory if I told you that you wrote in the police report that the defendant was carrying exactly two dollars and forty-three cents?"

If Terry had been asking the questions, by now he would have been pounding the podium and shouting. He liked being obvious with the jury. If he was going to make a point, he was going to be damn sure the jury knew it.

Zack liked keeping it calmer, especially when he felt like the jury was fully engaged. He also never wanted to seem like he was a bully. But if there was ever a witness that was begging to be bullied, it was this walking toothpaste commercial.

The detective tried to look reflective. "Two forty-three sounds about right."

"And after the defendant was arrested, you searched his house, didn't you?"

Detective Morrison took a deep breath. "Yes, we searched his apartment, but we didn't find any weapon, and we didn't find any stolen money."

"In fact, the only other money you found in the apartment was in the defendant's mother's purse, correct?"

"That's correct."

Zack again consulted the police report. "A five-dollar bill, three singles, and some spare change, totaling nine dollars and sixty-five cents, correct?"

"That's right."

"So, at this point, your investigation has not been able

to account for the money that was stolen from the convenience store?"

"We didn't find a hundred dollars under the defendant's mattress, if that's what you mean." Oh ho. A little bit of testiness was starting to ooze out of the witness stand. That was nice. Keep up that attitude, Spiffy, and Zack will eat you for lunch.

"Well, I didn't mean that exactly, Detective. I was more wondering if you asked any of the people working at the bars in Springfield if they saw Mr. Gardiner spend in the neighborhood of a hundred dollars that night."

Oooh. From the look on the poor detective's face, he suddenly wasn't having a very good morning. He knew that Zack knew that nobody asked anybody anything. The cops had a victim who clearly identified the robber, and then later, they had the robber's DNA on the victim's dead body. Why the hell would they waste their time running all over town, trying to find out where a hundred dollars went?

But because Zack was who he was, he was making that kind of investigation sound as logical as it seemed. And the lack of it sound like the sloppy police work that it was. And Detective Morrison was stuck with it.

"No. We did not make those inquiries."

"Oh." Zack paused, registering a slight disappointment in the police force that he so respected and appreciated. "I see." He took a breath and then asked, "But you did check for fingerprints in the convenience store, though, right?"

Morrison tightened his lips. Gone was the toothpaste commercial. "Yes. We checked for fingerprints in the convenience store."

Zack nodded. Then he turned a page in his notebook, peered down at it again, and turned it back. Looking back up at Detective Morrison, he asked, with just the right amount of incredulity, "But you didn't find any of the defendant's?"

"No."

"Not even on the cash register?"

"He might have been wearing gloves. You can't tell from the video."

Zack nodded again. "That's true. You can't tell from the video." Then he hesitated for a second and asked, "But you can't tell from the video that the defendant was the robber, either, can you?"

The jury was fascinated. The thin black man and the truck driver with the hearing aid looked bemused. Grandma one looked surprised. Grandma two looked a little scared. And the rest of the expressions in the box reflected intense interest.

Early in Morrison's testimony, the jury had heard him describe the clerk's identification of Babe, and their faces fell a little. What kind of a trial was this turning out to be? The guy who got robbed saw the robber and told Captain America who it was. The case was going to be over in five minutes.

But now the superhero witness with the million-dollar smile and all of the answers wasn't smiling, and didn't have all the answers. They were suddenly paying very close attention to everything.

So Zack gave them more.

"Detective Morrison, I'd like to draw your attention to that part of the police report where you describe the condition of the victim as he told you what had happened to him."

Morrison looked a little wary, but obviously relieved that they were shifting gears. The judge's clerk gave him a copy of the report, and he looked at it, and then back up at Zack. "Okay." The smile was back. He'd been writing police reports for years. There was no way he was going to get tripped up here.

"You wrote 'Mr. Hirsch was nervous and upset, and his hands were shaking.' That's correct, isn't it?"

Morrison checked his report. "That's correct." He was starting to look cocky.

Zack took a few steps to retrieve a book of Massachusetts court decisions that he'd placed on the defense table earlier. As he did, he asked, "Are you familiar with the doctrine of 'excited' or 'spontaneous utterances'?"

A falsely puzzled expression, and then an apologetic little smile crossed Morrison's face. "I'm afraid that's your department, Counselor. It's got something to do with hearsay, doesn't it? It's pretty technical stuff, I think." Subtext to the jury: *Hey, I'm just an ordinary guy. It's this slick lawyer that you need to watch out for.*

Zack was busy turning the pages of his big law book, and finally found what he was looking for. "So you are not familiar with the holding in the case of *Commonwealth v. Fagan,* in which the court wrote, 'because the victim was nervous and upset and his hands were shaking, the prosecution was able to avoid the hearsay rule entirely, and present evidence of the victim's statement, since the victim was not available to testify himself.'"

Morrison just sat there. This had never happened to him, and he didn't like it. Zack was making him look like a lying punk. Well, the truth hurts, Johnny. He cleared his throat and said, entirely unconvincingly, "I have never heard of that case before."

Another lawyer might have pounced, but Zack was going to play this right to the end as the respectful, but increasingly concerned, citizen. "So it's just a coincidence? The fact that the words 'nervous and upset and his hands were shaking' appear in your police report and are the *exact* words identified by the Massachusetts Supreme Judicial Court as the key to avoiding the hearsay rule for the prosecution? That's just a"—he paused, looking around for the right words—"a lucky break for Assistant District Attorney Lovell in this case?"

Morrison couldn't refuse the bait. His voice got louder. "Call it what you want, sir, but I had never heard of that case before."

Zack remained steady. "And of course, since you didn't know the importance of those exact words, you also had no idea that the only way they would come into play would be if Mr. Hirsch was not available to testify. But you couldn't have known that he wouldn't be at the trial when you spoke to him, correct?"

"Of course not," Morrison snapped. "What are you trying to imply, Counselor?"

And that's why Zack had stayed so calm. At Morrison's attack, all he had to do was look a little surprised, as if taken aback by the good police detective's sudden unpleasant tone. Zack didn't say a word, but every juror in the place got the message—this witness was acting awfully defensive for someone who was supposed to be the good guy. They were wide-eyed.

Sure, the A.D.A. was a smart lawyer, and he was going to be able to rehabilitate Morrison on redirect. It wasn't like just because Zack made a few points they had won the case.

But it was starting to look like Babe Gardiner actually had a chance.

TWENTY-TWO

CROSS-EXAMINATION BY ATTORNEY WILSON:

Q: *Dr. Trahn, are you familiar with fingernail scrapings?*

A: *Yes.*

Q: *Could you describe what fingernail scrapings are to the jury?*

A: *Fingernail scrapings are the materials collected from beneath the fingernails of victims of crime, or individuals who are suspected of committing crimes.*

Q: *And what are such scrapings typically used for?*

A: *Occasionally, the victim of a crime engages in a struggle with his or her assailant. And sometimes, especially if the victim manages to scratch the attacker, bits of skin, hair, or blood of the attacker are lodged beneath the victim's fingernails. Conversely, sometimes bits of such material are found under the attacker's fingernails, tying him to the victim.*

Q: *And in this case, did you find such material under the fingernails of the victim, Mr. Hirsch?*

A: *Yes.*

Q: *Can you describe for us your findings?*

A: *Yes. Under the fingernails of the victim's right index finger and ring finger, I found skin cells....*

(*Commonwealth v. Gardiner*, Trial Volume V, Pages 122–123)

"I DON'T GIVE A SHIT THAT SHE'S IN THE HOSPItal. You gotta get to her."

Elmo was supposed to be having dinner with Wally, but Wally was the only one eating anything. Elmo's stomach was too upset. Everything was falling apart. It was all he could do to drink his beer. And even that was a pain in the ass. Wally had insisted on getting a couple of six-packs of Heineken, and when they got back to Elmo's place, they couldn't find a bottle opener. Thank God Elmo remembered that his old Swiss Army knife had one.

They were sitting in the downstairs den, at the card table. Wally was working on his second slice. Elmo was working on making sure that his entire life didn't go down the shitter.

"They got too many people in there. No way to do it without getting caught." Wally lit up a cigarette, then opened up another Heinie and took a swig.

"Jesus H. Christ, Wally, you should have seen that trial today. No investigation on where the money went, no fingerprints—he couldn't even explain why he wrote the report the way he did. The whole thing was a goddamn disaster." Elmo stood up and walked into the next room, retrieved a bottle of Jack, and brought it back to the table. He'd need that in about fifteen seconds. "I gotta do something. You know they just found this Zwaggert asshole in the lake."

Wally chewed another slice of pizza thoughtfully. "I can still reach out to Gardiner. He doesn't know we can't hit his mom in the hospital."

"Yeah, but so far what's that got us? We gotta be ready with something more."

Wally washed down a bite of the crust with another swig of beer. "I been tailing the lawyers, like you said," he said.

Elmo laughed. "I didn't tell you to tail them so we could whack them. That's not gonna get me a guilty. I was just thinking we might find something we could use."

"That's what I'm saying," Wally said, opening another bottle. "The skinny one lives in this neighborhood with all these houses and people all over the place. He's got a kid, and he's all buttoned up by dark."

"So what are you saying?"

"The other one. He lives in these condos out by River-side, in the middle of nowhere. He's always out late, driving around by himself in his hot-shit car, going to movies, restaurants, whatever."

"So?"

"So, what about we wait for him back by the entrance to the condo complex, and grab him?"

"What for?"

"To blackmail the other lawyer. Lose the case, or you lose your partner."

Whoa. Elmo knew that Wally was good for muscle, but he hadn't counted on him coming up with a solid plan like this. "That might just work."

Wally shrugged. "It's risky," he said. "The guy's pretty big."

Elmo nodded and reached over for a slice of pizza. His stomach was feeling better. "I know. We'll save it for a last resort. But if this thing doesn't turn around soon, I wanna do it."

September 13, 2004
Day 5 of the Babe Gardiner trial

MARIA WATCHED AS ANTHONY SIGNALED AND then pulled into an empty parking lot near a small, overgrown playing field. "I've got to get something out of the trunk," he said, getting out of the car.

Maria was curious, so she got out, too, just in time to see Anthony open up a small box sitting next to the spare tire storage compartment. Inside was a scary-looking black pistol. "You've got a gun?" she asked, completely surprised.

Anthony took the weapon out of the box, checked something near the trigger, and then put it into the holster he was wearing under his sports jacket. "I've got a handgun, and a license to carry," he said, shutting the trunk and climbing back into the car. "Not that I've ever actually carried it before, but this seemed like a good time to start."

They were working their way down the list of people who had visited Roger Tedesco while he was in prison, starting with when he was there with Babe Gardiner. The list wasn't that long, which was good, because they didn't have much time. Babe's trial was already under way. If they were going to turn up anything useful, it was going to have to be in the next day or two.

They had decided to start with the people who had visited more than once. Two names topped the list: Jimmy Perez, who had come to the prison five times in five weeks to see Tedesco, and Angela Gannon, who had come to see him four times. Actually, she'd been to that prison a total of nine times, but five were in the month and a half before Tedesco had been transferred to that facility.

Neither had listed phone numbers, so they drove first to Jimmy Perez's apartment, since it was only about a half hour from the office. Angela Gannon lived in North

Babylon, which was more than twice as far away, in the other direction.

It was funny, but there were times when just thinking about her life insurance policy made Maria feel like she was wearing a bulletproof vest. Knowing that Felix and her mother would get a check for a half million dollars was so comforting that occasionally it calmed down the part of her that was terrified by the thought that somebody had threatened to shoot her.

Yet there were still times when the terrified part of her was in charge. Like the first time she returned to the office after the window had been replaced.

It was weird, because when she walked in that morning, there was really nothing different than any other morning. Anthony was already there, having coffee in his office. Maria went into the kitchen area, poured herself a cup, and then went to her desk.

But then she heard a car engine approach as it came down the street, and her heart started to race. She froze, and even flinched a little, as it drove past.

She had felt like a total fool.

Anthony, of course, had seen it, and had told her that it was going to take some time before she was back to normal. It was natural, he said, for someone who had gone through such a startling incident to be a little jumpy. He called it "hypervigilant."

That sounded about right, because she sure was hyper now. Her heart was pounding like a salsa band as Anthony pulled up in front of 1083 Maple Street, in Westhaven. "Let's go," he said.

Perez's home was on the left of a side-by-side, rundown two-family house. As they walked up the steps to the front porch, a cat jumped out from behind some overgrown shrubs that were on the side of the building and bolted across the street. Maria was so startled she nearly threw up.

Anthony tried the doorbell, but they didn't hear anything when he pressed the button, so he knocked on the door. They waited a few seconds, and he was just about to knock again, when it opened. A heavy old woman with very dark brown skin and gray hair opened the door. "*Que?*" she said.

Anthony looked at Maria, who suddenly felt very useful. Speaking in Spanish, she told the old woman that they were looking for Jimmy Perez, because he might be able to help them find a friend of his named Roger Tedesco.

Two minutes later, Anthony and Maria were in his car, driving like crazy toward North Babylon. From what the old woman said, it was obvious. Angela Gannon was the key.

LOUIS WASN'T INTERESTED IN GROSSING ANY-body out, but the facts were the facts. Whoever had done this crime had hit Steve Hirsch in the head hard enough to fracture his skull, then wrapped and taped him up in garbage bags, stuffed him in the trunk of a car, and then abandoned the car in the middle of the woods. The jury had to learn the facts in order to do their job.

He gathered the crime scene photographs together and brought them to Officer Cherry, who was his last witness. "I'd like to show you a series of photographs that has been marked for identification as items J, K, L, M, uh, J through T. Can you please tell me whether these photographs fairly and accurately depict the car and the body you discovered in that car on July 6?"

Officer Cherry looked through them all and then handed them back to Louis. "Yes."

Louis turned to the judge. "Your Honor, I'd like to offer these photographs into evidence."

The defense lawyers objected, and they all headed for the sidebar.

The conversation between the lawyers and Judge Park was predictable, and necessary. The defense attorneys didn't want him to inflame the jury with unnecessarily graphic and gory photos of decomposing flesh and bloody carnage. Conversely, the Commonwealth had to make sure that the jury had a full understanding of what had happened to that young man.

Louis had been through enough of these conferences to know how it would turn out. He'd been careful in selecting the pictures he wanted in the case. He had chosen color photos for all of them, except those depicting the victim after the plastic bags had been stripped away. Black-and-white shots of the badly damaged head and decomposed body were all Louis could expect anybody to handle. They were tough enough for him to take, and he was a pro at this.

And besides protecting the jury, Louis had no intention of giving the defense an issue to argue on appeal. Louis took a lot of pride in knowing that when the defendants in his trials were convicted, they stayed convicted.

To their credit, the defense attorneys recognized that Louis had taken pains to keep the worst photos out of the case. They knew that the judge was going to have to allow the jury to see some crime scene photos, and so they only tried to eliminate the ugliest ones of the victim.

The judge made his ruling, they stepped back from the bench, and Louis handed the admissible photos to the court officer.

"With the court's permission, I'd like to publish the exhibits to the jury, Your Honor."

"Very well," Judge Park replied.

Silently, the jurors passed the photographs from one to the next. In almost every face, you could see a series of emotions play out. First, curiosity, as they examined the pictures of the old, battered car, oddly parked in the middle of the woods. And then horror, as they saw the brutality reflected in the images of the decomposing body of a young man who had suffered a crushed skull.

The judge had allowed all of Louis's proposed photos into evidence except one—a close-up of the head injury. He felt that was too graphic, especially because there was another photo of the head and shoulders of the victim, clearly showing the injury.

Louis hadn't agreed, but that was all right. He had done his job, and the judge had done his job.

The last juror handed the photographs to the court officer, and Louis stood up. "Your Honor, the prosecution rests."

"BY NOW, YOU ALL KNOW THAT THERE IS SOME-thing very unusual about this case."

Terry watched the jury as Zack began his opening statement.

Zack had established a great deal of rapport with many of them over the course of the trial, especially during his cross-examination of Detective Morrison. But now that the prosecution's case was closed, and the reality of the murder and Babe's possible connection had been presented to them, they were obviously very torn.

The evidence against Babe was pretty strong. Not perfect, by a long shot. No one could deny that it was weird that there were so many unanswered questions about things like the fingerprints, the stolen money, the fingernail scrapings, and the language of the police report. And Zack was planning to get into the fact that there seemed to be absolutely no motive for this crime when he questioned Babe.

But Morrison testified that the victim had told him

that Babe was the robber, and that Babe had threatened to kill him. And then sure enough, when the cops found the victim's dead body, it had Babe's hair on it.

The jury was not unaffected. Many, if not all, if pressed to vote right after they had seen the pictures of the dead body, would probably have voted guilty. And might well have convinced the others to go along.

But Zack was really on today. The man always had a way with people, but something unusually powerful was working inside him now. As he described how Babe intended to defend himself against the accusations, he managed to reconnect with just about every single person on the jury, presenting himself as just another person trying to make sense of it all. So calm, so confident.

Why would an otherwise gentle man suddenly commit armed robbery—and then murder? How could he be so cunning as to commit an armed robbery without a trace of fingerprints or any other evidence, and yet be so sloppy as to leave his own hairs on the body of the victim? What did he do with the money he supposedly stole? And how about the weapon?

As Zack calmly and logically went through the defense—essentially arguing a lack of motive, supported by the defendant's denials—even if you weren't looking at the jury, you'd know he was making some serious headway. And when you actually saw the faces of the jury, you could see that by the end of his opening statement, this case was Zack's to lose.

Sweet grandma number one and the cute schoolteacher had remained two definite allies. They were following everything Zack said during his opening carefully, smiling, nodding sympathetically. The old black man was also in the defendant's camp. Sweet grandma number two, the hearing-impaired truck driver, and the Hispanic phone worker had started on the fence when Zack began, but by the time he was ready to question Babe, they had returned to the fold.

Most of the others were harder to read, but everyone was paying very close attention. Except for one woman on the top row, who looked pretty disgusted with the whole thing. At this point, she looked like a guilty for sure.

But for a defense attorney, that was an outstanding position to be in before you even started to present your case.

Of course, any enthusiasm about how they were doing had to be tempered by the knowledge that the case they were about to present was essentially the testimony of Babe Gardiner.

And true to form, as he took the stand, Babe looked just awful. The pumpkin-orange jumpsuit was badly wrinkled, and he had acquired a slight bruise on his chin and the hint of a fat lip since yesterday. For one of the meekest persons Terry had ever known, the guy couldn't go two days without getting into a fight.

And with the terrible posture, shifty eyes, and atrocious hair, it was a safe bet that Babe was going to have to rely on something other than sex appeal to connect with the jury.

There was a sense of anticipation as Zack stood at the podium, waited for Babe to finish taking his oath, turned a page of his notebook, and prepared to ask his first question.

There hadn't been a lot they could do with Babe to prepare him for his testimony. Every time they tried to speak to him about how to present himself at trial, he got overwhelmed.

So they had focused on what they thought they might be able to control. They told him what the first question would be. And they made him practice the answer, until he looked straight ahead, and said it in a clear and confident voice.

Good afternoon. Would you state your name for the record, please?

My name is Rufus Gardiner.

Good afternoon. Would you state your name for the record, please?

My name is Rufus Gardiner.

Good afternoon. Would you state your name for the record, please?

My name is Rufus Gardiner.

And so here they were. Time for Babe's big shot at making that solid, positive first impression. The one he'd never get a chance to make again. Zack looked up, smiled his most winning, relaxing smile, and said, in a clear and confident voice, "Good afternoon. Would you state your name for the record, please?"

And Babe just sat there. Then he swallowed, blinked a few times, looked up, looked away, and finally muttered to no one in particular, "Uh, Babe, uh, Rufus, uh, Babe Gardiner."

They were off to a great start.

TWENTY-THREE

DIRECT EXAMINATION BY ATTORNEY WILSON:

Q: *It's getting late, Babe, so I'd like to ask you just two more very important questions before we break for the day. First, did you, on March 19, 2004, enter the Nite & Day Convenience Store and rob Steve Hirsch at knifepoint?*

(*Commonwealth v. Gardiner*, Trial Volume V, Page 240)

"BY NOW, YOU ALL KNOW THAT THERE IS SOMEthing very unusual about this case."

Elmo sat and watched as the blond lawyer did his opening.

And he was goddamn terrific. Openings weren't supposed to be any big thing, but you had to be an idiot to think that Gardiner didn't have a real chance at beating this.

He turned off the TV, got up, and went to his car. He'd call on the cell phone on the way over to Wally's house. They were going to have to grab the lawyer.

* * *

VERA'S CONVERSATION WITH ROGER TEDESCO'S mother had generated a list of about a dozen people who Roger had been in contact with over the past several years.

The problem was that Roger was so bad at staying in touch with his mother, most of the contacts she was able to remember were either old, or were only first names—like Jenny from high school. But they were the only leads Vera had. The uniformed patrols were canvassing the area around the lake to see if anybody had noticed anything unusual five or six months ago, when they thought the body might have been dumped. But there wasn't much hope that anything was going to come of that.

Vera had decided to start with the contacts that were nearest to the lake. First on the list was Phyllis Krantz. According to Roger's mother, she was an old girlfriend who was a hairdresser on Main Street up in Overton.

Remarkably, when Vera had checked, not only was Hair Today the only hair salon in Overton on Main Street, but Phyllis Krantz worked there on Mondays, Tuesdays, Wednesdays, and Saturdays. So Vera made an appointment to speak to her during Phyllis's lunch break, and drove up to Overton.

Hair Today consisted of a big room with four stations for stylists in the back, and a reception desk and waiting area in the front. Only two stylists were working when Vera arrived—a large woman with red hair who was doing a foil coloring job on a teenage girl, and Phyllis.

Phyllis Krantz had a Goth look—black clothes, jet black hair, straight bangs, heavy makeup. She was small, and moved quickly, grabbing some personal things from her counter and putting them in her bag. They turned left out of the salon and went into the little deli next door. They ordered a couple of salads and drinks, and sat down at one of the tables along the back wall to eat.

Phyllis picked up a piece of lettuce, dipped the end of it into the little plastic container of salad dressing that had come with the meal, and put it into her mouth. "Sorry," she said with a little shrug and a sheepish grin. "I'm a salad picker." The words came out of her mouth like she spoke through a speeded-up tape recorder. She wiped her hands on her napkin. "I try to eat vegetables with a fork, and it turns into a mess. Give me a pair of scissors and I'm a miracle worker. But utensils make me look like a three-year-old. So what's Roger done now?"

It took Vera a second to catch up to Phyllis's shift in conversational direction, but then she told the young woman about what had happened to Davy Zwaggert, his connection to Roger Tedesco, and how Roger had recently gone missing.

Phyllis nodded. "Sounds just like Roger. Not that I think he'd do anything to this guy—what was his name?—Davy," she added, even more quickly than normal. "But Roger is a trouble magnet, if you know what I mean. I used to go out with him. He was fun, kind of, in a, I don't know, never-know-what's-going-to-happen-next kind of way."

"When's the last time you saw Roger?" Vera asked. "This is a homicide investigation. We can't afford to assume anything." Phyllis didn't seem like the kind of person she needed to coddle. Vera could be direct. The young hairdresser was nobody's fool.

"That's fine, I totally understand," Phyllis replied. "We started going out a couple of years ago, and the last time I saw him was the night before he got arrested and thrown in jail for some stupid drug crime. I don't have a lot of rules about guys, but one of them is that I do not need a boyfriend who gets himself arrested. So after about a week, when I finally found out where he'd disappeared to, I wrote him a letter, telling him we were done." She rolled her eyes. "Of course, about a month later, I found out he'd been screwing around with this other girl behind my back, anyway."

"Oh. I'm sorry," Vera said.

Phyllis took a sip of her iced tea and waved her hand back and forth. "It's okay. We weren't that serious, anyway. It was just kind of, I don't know. Surprising, I guess. That doesn't usually happen to me. But you go out with those kinds of guys..." She shrugged.

"And you haven't had any contact with him after that letter?"

"Oh, he wrote me back. This was what—three, four years ago? Anyway, I didn't bother opening it. I just threw it away. I figured if I wanted the thrill of a cheating boyfriend in jail, I could probably find it on TV somewhere."

"But that was it? He didn't write again? Or call?"

"About a week after the letter, he tried to call collect from the jail, and I didn't accept the charges. And that was it. I haven't seen or heard from him since then. I'm sorry about that." She took a bite of a thin piece of green pepper. She really did seem sad that she couldn't help.

"I know this must be awkward—" Vera began, but light-speed Phyllis was two steps ahead of her.

"The girl he was cheating on me with—her name was Angela Gannon. I think she lived in Babylon, or North Babylon, somewhere up there. Thank God I didn't know her. That would have been really awful. It was bad enough as it was."

Vera wrote the name down. She'd return to the squad, make some calls, see what she could find out, and then drive out there tomorrow. Babylon and North Babylon were too far for her to make today, especially since she had that dinner in town tonight for that ethics thing that the judge was hosting. The lieutenant had suggested that she go, because it would be a chance to meet some people, including a lot of the local prosecutors. She had met one of them the other day, when he'd come to the station to talk to John Morrison. He seemed like a nice guy. He'd offered to buy her a cup of coffee the next time he was in the neighborhood. Maybe he'd be there.

It didn't matter, though. Vera liked meeting new people. She was really looking forward to it.

"AND WHERE WERE YOU EMPLOYED?"

"I used to be employed," Babe said. "Now I'm in jail."

Zack had never worked so hard on a direct examination in his life.

Normally, this was a fairly easy part of the trial. The defendant had a story to tell, and all Zack had to do was facilitate the process with some open-ended questions and get out of the way.

Can you describe what happened that night?

What happened next?

What was going through your mind at the time?

It was true that even the simple direct examinations of defendants required some skill, because when you asked the jackpot question—*Did you do it?*—you had to do it in a way that was timed and phrased for maximum impact.

But in Babe's case, everything was hard. Not only was it a major effort to get a straight answer to the simplest question—it took four tries before the jury knew the address of the house Babe was living in at the time he was arrested—but Zack had to put a huge amount of energy into counteracting the overarching impression of guilt and deceit that suffused Babe's every word and gesture.

It would be funny, if it wasn't so pathetic.

And important.

Right now, it was late afternoon. Zack wouldn't finish by the time the judge recessed for the end of the day, but he was going to go for the jackpot anyway, as his last question. So the jury would have Babe's ringing denial as the last thing they heard from the witness stand before they went home tonight.

But before he asked the big question, he needed Babe to establish that he had an income and that there was no reason for him to rob a convenience store. "In the days and weeks immediately preceding your arrest, where did you work?"

"At Ibis Industries."

"I see. And where is Ibis Industries?"

"In Laurelton."

"And what were your duties—what was your job at Ibis Industries?"

"I was a janitor."

For late in the afternoon, the jury was really paying close attention, which was very important. Babe needed to establish himself as a sympathetic person who would never rob or murder anyone. It had started when the questioning was focused on his relationship with his mother, and on his attitude toward his two prior crimes.

It would continue here, with his sense of responsibility toward his job. There was nothing wrong with being a janitor, especially if you did your job well, and honestly. There were plenty of blue-collar workers on the jury. They could respect a janitor as much as anyone.

Whether they would respect Babe, of course, was entirely another thing.

"How long were you working as a janitor before you were arrested?"

"I worked that whole day."

There was a moment of silence, then Terry exhaled forcefully. Every once in a while, Babe dropped such a stunningly stupid answer on them all that the entire courtroom froze for a second or two. These Babe moments were coming frequently enough that Zack was now prepared—he made sure that his face remained neutral, and maybe even a little apologetic. Then he started again.

"No. I'm sorry. I meant, um, I know. I'll ask it this way. When did you begin—" Zack smiled, and stopped once more. He almost messed up again. But that was okay. The jury was with him. Three of them were smiling, too. "Sorry. What month and year did you begin your employment at Ibis Industries?"

"April 2002."

"Great. And focusing on the days and weeks immediately before you were arrested for this robbery, were you working full time?"

"What do you mean by full time?"

Terry groaned softly.

"Let me ask another question. During the weeks immediately prior to your arrest, did you work a set number of hours per week?"

"Yes."

Zack waited, and then realized that Babe had finished his answer.

"And how many hours per week was that?"

"Thirty-five."

Zack turned the page in his notebook that summarized Babe's employment records. He worked thirty-five hours per week, and was paid eleven dollars and sixty cents per hour.

"And what was your hourly wage at that time?"

"Three hundred sixteen dollars and sixty-eight cents."

Zack blinked, but then looked down, and thank goodness for the notebook, because if Zack had tried to process that answer without it, he wouldn't have had any idea what to do.

"Is that the amount of money that you would take home each week in your paycheck?"

"Yes."

"Great." Zack took a moment, so his point would sink in. "So your take-home pay each week was a little more than three hundred sixteen dollars."

"And sixty-eight cents."

Zack turned a page in the notebook. "And how much was the rent for you and your mother?"

"We pay nine hundred dollars per month."

"I see. And who—did your mother also work, during the time before you were arrested?"

"Yes. She had a job at the mall."

"Do you know what her weekly take-home pay was?"

"Ten dollars an hour."

A small part of Zack wanted to laugh out loud. It was like Babe had the gift of misunderstanding.

"And how many hours per week did she work, approximately, during the time before you were arrested?"

"About twenty-five or thirty, depending. Christmastime she worked a lot of overtime."

Zack nodded, and turned a page in his book, more to stall than for any other reason. Christmastime? Normally, it was dangerous for any witness to start volunteering information beyond the scope of the question. If Babe suddenly started talking about Christmastime, or whatever else was zinging around inside that mysterious head of his, there was no telling what damage he might start doing.

But there wasn't much else to ask, at least today. It was as good a time as any to finish up with the jackpot question.

They had gone over this with Babe several times. The way the facts of the case lined up, the focus had to be on the robbery. If the jury didn't believe that Babe committed the robbery, it was extremely unlikely that they'd believe he committed the murder. It just didn't make any sense.

So Zack would ask two jackpot questions. First the robbery, and then the murder.

The important thing was to set it up right and make sure that Babe nailed the answer. He didn't want to over-sell it to the jury. They knew the stakes, and by now, they knew Zack. Too much drama, and he'd sound like he was a phony. He wasn't, and it would be stupid to come across like one now.

"It's getting late, Babe, so I'd like to ask you just two more very important questions before we break for the day. First, did you, on March 19, 2004, enter the Nite & Day Convenience Store and rob Steve Hirsch at knife-point?"

Babe had known that the question was coming, but as Zack was asking it, he still managed to look like he was just about to jump through the roof. He looked down, he looked up, he looked down again, he inhaled, closed his eyes, and then opened them and looked from side to side. Finally, he swallowed and said, "I did rob him, but I didn't kill him. I absolutely did not kill him. I did rob him, though. At the store. That was me."

There was no question that what immediately fol-lowed was the biggest Babe moment of them all. For what seemed like minutes, the entire courtroom stood dead still, as Babe's words hung there, almost incomprehensi-ble, yet ultimately quite clear, and entirely damning.

And then, from behind Zack's left shoulder, the soli-tary voice of Terry broke the silence. "You have got to be shitting me."

TWENTY-FOUR

THE COURT: *What is your name?*

THE DEFENDANT: *Um. My real name is Rufus, but I nicknamed myself Babe.*

THE COURT: *What is your last name?*

THE DEFENDANT: *Gardiner.*

THE COURT: *Thank you. And how old are you?*

THE DEFENDANT: *Thirty.*

THE COURT: *How far did you get in school, Mr. Gardiner?*

THE DEFENDANT: *Uh, I'm not sure what you mean.*

THE COURT: *For example, did you graduate from high school?*

THE DEFENDANT: *No. I went to high school, though.*

THE COURT: *I see. Did you finish ninth grade?*

THE DEFENDANT: *Yes. And I finished tenth grade, too.*

THE COURT: *Good. Did you finish eleventh grade?*

THE DEFENDANT: *No. I dropped out.*

THE COURT: *Yesterday, there were fourteen people sitting in those seats over there. Can you tell me what those people were doing?*

THE DEFENDANT: *They were listening to the trial.*

THE COURT: *Yes. And who are they?*

THE DEFENDANT: *The jury.*

THE COURT: *That's right. Do you know what their role is in a trial?*

THE DEFENDANT: *They get to say guilty or not guilty.*

THE COURT: *Right. They decide whether the Common-wealth has proved beyond a reasonable doubt that you are guilty of the crimes you've been charged with. Now, who are your attorneys?*

THE DEFENDANT: *Mr. Wilson and Mr. Tallach.*

THE COURT: *Before the trial began, did you speak to them about the trial?*

THE DEFENDANT: *Yes. A lot.*

(*Commonwealth v. Gardiner*, Volume VI, Pages 12–16)

TERRY CLIMBED INTO HIS CAR, TURNED THE CD player on, and turned the volume up until Stevie Wonder was filling the car with music, then pulled out of the courthouse parking lot and headed down Spring Street. It really was best for everyone that he already had plans to attend this ethics dinner with Judge Baumgartner tonight. Earlier in the day he'd considered bailing on it, but now he was all about getting together with a bunch of other tired lawyers and cops and A.D.A.s and eating not very good food and talking about bad behavior in criminal law. Otherwise, he'd be in the courthouse lockup now, wrestling with Zack and Sean, because they'd want to try to keep him from killing their client.

It wasn't just that Babe got on the stand and admitted to the robbery. Terry had represented plenty of people who were guilty, and plenty who had pleaded guilty. That was part of the deal of being a criminal defense lawyer. Some, if not many, of your clients were going to be factually guilty of the crimes they were charged with. The cops weren't idiots. Well, at least most of them weren't. When they arrested somebody, they usually had a pretty good reason for it.

But representing Babe had been such a relentless exercise in getting your balls broken that to endure all of his bullshit, only to have him blow himself up right there in the middle of the trial, without any warning, really sucked ass. He could have spared them a lot of aggravation if he'd just told them from the start that he did it and that he wanted to admit it.

As always, Babe's motives were incomprehensible. What was he thinking? That the jury would believe that he did the robbery and didn't murder the guy? That was pretty damn stupid, even for Babe. Maybe he thought if he admitted something they would cut him a break. Terry could just hear sweet grandma one talking to sweet grandma two in the deliberation room: "He already said he did the robbery—let's not be too hard on the poor boy. Maybe we should acquit him of the murder."

Terry pulled into the parking lot of the restaurant where the judge was holding his meeting. There weren't that many cars there, which wasn't exactly the biggest surprise.

Judge Baumgartner had been holding these things about every six months for the past three or four years. He was getting close to retirement age, and he had hoped that he could help everybody in the criminal justice system— cops, prosecutors, judges, and defense attorneys—get a good working agreement on ethical conduct in the prosecution of crimes.

Lately, it seemed that he'd given up on that, and

simply was hoping that people would at least talk about ethical conduct in the prosecution of crimes.

And he hadn't been having a lot of luck with that.

So far, Terry had been to three of them in the past two years. In one, he'd gotten into a lively debate with an asshole assistant attorney general who was actually arguing with a straight face that the attorney-client privilege made criminal defense lawyers nothing more than well-educated accessories-after-the-fact of whatever crime their clients were charged with.

But other than that, the conferences had been pretty dead. Terry didn't have particularly high hopes for this one, either.

He entered the restaurant and walked through the lobby to the dining room that had been reserved for the meeting. A couple of tables had been set up on either side of the long room, with a podium between them at one end. Somewhere between fifteen and twenty people were milling around with drinks, many with familiar faces.

And then suddenly, the conference got a whole lot better. Because standing there, talking with a couple of the local A.D.A.s, including Louis Lovell, was Springfield Police Detective Vera Demopolous.

"SO YOU'RE TELLING ME THAT HE CONFESSED TO the crime, but we're still chasing after this woman?"

Maria watched as Anthony put his cell phone back into a slot in the dashboard. "Yeah. Zack says that as long as we're this close, we might as well talk to her. The trial is going to be over tomorrow, so if we don't turn up anything now, we're finished with this case. But he still thinks there's more going on than his client is telling him."

Maria shook her head as the two of them pulled up to a tired-looking house on the outskirts of North Babylon.

This was exactly the kind of thing she was afraid of. The case should be over, and the danger should be past. But no. They keep working on it, and then bang. Somebody starts shooting.

That would be just her luck. To get shot after they should have been finished with their assignment. Jesus, Mary, and Joseph.

Anthony got out of the car and headed toward the front door. Maria scanned the face of the house as she approached, about five feet behind him. There were windows everywhere, on both the first and second floor. If anyone had wanted to, they'd have a clear shot at either or both of them as they came up the walkway.

Anthony reached the house and rang the bell. Maria joined him. No shots rang out. No windows broke. Instead, hurried footsteps got louder as someone came to the door.

Then it opened. A small woman, about twenty-four years old, stood there, in a T-shirt and jeans. Her hair looked badly rumpled, like she'd just been sleeping. Her makeup was a mess. She looked like she might have fallen asleep after she had been crying for a while. She smiled. "Can I help you?"

Anthony smiled back and said, "Angela?"

The young woman said, "Angela's working right now. I'm her sister. Can I help you?" The smile was a little tentative now. Maria felt herself tense. What if there was somebody behind the door?

Anthony said, "We're private investigators, and we're trying to find a witness named Roger Tedesco who might be able to help our client. I'm wondering if you could—"

"Oh my God," the young woman gasped, holding her hand up to her mouth. "Are you looking for Davy?"

Anthony stole a quick look at Maria and then cocked his head. "No, we're looking for Roger, because a guy named Babe Gardiner might be able to use him as an alibi witness. We were hoping—"

"Thank God you got here," she interrupted. "Angela's been going crazy about this. She kept asking me what to do and I kept saying call the cops, but she said she couldn't. She'll be back from work at around eleven."

EVEN THOUGH VERA HAD BEEN LOOKING FOR-ward to it, the ethics buffet dinner was turning out to be even more fun than she had expected. Judge Baumgartner reminded her of her grandfather—smart, funny, and somebody she wished she knew when he was young. And even though Louis and a couple of the other A.D.A.s had to leave early, two of the others—both young women who had started with the D.A.'s office about a year ago—had invited her to a kickboxing class they were taking at their health club this Saturday.

But the highlight of the evening was Terry Tallach, the big, loud lawyer who represented the inmate she'd inter-viewed when she was looking for that fugitive Tedesco in the Davy Zwaggert investigation. Sitting next to Terry during dinner was like going fishing with her uncle Max up near Moose Rock. She wasn't sure that anything he said was actually true, but it was a blast to listen.

A tall thin man with a sparse gray beard got up to get some more bread. "Did you meet Dick Danniker? Good lawyer, but I swear to Jesus—what a load. If Dick starts telling you about his big Texas death penalty case, pretend to faint, or have a seizure or something."

It went on like that all night. Mary Franco was a de-cent judge for civil cases, but in a criminal trial, you might as well stick a Magic 8-Ball up on the bench. Ralph Katz was a killer A.D.A., but give him two beers, and suddenly he can't do anything but giggle and urinate. Police Captain

Sandy Kasperian had only two jokes—both dirty, neither funny.

At the end of the dinner, as they walked out toward their cars, Vera said with a smile, "Well, thanks so much for letting me know all of the horrible things about the people I'll be working with. You are so full of information, it's..."

"I'm sure full of something," Terry said, smiling apologetically. "Sorry about talking so much. Sometimes when I get going..." He kind of shrugged, rather than finishing the sentence. He was so tall that she had to tip her head back to look up at his face. "I love Harry Baumgartner, and I try to come to as many of these things as I can, but sometimes they're, well..." He sighed. "Not the greatest way to spend an evening."

"Oh, please. Don't worry. For somebody who's pretty new in town, this was a great time," Vera said. "And what made it even better was that it's my birthday. So I got to do something a little special—"

"You're kidding!" he interrupted. "Today's your birthday, and you spend it with Harry Baumgartner on Good and Evil Night? Well, happy freakin' birthday to you." He shook his head. "No song, no cake—you didn't even have any dessert. Not that you were missing much—the ice cream at that place tastes like ass. Are you sure you don't want to go somewhere for a real piece of birthday cake, or something? On me? I know a great Italian pastry shop—"

"No, I can't, really," Vera said. "I'd love to, but I've got a health thing. Believe it or not, I've really got to watch my—wow, it sounds so trendy—but I can't have a lot of carbohydrates. Especially things like desserts and cakes. I'm diabetic."

He didn't miss a beat, which was kind of refreshing. "Oh. Well, that doesn't matter. I had an aunt who was diabetic. Scared the shit out of me thinking about those shots, until one day she showed me, and then it was kind of cool. You can have fruit, can't you?"

Vera was a little taken aback, but she nodded. "Uh, yes, but—"

"I know the perfect place," Terry said. "It's this natural foods restaurant. They stay open late with live music, and they have lots of desserts on the menu that are perfect for you. We stick a candle in one of those babies and bingo! You got yourself a real birthday mango sorbet banana split."

It sounded tempting. Especially with somebody as fun as Terry. "Okay, if you're sure you don't have to get home," she said.

"Oh yeah, I forgot how much I'm dying to hurry home and think about how Babe Gardiner is single-handedly screwing himself in his trial." Vera was about to ask him about that, but he cut her off. "Let's just say that having dessert with you would be great, and leave it at that," he continued. "The restaurant is about two blocks down from here. Want to walk? I wanted to tell you something."

They started down the sidewalk and turned left at the corner, down a well-lit street with lots of little shops. The night sky was clear and the moon was full. As they walked along, there was a short period of silence, which seemed to be unusual for Terry. But it ended abruptly.

"I need to tell you this because, well, I don't know. It's just my thing, I guess. I tell people stuff." He paused to look at a window display of a local artist's pottery. "So here it is. I think you are an incredibly attractive woman, and in just about any other circumstances, I would be asking you for your phone number."

Wow. If that wasn't the biggest lead-in to a "but" in history, it was definitely getting an honorable mention. *But I'm married. But I'm on the rebound. But I'm gay.*

"But I'm a criminal lawyer, and you're a cop. And my partner, Zack, well, he tells me I'm crazy, but I don't think it's right. I just can't see dating a cop. It's too—I don't know. It just seems wrong. Being your friend seems fine. I'm just talking about anything more. I wish I didn't, but I've got this problem with it."

Vera had never heard that one before.

She was surprised that Terry's assumption that she wasn't seeing anyone didn't bother her. Of course, in the end, it didn't matter. They'd be friends, which would work out fine.

"Well," she said, "since it's my birthday, I think I'm going to just take that as, I guess, an unusual compliment." They came to the door of a funky-looking little place called Camille's. The sounds of a jazz saxophone were making their way out to the street. "And then I'm going to enjoy some birthday mango sorbet with my new friend."

ELMO LOOKED OUT THE VAN WINDOW AND SAW that the lawyer had a girlfriend. He watched them enter the restaurant, smiled at Wally, and said, "Change of plans."

TWENTY-FIVE

THE COURT: *Good morning, ladies and gentlemen of the jury. I hope you had a pleasant evening. Before we begin, as always, I'd like to start the day by asking you if you complied with my instructions....*

ATTORNEY WILSON: *Babe, when we left off yesterday, we were talking about the robbery, and I'd like to pick it up there, if you don't mind.*

THE DEFENDANT: *I don't mind.*

Q: *Good. So, just so that we're all on the same page, I'd like to ask you again. Did you, on March 19, 2004, enter the Nite & Day Convenience Store and rob Steve Hirsch at knifepoint?*

A: *Yes. I told you that yesterday. I robbed that man at the convenience store. But I didn't kill him.*

Q: *And you understand that you are under oath, and that lying while under oath is itself a crime.*

A: *Yes. I understand that. I ain't lying. I robbed him.*

ATTORNEY WILSON: *Your Honor, may I have a moment to confer with cocounsel?*

THE COURT: *Of course. [Defense counsel conferring.]*

ATTORNEY WILSON: *May we be seen at sidebar, please?*

(*Commonwealth v. Gardiner*, Volume VI, Pages 51–52)

* * *

ZACK WAS HOME WITH HIS SON, JUSTIN, PLAYING a game of Go Fish. Justin was winning, big.

"Do you have any fives?" Justin asked with an expectant smile.

Babe Gardiner's case had to be the most perplexing one that Zack had ever encountered. The A.D.A. was solid, and fair, and the jury was also fair. And there were some significant holes in the case against the defendant.

Yet, for reasons completely unknown to Zack, his client had completely sandbagged him on the witness stand, and admitted to the robbery.

Which virtually locked up the conviction on the murder. If Babe had robbed the clerk, then the jury was sure to believe that he had threatened him. Add the robbery, the threat, and the hairs on the dead body together, and you've got yourself a first-degree-murder conviction.

"Daddy, do you have any fives?" Justin asked again, a little more insistently this time.

"Oh, sorry, buddy. I got distracted again by this trial I'm having a problem with." Babe's case had been pulling Zack's attention away from Justin ever since he'd gotten home tonight. "Here you go." Zack handed over a pair of sixes to his son.

Justin rolled his eyes and gave them back to his father. "Daddy. I said, 'Do you have any *fives*?' Not *sixes*."

Zack took back the pair and sighed. "I'm sorry, Justin. I am such a loser today."

"Did you get distracted again by your problem trial?" Justin asked.

Zack put down his cards and opened his arms for Justin to come in for a hug. "Yes, I did."

" 'You know, sometimes big problems get smaller

when you talk about them,'" Justin said as he crawled into Zack's arms.

Hearing his own words come back to him that way startled Zack a little. Last week, Justin had been frustrated to the point of tears as he tried to put together a puzzle. Finally, completely overwrought, he went to Zack, who discovered that there were pieces missing, which had made completing the puzzle impossible. And then Zack told Justin that it was better to ask for help than to get overly upset by a problem. Using the words just now quoted by the boy.

It was somewhat embarrassing being counseled by a six-year-old, but there was no denying it. Zack needed to talk to somebody about this. The problem was that the most likely candidates—Terry and Sean—were unavailable. Terry was at Judge Baumgartner's ethics conference. Sean had TiVo'd the trial, and was watching it over again on television, and revising his notes.

"Do you want to talk about it, Daddy?" Justin asked.

Zack smiled, and hugged Justin tight. Sometimes, like right now, he loved his son so much that nothing else mattered. "Sure. Shall I tell you the problem?"

The little boy turned so that he could look directly into Zack's eyes. "Okay."

"Okay. Here's my problem. My client in this trial was testifying today, and right in front of everybody, I think he told a lie."

Justin gasped. Zack had worked very hard impressing upon the little guy how important honesty was. There wasn't much in Justin's world that was worse than a lie.

"So you see why I'm so upset."

Justin nodded, fully serious. Clearly, this was a bigger problem than he had expected. But then suddenly, his face brightened. "I know, Daddy! You can tell the judge he's lying."

Zack smiled and pushed a stray strand of hair back off the little boy's forehead. "Oh, buddy, I wish it were that simple."

September 14, 2004
Day 6 of the Babe Gardiner trial

MARIA WAS EXHAUSTED THE NEXT MORNING when she and Anthony reached the courthouse to meet with the lawyers and report what they had found.

By the time they had gotten home after speaking to Angela Gannon it was after two A.M. And Maria had to be up before seven to make sure that Felix and her mother had everything they needed before Anthony picked her up. Thank God he had stopped at Starbucks on the way.

Now they were sitting in a small conference room, about five minutes before the trial was supposed to start up again. Zack and Terry had just come up from visiting with their client in the basement holding cell.

"Sorry we couldn't get here before now," Zack said as they pulled up chairs on the other side of the table. Terry was dressed in a sharp-looking dark suit, with a white shirt and a yellow tie with dark blue stripes. Zack looked a little disheveled. His light blue tie was already loosened, and his gray, pin-striped suit just didn't look quite as crisp as Terry's. "Did you finally find Tedesco?"

"Not exactly," Anthony responded. "But we did find his girlfriend. Sort of. I guess the most important thing, though, is that we might have found an alibi for Babe."

Terry took a deep breath and closed his eyes. "I'll go check the barn door."

Zack was more upbeat. "Really? Maybe we'll be able to voir dire you, and get a continuance—"

"Zack, uh, not to be a downer or anything," Terry

said. "But I'm not sure how the whole post-confession alibi thing plays out."

"Me, neither," Zack said, "but I still want to hear about it." He turned to Anthony. "What did you find out?"

Anthony looked quickly at Maria and then began to speak. "I don't really think you can use this," he said, "but anyway, here it is. As far as I can tell, Babe's alibi would be that he couldn't have robbed and murdered that convenience store clerk that night because while that was happening, he was on the other side of town, shooting Davy Zwaggert."

TERRY WAS MENTALLY DESIGNING HIS CLIENT'S new business cards: *Babe Gardiner—Village Idiot, One-Man Crime Wave*.

It was less depressing than paying full attention to what the private investigator was saying.

Even so, he couldn't stop himself from listening.

According to Angela Gannon, she was Davy Zwaggert's girlfriend when he got arrested, and she first heard about Roger Tedesco and Babe when she visited Davy in prison.

Babe, Roger, and Davy were cell mates for a while at MCI–Bayview, and the three had formed a kind of bond. So when Roger got out of jail, he looked up Babe and, through him, got a job at Ibis Industries. And when Davy got his release, he called Roger, supposedly to celebrate his new freedom. Naturally, Roger invited Babe along.

But Davy wasn't really about celebrating. He was about Angela Gannon. Because although Angela was Davy's girlfriend when he went into prison, by the time he got out of prison, she was Roger's girlfriend.

And that didn't sit well with Davy.

Angela had written to Davy to inform him of the bad—for him—news, and then visited him in prison a month later, just to be sure that they all could still be friends. She thought she had handled it perfectly, and that everything was totally okay. And maybe it was, while Davy was in jail, not drinking, and not really able to do anything about it anyway.

Anthony continued his story. After Davy was released, and after he allowed himself to get drunk enough to unlock whatever emotional clamp he had put on himself, the feelings that emerged were—surprise—rage and betrayal.

The night Davy got together with Angela, Roger, and Babe, the four of them met at a bar in North Babylon and started drinking. But then they decided that it was such a nice night they'd pick up a case of beer and some raspberry vodka, and head to Glass Lake to hang out.

When Roger pulled to the side of the private road that led to the lake, and parked, Davy decided that the first thing he had to do was pee. So he jumped out of the car and went into the woods behind a tree.

A moment later, Roger decided to join him.

But before Roger made it into the woods, Davy emerged, pointing a gun at Roger and loudly accusing him of stealing his girlfriend while he was incarcerated.

Babe decided that what this situation needed was another drunken moron, so he jumped out of the car and ran toward them, just as Roger and Davy began to wrestle.

Angela watched with horror as the three stooges struggled with each other and the laws of physics. Then she heard a muffled pop, and before she knew it, Babe was running back to the car, while Roger stood frozen to his spot with the gun in his hand as Davy collapsed to the ground at his feet.

"I shot Davy! I shot Davy!" shouted Babe as he scrambled into the passenger seat. "Oh my God! I shot Davy!"

Roger, ever the brains of the operation, assessed the

situation: three ex-cons, two parolees, and one dead body. He decided the prudent course of action was to use some old rope he had in the trunk of the car, tie a big rock to Davy's body, and dump it into the lake with the gun.

Then he told Babe and Angela never to talk to anyone about what happened, drove Babe to his car, dropped Angela off, and disappeared, never to be heard from again.

A court officer poked his head into the conference room. "Judge will be on the bench in one minute," he said.

LOUIS LOVELL DIDN'T BLAME THE DEFENDANT'S attorney Zack Wilson. If he'd been in Wilson's shoes, he probably would have asked, too.

Right after Wilson had met with the defendant in the lockup, he'd come over to Louis and asked him if he'd consider accepting a guilty plea to the robbery, with a rec-ommended sentence of twenty years, in exchange for dropping the murder charge.

But Louis couldn't possibly accept that deal. It wasn't about the "Case Closed" program, or his boss, or anything other than the fact that it just flew in the face of common sense.

Yesterday, the defendant had gotten on the stand and admitted to the robbery. His entire testimony was bizarre—it was hard to believe almost anything that the man said—but even though the body language was wildly contradictory, the words came out straightforward.

And if Gardiner robbed the clerk, he had to have killed the clerk. And there was no way that Louis could let him off on that murder. If he committed murder, he needed to be held responsible for it.

Louis knew that there was a chance that he'd suffer for the decision. If some miracle arose, and Gardiner was found innocent, he'd surely be fired. But he was okay with that.

He wasn't okay with letting someone get away with murder.

"Court!" shouted one of the court officers, as the judge took the bench.

TERRY WAS HAVING A HARD TIME SITTING STILL while Judge Park asked the jury whether they saw or heard anything in the news about the case last night. It wouldn't matter. Babe was done.

Trust this blockhead to hide the truth from them so successfully that even when they finally uncovered an alibi, it was too late to use it. What were they going to say? "Uh, ladies and gentlemen of the jury. You know how our client said he did the crime? He was lying when he said that. What he really meant to say was that he didn't do *that* crime, because he was busy doing another one."

There was a topic for one of Judge Baumgartner's ethics conferences. What do you do when you can get your guy off on crime #1 by implicating him in crime #2?

It was one thing to fight a losing battle. It was another one entirely to fight for somebody who was determined to lose.

Zack got up and headed for the podium, to continue whatever it was they were doing. This was going to be hard to bear. He looked down, and his attention was drawn to Babe's legal folder. Some of the papers were spilling onto the table, and Terry reached over to straighten them.

He pulled the entire folder over in front of him and began to read what Babe had scrawled in the margin of some case out of the Hawaii Supreme Court.

These weren't the kinds of doodles that Terry had seen Babe making before—lame drawings of dogs, planets, and rocket ships. These were words.

Coherent, important words.

Holy shit.

And then he was on his feet, tapping Zack on the shoulder, just as Babe said, with about the least amount of conviction Terry had ever seen in a witness, "I understand that. I ain't lying. I robbed him."

TWENTY-SIX

[Sidebar conference.]

ATTORNEY WILSON: At this point, Your Honor, I'd like to move that the court declare this to be a hostile witness, so that I may propound leading questions.

THE COURT: I'm sorry. Did you say that the defendant was a hostile witness?

ATTORNEY WILSON: Yes, Your Honor. I suspect that the defendant is not being honest in his testimony. But unfortunately, I cannot be sure, and so I cannot invoke the ethical guideline by which I would simply cease asking the defendant questions, and let him testify in the narrative. Judge, I just don't know what's going on up there. He pleaded not guilty, and then testified that he committed the crime he is charged with. By definition, the defendant has aligned himself with the Commonwealth and made himself an adverse, hostile witness. I merely seek permission at this time to ask him leading questions.

THE COURT: Forgive me, Mr. Lovell. I have never heard of anything like this, and I'm a little at a loss. What is the Commonwealth's position?

ASSISTANT DISTRICT ATTORNEY LOVELL: Your Honor, the Commonwealth's interest is in a full disclosure of the truth. . . .

* * *

ZACK TRULY ADMIRED LOUIS LOVELL. THE GUY really walked his talk.

It would have been easy for him to object to this crazy business, and Judge Park probably would have sustained the objection and forbidden him from asking Babe leading questions. Who had ever heard of the defense attorney treating his own client in a criminal trial as a hostile, adverse witness?

But then again, who had ever seen Babe Gardiner in a trial?

To protect himself, Lovell had reserved the right to raise an objection if it seemed to him that Zack's questions were being used to distort the truth. That was totally understandable, of course.

Although it was going to take some doing to know when the truth was being distorted and when it wasn't, with Babe on the stand.

Zack stood at the podium, with some of Babe's legal file open before him. Terry was sifting through the rest of it to see if there was anything else in there that they could use.

Zack began by picking up Babe's legal folder. "Mr. Gardiner, do you know what I am holding in my hand?"

Babe was bewildered for a second, and then as the folder cleared the top of the podium, recognition crossed his face. This was the battered manila folder with BABE in gigantic handwritten lettering across both its front and its back that he had been carting around to every trial appearance and every meeting with his lawyers he'd had since the beginning of the case. "Yeah," he said. "That's my legal folder."

"And do you sometimes make drawings on some of the papers in your legal folder?"

Babe nodded. "Yes."

"Little doodles, right, of things like animals, and geometric shapes, and things like that?"

"Uh-huh."

"And sometimes, do you write things in your folder? Like words, and sentences?"

Babe looked off to the side, and then down. Something wasn't right, but he couldn't quite put his finger on it. "Uh, yeah. Sometimes."

"Great. Now, can you tell me whether, throughout the course of this trial, you were and you are still being threatened by someone in prison by the name or the nickname of 'Rock'?"

AS TERRY WATCHED HIS CLIENT'S EXPRESSION, HE knew what everyone in the court knew.

No matter what Babe said in response to Zack's question, the real answer was "Yes."

"No."

"Oh," Zack said with a puzzled look. Then he picked up one of the pieces of paper from the folder, held it up, made a big show of reading something in the margin, and then asked, "But you wrote in the margin of one of the pages in your folder, 'Rock says I'm guilty, or Mom is dead,' didn't you?"

The jury was absolutely fascinated. The cute schoolteacher was staring with her mouth open. Sweet grandma one and sweet grandma two were mirror images of each other, heads back, shocked, mesmerized. Every single person on that jury knew that Babe had written it. Regardless of what he said.

"No. I didn't write that. What are you talking about?"

By now, Babe's body language was so chaotic that it was absolutely certain that he was lying through his teeth. He was breathing rapidly, shifting his eyes left, right, down, every which way but directly at Zack. Everything he

said in response to Zack's questions was going to be reinterpreted, one hundred eighty degrees, by the jury.

"Well, I'm talking about whether you are being pres-
sured to accept guilt for these crimes by someone named
Rock, who has threatened to hurt your mother if you
don't. Is that what is happening?"

"No. That is not what is happening. Not at all." Babe
was starting to stammer. "Rock n-never threatened me.
He n-never did."

If there had been any doubt in the jury's mind that
Babe was being threatened, it was gone now.

"I see," said Zack quietly. He held up another piece of
paper. "So the words 'No way out must save Mom.' Did
you write that?"

"N-no. I didn't write that. I didn't write anything like
that."

Zack nodded, all seriousness. "Okay, Babe. Let's shift
gears for a minute. Can you tell me who Davy Zwaggert is?"

That one really shook him.

He looked away, he ran his hand through his stringy
hair, he sniffed, and then he blinked. He looked like he was
about to cry. When he answered, his voice was shaky. "No.
I can't."

"How about Roger Tedesco?"

Babe started to weep. "Why are you doing this to
me? I told you I robbed the convenience store. And you
know what else? I killed him, too. I killed that man after I
robbed him."

If anyone else had been asking the questions, he
might have come off like some kind of sadistic monster,
goading his own client into the tearful admission of guilt
of an unforgivable felony. But not Zack. There was nothing pleasurable about this for him. He was just a man
committed to taking the only course he knew that would
lead them all to the truth, no matter how difficult. Because

he knew what the jury was seeing and hearing. And he knew that whatever Babe was saying, the jury was hearing the opposite.

"So your testimony is that on March 19, at 11:45 in the evening, you went into the Nite & Day Convenience Store with a knife, intending to rob it?"

"That's right, I did," Babe sniffed defiantly, and completely untruthfully.

"And then you robbed the store of approximately one hundred dollars, is that correct?"

"Yes, that's correct. Exactly correct. Approximately one hundred dollars." Still no eye contact.

"And where did that money go?" Zack asked. "What happened to the money that you stole?"

Babe hadn't thought that far ahead, and the question clearly stumped him. His next lie sounded worse than all of the others. "I don't remember," he said, wiping his eyes.

"I see," said Zack, nodding respectfully. "But you do remember that after the robbery, you killed the convenience store clerk, is that correct?"

It took a minute for Babe to process that one. He didn't want to get tricked again. He cleared his throat, and once again, in a manner that no one on earth would ever believe, admitted to murder.

It was incredible. By now, several members of the jury, including sweet grandma two and the teacher, actually looked like they might start to cry, too. The truck driver with the hearing aid looked over at the thin black man, met his eyes, and they shared a smile.

Despite everything he had done to try to hide the truth and to sabotage himself, Babe Gardiner was about to be found innocent.

There was a movement to Terry's left, which was annoying, because he wanted to keep looking at the faces of the jurors. But he couldn't ignore it, and he turned to see one of the court officers handing an envelope to Sean, who opened it and showed it to Terry.

And then everything went straight to hell.

THE JUDGE CALLED THE MORNING RECESS, AND before Zack even had a chance to sit down, he felt Terry's hand on his shoulder and heard him say, in a low voice, "Zack, you've got to look at this right away."

Zack turned to face his friend, who was holding a letter and a photo.

"This can't be right," Terry said, his hand literally shaking as he held the picture of the police detective that had questioned Babe a month ago. "Jesus Christ, Zack, I was with her last night. They must have taken her after I left her. What the fuck is going on? What are we going to do?"

The picture was a Polaroid of Vera with a copy of today's *Boston Globe* in front of her. She was bound and gagged, and had been beaten badly—she had a swollen eye and her hair was matted with blood. It wasn't clear whether she was conscious or even alive.

What was worse was the letter. It had obviously come off a computer printer.

Attorney Wilson and Attorney Tallach

Make sure the jury finds your client Babe Gardiner guilty, or else the woman dies.

I'm watching the trial on TV, so I'll know if you try anything. If they stop TV coverage of the trial, or if the judge stops the trial for any reason, she dies.

Even if the judge recesses for a long time, she dies. I've been watching, and I know when he takes breaks. If there's any change in his schedule, she dies.

It's on you.

Zack's brain began to race. He had an ethical obligation to protect the rights of his client. There was no way he could throw a trial, or even try to throw one.

But if he didn't, that police detective would be killed.

And even if he wanted to, how in the world was he going to be sure he'd lose? Incredibly, right now, things looked pretty good for Babe.

From behind him, a court officer shouted, "Court! All rise! Court is in session!" and Judge Park took the bench.

He grabbed Terry and whispered frantically into his ear.

THEY WERE SCREWED.

Holy motherfucking shit. They were so completely and royally screwed.

The A.D.A.—Lovell—was cross-examining Babe, but the case was over, and he knew it.

Zack's direct examination of Babe had been incredible. By confronting him with the truth—and, at times, even a suggestion of the truth—Babe's lies had become spectacularly obvious to the jury, and to everyone else in the courtroom. The only question that remained was whether the prosecutor was going to try to indict him for perjury.

But as for the robbery and the murder of Steve Hirsch, that was not Babe Gardiner.

And thanks to the great job they'd done, Vera Demopolous was doomed.

Unless Zack's plan worked, which was a freakin' long shot if he'd ever heard one.

Terry leaned over and began writing a note to Sean.

As soon as the judge recesses for lunch, I've got to run out of here. You need to go with Zack and meet with Babe.

TWENTY-SEVEN

THE COURT: *I understand that the defense wishes to address the court.*

ATTORNEY WILSON: *Yes, Your Honor. As a result of the, um, unusual nature of the defendant's testimony yesterday and this morning, I spoke to him during the lunch break, and came to the conclusion that it would be best if we approached the court with a request.*

(*Commonwealth v. Gardiner*, Volume VI, Pages 110–111)

LOUIS LOVELL FINISHED HIS CROSS-EXAMINATION, and Judge Park recessed for lunch. Lovell had lost the case, and with it, his job. It didn't matter that Gardiner should be found not guilty. F.X. O'Neill was going to have his head after this catastrophe.

The only possible way he could hang on to his job was to get a plea bargain, and there was absolutely no chance of that, especially after he had rejected the defendant's offer only a few hours ago.

And then, just as he was leaving the courthouse to walk to a deli and get some lunch, one of the court officers ran up to him and gave him a note.

Five seconds later, he was running back into the courthouse.

AS HE WENT DOWN THE ELEVATOR WITH SEAN TO meet with Babe in the courthouse lockup, Zack knew there was an easy way out.

All Babe had to do was change his plea to guilty.

After all, Babe had already confessed, during his testimony, to everything that he had been charged with. All they needed to do was to come back from lunch, go through the new, streamlined version of the guilty plea hearing, and everyone would get what they wanted.

Babe would appease the person threatening his mother, Zack and Terry would comply with the kidnapper's demands and hopefully save Vera, and the Commonwealth would have another case closed.

The problem with that solution, of course, was that Babe was not guilty.

So either Zack was going to advise his client to plead guilty to crimes he didn't commit, or Vera, and possibly Babe's mother, were going to be harmed or killed.

They signed in at the guard's desk and then joined Babe at his cell. "Babe," Zack said, glancing first at his client and then over at Sean. "I've got an unusual suggestion."

TERRY COULDN'T FIND THE PRIVATE DETECTIVES when the lunch recess was called, so he ran out of the building and down the street, praying that the store was open. He had just about enough time to get there and back on foot.

Shit. Even if it was open, he had no idea if the plan would actually work.

By the time he reached the store, he was sweating like

a pig in a really nice suit. He was sure that he looked like a total freak as he charged up and down the aisles.

But five minutes later, he was running back to the courthouse, calling Zack on his cell phone, saying, "I got it."

Zack merely responded, "Hurry."

ELMO WOKE UP TO THE SMELL OF VOMIT. SHIT. He didn't remember puking.

He sat up, still with a pretty good buzz going.

And then he saw the television, and focused on what they were saying.

He'd won. Goddammit, he'd *won*.

He clapped his hands together once, loudly. "Yeah!" he shouted at the TV.

That asshole Gardiner and his lawyer were standing there at the defense table, their backs to the camera, facing the judge, who was looking at them from the bench.

"I understand that you wish to plead guilty, sir," the judge said.

"Yes, Your Honor," Gardiner mumbled. His long, stringy hair looked even uglier than normal. But his prison jumpsuit looked just the same as it always looked. Better on him than on Elmo.

"I'm going to ask you a series of questions, starting with this: Are you mentally competent and do you understand the rights you are waiving by pleading guilty?"

"Yes."

"Has your attorney explained the charges and allegations against you?"

"Yes, sir."

The judge shifted some papers around on his desk and picked up a few stapled sheets. "Now I'm going to ask you an extremely important question, which I need you to answer after very careful thought."

"Okay with me," Gardiner responded. His lawyer looked over at him, cleared his throat as if he was going to say something, but then turned back to the judge without comment.

"Are you guilty of the charges and allegations made against you in this case?"

"Yes, sir."

"Very well, then." The judge flipped over one of the pieces of paper and began to read. "The court accepts the plea of guilty to the following two charges: armed robbery and, pursuant to a plea agreement reached with the Commonwealth, second-degree murder."

TERRY FOUND ANTHONY AND MARIA AND WAS running out of the courthouse with them when they almost stampeded John Morrison, the detective that Zack had done a number on last week on cross-examination. "Hey, what's the big hurry?" the cop demanded, in a blustering, good-looking asshole kind of way.

Terry had already pulled out his cell phone and was in the middle of a call. He quickly said into the phone, "Hold on," pulled the letter and the photo of Vera out of his pocket and shoved them into Morrison's hands. "They took Vera. I was just calling 911."

Morrison looked at the letter and then the picture. Then his gaze seemed to sharpen as he looked closer at the photo, and he reached for Terry's phone. "Give me that," he said, turning away from the building and hurrying down the steps to the street.

Terry and the private detectives followed him. "Hey, that's my phone," Terry said.

Morrison ignored him. "This is Detective John

Morrison. I'm on my way to 45 Widener Drive, and I need backup. Possible kidnapping, with injuries. Code Red. Hurry."

He turned back to Terry and tossed him the phone. "Thanks," he said, then he turned and ran down the street toward a parking garage.

Terry turned to Anthony. "You parked around here?"

Anthony pulled car keys out of his pocket, deactivated the alarm on a sharp little Audi parked three spaces from where they were standing, and said, "Let's go."

VERA HAD LOST CONTROL OF HER BLADDER when she vomited, and so her pants were wet. And her headache was so severe that she couldn't move her feet.

Never give up, because you can't know who's just around the corner.

Unfortunately, Grandma Burke, this time she did know. It was a madman with a crowbar, who was now awake, and who intended to kill her.

Vera was minutes—maybe seconds—from passing out. If she didn't get to somebody with some insulin soon, she would die.

Because the chair had been backed up against the doorway, Vera couldn't really get a good swing at her kidnapper. She was going to have to hope that he was still sitting there, and see if she could use her trusty floor lamp like a lance. If she was lucky, she would be able to hit him hard enough with it to stun him, and then she could climb over the chair and run to safety.

That is, if she could actually move from the spot she was on.

Mustering the very last of her strength, she picked up the lamp and staggered toward the door to the other room, listening for any clue as to where her attacker might be. Then she heard him clap, and shout, "Yeah!"

He was still right there on the other side of the door.

As she got closer, she heard a voice from the television say, *"Now I'm going to ask you an extremely important question, which I need you to answer after very careful thought...."*

But just as she reached the door, another severe surge of dizziness and nausea overtook her. She couldn't afford to wait. She was on the verge of slipping into a coma.

A tiny charge of energy went through her, and, holding the lamp with both hands, she hooked her foot around the edge of the door and pulled it back. Then she took a breath and, as the door swung open, charged forward.

It was as good as she could have hoped for. He was sitting forward on the chair, transfixed by the television. He hadn't been paying attention to anything behind him at all. As she lunged forward, the lamp base connected squarely with the back side of his head, and he fell forward onto his hands and knees on the floor, screaming, "Fuck!"

Now Vera was faced with getting over the chair fast enough to get past him. She dropped the lamp, grabbed the back of the seat with both hands, and suddenly got hit with the worst abdominal cramp she'd ever experienced. It was as if she had been speared by a harpoon right in the navel. She clutched her stomach and stumbled backward, away from the doorway, into the room where she'd been held hostage.

She looked up into the other room and saw the kidnapper walking toward the recliner that stood in the doorway. He was looking at her as he approached, holding the back of his head with his left hand and a handgun in his right.

This was it. He was going to shoot her.

A tide of vertigo rushed her, and her field of vision narrowed. Then there was the sound of a door opening from behind the kidnapper. Suddenly there were two gunshots, and the sound of a window breaking, and another searing pain in her stomach.

Someone said, "Dad? Why?"

And then the world went black.

MARIA BARELY HAD A CHANCE TO ABSORB WHAT was going on before Anthony had driven her and Terry, the big lawyer, to the address that the good-looking detective had given to the 911 operator.

They were just pulling up when Terry suddenly said, "Holy shit, I forgot she's diabetic!" As Anthony stopped the car, Terry jumped out, calling over his shoulder, "Tell 911 she might need insulin!"

Maria started to pull her phone out of her purse, but Anthony was already dialing. As Terry ran toward the house, the good-looking detective was entering the front door. Just as Maria turned to ask Anthony if he'd gotten through, the car's windows exploded and Maria felt someone punch her in the back.

Anthony shouted something, but Maria didn't really understand what he was saying. She felt something strange near her right breast, and she looked down. A red stain was starting to spread across the front of her shirt.

Sirens were approaching, and Anthony was still shouting. She needed to tell him something, but he wouldn't stop shouting. Somehow he had gotten into the backseat with her, and was pulling her out of the back door on the driver's side, into the street.

And then she was on her back, and Anthony was

above her. Finally. Her chance. She motioned with her left hand for Anthony to come closer. Her right hand felt funny, and wasn't working.

"Tell Felix that everything is going to be all right," she said.

TERRY REACHED THE FRONT DOOR AT THE PRE-cise moment that somebody started shooting a gun. A nearby window shattered into what sounded like a million pieces.

He ducked. Holy shit. How the fuck was he going to get in there with bullets flying all over the place?

And then Anthony was screaming, "She's hit! She's hit!" over the sound of rapidly approaching sirens.

Jesus Christ. Vera was wounded and he was standing out here with his head up his ass. He had to get in there, flying bullets or not. He put his hand on the doorknob just as a car came tearing up the driveway and a cop jumped out, pointing a gun at him, shouting, "Freeze!"

Terry put his hands up over his head. "Not *me*, you idiot! The guy with the gun is in there!" he shouted, pointing to the house as more cars flew up to it and a dozen policemen surrounded him and pulled him face first to the ground. "And there's a diabetic woman in there, too!" he groaned into the lawn, as handcuffs snapped around his wrists. Fuckshit. While these morons were dicking around with him, Vera was in there bleeding to death.

Just then, the door burst open and another fifty cops yelled, "Freeze!"

And then the voice of an old man who sounded like he was crying said, "Don't shoot."

There was a flurry of activity at the door, and then a couple of cops hauled Terry up just in time for him to see another hundred or so fly through the door. Seconds later, two stretchers were being rushed into the house.

Detective Morrison was pulled out on the first stretcher. Blood was everywhere. He looked awful. And after an eternity, finally, Vera was brought out. And she looked worse.

TWENTY-EIGHT

THE CLERK: *Defendant, please rise.*

Members of the jury, harken to the indictments returned against this defendant by the grand inquest by the body of the County of Hampden.

Indictment 79443, Laurence "Elmo" Morrison.

At the Superior Court begun and holden at the City of Springfield within and for the County of Hampden, on the first Monday in October in this year, the Grand Jurors for the Commonwealth of Massachusetts on their oath present that Laurence Morrison on or about the fourteenth day of September at Springfield, in the County of Hampden aforesaid, did kidnap Vera Demopolous... did assault and beat with a dangerous weapon Maria Gallegos, and did assault and beat with intent to murder John Morrison, and by such assault and beating did kill and murder the said John Morrison.

Against the peace of said Commonwealth and contrary to the form of the statute.

To these indictments, members of the jury, the defendant has pleaded not guilty and for trial thereof he has placed himself upon the county, which county you are.

You are now sworn to try the issues.

October 5, 2004

ZACK WAS SUPPOSED TO BE READING A NEW CASE that had just been released by the S.J.C. on plea bargaining, but what he was really doing was thinking about the Babe Gardiner case.

"You're thinking about the Babe Gardiner case, aren't you?" Terry asked from the easy chair on the other side of the room. He was supposed to be reading the same case.

"No," Zack answered. "I'm enjoying the prose of one of our most gifted jurists."

"Yeah, me, too." Terry put down the file on the arm of the chair and laced his fingers behind his head. "So what would you have done if the costume shop hadn't carried shitty long-hair wigs and Sean hadn't been able to pull off a Babe Gardiner impression?"

"I don't know," Zack answered. "That was the only hopeless, desperate idea I had."

"Speaking of hopeless, I really fucked it up with that detective, Vera, you know. When we went out for dessert the night before she got grabbed, I told her that there was no way we could be a couple."

Sometimes Terry made things harder for himself than they needed to be. "Yeah," Zack replied. "That was dumb-ass dumb."

"Thanks for your understanding."

"I'm just saying."

For some reason, Terry had decided that defense lawyers couldn't go out with cops. It was clearly based on some ethical principle, but it was so misguided that it was comical. Except for Terry.

"So I decided that I was wrong. I made a few calls, and I hear that Vera's going to be at that retirement party they're throwing for Gloria down at the courthouse."

"She's already up and around?"

"Yeah." Terry got up and started to pace. "The diabetic thing is weird. I talked to somebody down at the police station, and I guess as soon as your body chemistry gets back into sync, as long as there's no permanent damage, you're okay. And the injuries from the attack were bad—bruises and a concussion—but no fracture. She should be back to normal pretty quick."

"That's great."

He had found his way to the window that overlooked the side yard, and was watching Justin play with his new puppy, Kermit. "So I'm going to put in an appearance at the party, and ask her out."

"About time, Elvis."

"Don't call me Elvis."

MARIA SAT UP AND TRIED TO LOOK PRESENTABLE as the hospital door swung open.

She felt a lot better, now that some time had passed after the surgery, but without being able to fix her hair and her makeup, she still looked like an old plate of beans.

The bullet had broken her collarbone, torn some muscle, and caused some nerve damage. She'd also lost a good amount of blood, but all in all, she had been very lucky. If the gun hadn't been fired from so far away, if the bullet hadn't crashed through two windows before it reached her, if it had hit her just a few inches lower or to the left...Whatever. That kind of thinking was going to drive her crazy.

"Hello? Are you awake?"

It was Anthony. Carrying a huge vase of bright, beautiful flowers.

"Anthony. You already sent me too many flowers."

He put the vase down and moved a couple of the

blooms around a little. "I know. But these are from my garden. I arranged them myself."

"You grew these? And arranged them?"

He gave her a look. "What can I tell you? I'm gay."

She smiled. "If my arm weren't in this sling, and I weren't hooked up to all these tubes, I'd give you a hug."

He nodded, and sat down in the chair next to her bed. "Listen. When you get a little better, we need to talk about work after you are out of the hospital."

Maria knew this was coming. The doctors said that they expected her to recover from the nerve damage, but that they would only know for sure after many months of therapy. Until then, she was going to have trouble using her right arm. And although she was overjoyed to be alive, it was going to be very hard if she couldn't get work. What a trip—no matter what she did, she always seemed to fall a little short. Enough money to move into a different neighborhood, but not quite enough money to pay the bills. Shot badly enough to lose her job, but not shot badly enough for her family to collect the life insurance that would set them up forever.

"I understand," she said. "The doctors say that it's possible—" But he cut her off.

"I just want you to know that this job is turning out to be something that neither of us had thought it was going to be when I first hired you."

And here it was. The ultimate irony. Being fired by the nicest boss in the world after he'd promised her that, no matter what, he'd never fire her.

"So, whatever the doctors say," Anthony continued, "and whatever ends up happening with your recovery, when you are ready to get out of here, I intend to offer you a raise in pay and a promotion to partner."

That took a minute to sink in, but when it did, Maria couldn't find any words to say.

Which was probably just as well, because she couldn't seem to stop crying.

TERRY WAS FIVE MINUTES FROM THE COURT-house. It wouldn't be too long before that jerk Larry Morrison, nickname Elmo, or more properly "L.Mo."—God, a sixty-three-year-old ex-cop with a street name—would appear there for his moment in the spotlight, to get tried for Vera's kidnapping, the killing of his son, and the near killing of the private detective's assistant, Maria. What a schmuck.

From what Terry had heard, Elmo had pretty much confessed to just about everything.

It all flowed from the fact that Elmo was an alcoholic and a cokehead. What a surprise.

Apparently, Steve Hirsch was his dealer. The night when everything blew up, Elmo went to the convenience store to make a buy, but Steve held out on him. Elmo pushed him into the back room, where Steve normally had some of his stash, but when it turned out that Steve really didn't have any drugs to sell, Elmo snapped and killed the kid right there.

Back before he had been thrown off the force for dis-charging his weapon while drunk off his ass, Elmo had learned about things like surveillance camera angles, so he pulled his hat down over his face, returned to the main part of the store from the back room, and took money from the cash register to make it look like a robbery. Thanks to his alcohol-soaked brain, Elmo was afraid to leave the body there, so he lugged it back to his house in the trunk of his car and started wrapping it in plastic bags.

That's when Detective Morrison found out about everything. He lived next door to his father, partly because the two houses had been in the family for generations, and partly to keep an eye on his father the drunk. So that night, Morrison saw a light on in the garage, popped in unannounced, and hello Mr. Felony. There was Daddy Dumbshit, right in the middle of drunkenly trying to prepare Hirsch's body for abandonment in some car trunk in the woods.

Terry turned onto Spring Street and passed the costume shop where he'd bought the hair that Sean had worn during the fake guilty plea hearing. There had been a few tense moments when he first thought that his only choice was a "Cher" wig. He pulled up to the next intersection, where the light was red.

Anyway, according to Elmo, when Detective Morrison found his father trying to wrap a corpse in plastic bags and duct tape, he went apeshit, telling him that he was a lousy drunk and that he'd have to haul him in for murder. Before Elmo got a chance to explain why he shouldn't be treated like any other homicidal drug addict, his son's cell phone rang.

One of Morrison's best skills as a cop was keeping so close to what was happening in the city's underground. No one ever found out for sure who called Morrison that night, but they did find out that the call came from a pay phone way the fuck up near Yancy, a good forty miles north of Glass Lake.

The smart money was on Roger Tedesco.

The theory was that Roger decided to call Morrison to turn Babe in for the murder of Davy Zwaggert. The cops thought that Roger probably called to deflect any guilt, figuring that sooner or later somebody would turn up who remembered seeing Roger's car driving around near the lake on the same night that Zwaggert disappeared.

Whether Morrison really believed that Babe had done

it or whether he knew that Roger was just making sure that the blame fell on someone else, no one would ever know. What was known, though, was that Morrison and dear old Dad had just been handed a patsy on a plate. Elmo thought of it as a miracle.

Which makes sense, if you are a self-absorbed, alcoholic loser, living three feet up your own ass.

Anyway, whatever else Detective Morrison thought, he knew Babe was dumb as a stone, and probably figured that if he and his father could hide Hirsch's body and point the finger at Babe for the robbery, things wouldn't be too out of whack. After all, Babe had been involved in Zwaggert's death, so if he got hooked for robbery, the guy was really getting off easy, right?

So Morrison went to the store, which was still open but unmanned, grabbed the surveillance tape, and then drove home, where he erased everything on the tape after the robbery.

The traffic light turned green, and Terry headed for the parking garage on the far side of the courthouse. He and Zack should have realized that there was something fishy about that tape. They were too busy fussing with trigonometry to see what was right in front of their faces. A normal tape wouldn't have stopped right after the crime—it would have gone on for much longer, until someone shut it off to give to the police.

Anyway, after Morrison got back to his house, he called the station, reported the robbery and his "conversation" with Hirsch, and headed for Babe's house to arrest him.

Of course Babe, being Babe, never told his lawyers that while arresting him, Morrison had grabbed him by the hair, which is surely how Babe's DNA ended up on Hirsch's body. Whether Morrison did it accidentally when he helped his father throw the body into the trunk of the car that Elmo had borrowed from the junkyard, or whether he was planting evidence against Babe in case the body was found would never be known.

Anyway, things looked pretty good for criminal mastermind Elmo, until the combination of Zack's great lawyering, Louis Lovell's commitment to the truth, and Babe's pathetic inability to lie convincingly started to make it seem that he might beat the charges.

Even before the trial, Elmo had been trying to intimidate Babe and Anthony, through Inmate Roderick "Rock" Rolle and some other, as yet unnamed, coconspirators. But as the trial got down to the last day, Elmo panicked and decided to kidnap Terry. When the killer followed him and found him together with Vera—a woman Elmo thought was his girlfriend—he went for what he thought was the easier target.

Terry ground his teeth as he parked and slammed the door shut too hard. Vera was very lucky to be alive. Elmo was, too.

As Terry entered the lobby, he was immediately treated to the happy sounds of friendly people partying. A boom box was pounding out something from the seventies.

The hall was decorated with colored crepe paper, pictures of Gloria through the many years of her service as a court officer, signs wishing her well. Lawyers, cops, A.D.A.s, judges, clerks, court administrators, tons of people were there.

Including Louis Lovell, who still had his job, even though he'd *nol prossed*—dropped—the charges against Babe. The judge had suspended the trial pending an investigation, and yesterday, Lovell had made it official. Babe was going home. Even his stupid boss, that dope F.X.

O'Neill, knew that the "Case Closed" program wouldn't benefit from the publicity of railroading an innocent man into jail.

And then, from a group of people to his right, Vera appeared, looking almost as good as ever. If Terry hadn't known about her ordeal, he might not have noticed the fading bruising around her head and eye. Her smile was undiminished and dazzling.

And was aimed directly at Louis Lovell.

When she reached him, they joined hands, and then she tipped her head slightly and leaned in to kiss him.

And Lovell kissed back. For a while.

This was not a hey-this-is-sort-of-a-fun-get-together kind of kiss. It was more like a hey-it's-really-nice-being-with-you-now-and-it-will-be-*really*-nice-being-with-you-later kind of kiss.

Damn. Terry had definitely arrived a little late to the party.

ZACK PULLED INTO THE PARKING AREA IN FRONT of the administration building at MCI–Wakefield. This would be the last thing he did on the Babe Gardiner case.

For reasons Zack still didn't understand, prisoners were released from custody at two times in the day— between one and two in the afternoon, and between seven and eight at night.

Babe got the evening time.

He was sitting on one of the benches outside the front doors, and stood as Zack pulled up to the curb.

"I spoke to your mother, Babe," Zack explained. "I offered to give you a ride to the rehab center to see her."

Babe processed that as he climbed into the car. "Oh," he replied. "Okay."

They rode in silence until Zack reached the main road. Then he looked over at his former client. The poor guy had been pathetically mistaken about the consequences of Davy Zwaggert's death. By rushing in to attempt to defuse a lethal situation, Babe did not commit a crime, even though Zwaggert had been shot. But Babe was so mistrustful that he was afraid to ask his lawyers about it. And then when he walked in on them discussing the excited utterance exception to the hearsay rule, he assumed that because he shouted, "Oh my God! I shot Davy!" he was automatically guilty of murder. So he misled them right to the end, and almost wound up with a conviction for something he had nothing to do with.

"Hey, Babe, can I ask you something? Totally confidentially?"

Babe took a minute to respond. "You mean it will be a secret between us?"

"That's right."

He hesitated again. "Okay, I guess."

"I wanted to ask you if the reason you tried to steal that car radio was because you wanted to give it to your mother."

Babe inhaled quickly. "How did you know?"

"I guess I figured it out the other day, while I was talking to my son."

Babe was surprised. "You have a son?"

Zack nodded as he merged onto Route 44 and headed north. "Yeah. He's six. And he wanted me to tell you that you shouldn't be afraid to tell the truth anymore."

Babe didn't respond for a while. He just stared ahead through the windshield, as they approached the exit they would take to get to his mother. When they were a few minutes from arriving, he said, "Tell your son that I think he'd make a good lawyer."

Zack drove on quietly, silenced by the man who was always wrong. Then he smiled, realizing that this would be his last, and most unusual, Babe moment.

Because this time, Babe had finally gotten something right.

ABOUT THE AUTHOR

ED GAFFNEY took ten years of work as a criminal lawyer, added an overactive imagination, and came up with a new career as a novelist. This has led to an unexpected number of requests from his softball teammates to appear with Terry and Zack in future books.

Ed lives west of Boston with his wife, *New York Times* bestselling author Suzanne Brockmann, and their anxious but everloyal dog, Sugar. *Suffering Fools* is his second novel.

If you enjoyed Ed Gaffney's SUFFERING FOOLS, you won't want to miss his electrifying crime novel debut, PREMEDITATED MURDER, available in paperback from Dell. Look for it at your favorite bookseller's.

And coming soon from Dell, the third mystery in the series praised by critics as "full to the brim with thrills, spills, and chills . . . electric, tingling fare!"*

DIARY
of a
SERIAL KILLER

by

Ed Gaffney

*Los Angeles Times